Bullwhip Justice

Bullwhip Justice

GEORGE RICHARD KNIGHT

authorHOUSE®

AuthorHouse™
1663 Liberty Drive
Bloomington, IN 47403
www.authorhouse.com
Phone: 1-800-839-8640

First published by AuthorHouse   11/29/2011

ISBN: 978-1-4685-0772-0 (sc)
ISBN: 978-1-4685-0771-3 (hc)
ISBN: 978-1-4685-0770-6 (ebk)

Library of Congress Control Number: 2011961422

Printed in the United States of America

FOREWORD

Guided by the arm of adventure, James Alburn Knight, again leaves the reader asking for more in this second glimpse of his life written by the author and descendent, George Richard Knight. Following in the footsteps of West by Bullwhip, George's first novel about the life of James Alburn Knight, within these subsequent pages, the whole Knight family experiences highs and lows, gains and losses, ups and downs, but never do they give up, let go or stop striving forward. Here you will find snapshots of true and realistic 1800's everyday living embraced by each of the characters of this story. The most surprising and pleasing of all is the author's glimpses into the mind of James better known as Jack in the story. It is here in his innermost thoughts that you will find the force that reckons with the challenges and blessings of life and the joys and pains of just living it.

Crossing, or rather crisscrossing, the west, Jack touches the lives of so many people and greets each day and each place with such a hunger for all life has to offer. With George's attention to detail and historical accuracy, I often felt transported to the very place and time described in this book. Blending true family accounts with actual events in our country's timeline has been outstandingly portrayed in this second volume. Although, I must add, I was informed that the love story which is a major, climatic part of the novel was actually not factual in James' life; however, realistic it was portrayed.

Even so, George has for a second time painted a picture that causes us to want to know more about the Knight family and more about our country's growing pains during its expansion and settlement of the old west. He has intimated that there may be another novel following that will include an incident with his own father who was James' only son.

On a more personal note, I happily found many similarities between Jack and George. Not because he is the author and creator of this book, but because the Knight family spirit is alive and well after all these generations. George, himself, has that same altruistic yearning to learn more, meet new challenges" and 'give it all" spirit in everything he endeavors. He'll even carry you along with him if you're willing. Just like Jack, he makes you want more than the average. Thanks George. I am honored to know and love you.

You make a difference . . . everyday.

Mrs. D. L. Branham, Editor, Stepdaughter

CHAPTER 1

The trip from Portland, Oregon on the SS Yosemite side-wheeler was pleasant and uneventful. It was mid-November, 1872, and I was not sure at the moment what lay ahead for me; but there is an excitement in the air that was catching.

Looking out onto the crowded dock as passengers were getting ready to leave the side wheeler to enter the growing city of San Francisco, my mind drifted back over the events of the past 13 years that had brought me to this point in my life.

I had been an adventurer with time in the saddle, driven wagons with either mules, oxen or horses pulling them, fought Indians, and experienced extreme cold and hot weather, wet and dry conditions. Stampedes of cattle and buffalo have tried to kick the breath from me, and I have had the reward of helping put a railroad into operation. Along the way, I have met some of life's memorable people.

While all of these past events flashed through my mind, I saw my brother, Edwin, standing on a buckboard on the dock waiting for me to walk down the gangway into the crowded mass of people. We made eye contact and he followed my progress to his buckboard.

"Jack, you dress more sophisticated as compared to when you left San Francisco almost three years ago. Looks like Ben Holladay had a heavy influence on your appearance and has added some culture to my little brother."

"You would not believe what has happened since we last spoke, Edwin. I'm sure I have changed since gaining the confidence of a successful man and no one can take that from me. My time in Oregon has been nothing but a grand ride. The accomplishment I felt was enormous and the life style as enlightening, but I probably will never live that way again. Well, big brother, how has life been treating you? Are you still putting big deals together and helping to make the world go round?"

"As a matter of fact, the world is still turning, but the economic tide is slowing as I am sure Ben told you before you left Portland. I heard he had to put the Oregon and California railroad into bankrupt status to protect his other holdings. His timber holdings are worth much more than the railroad. How far did you get the line completed before the banks shut it down?"

"We got the line to Roseburg in southern Oregon, big brother. Our next challenge would have been to get into California. Ben was over extended because of several things. He was expanding the mill outside of Milwaukie, he had purchased the western Oregon railroad and ran it to McMinnville, and the last year we spent getting to Roseburg from Eugene was much more expensive than the previous two years because of the terrain. Even though we had revenue from the route to Eugene, more men were hired for the crews and we were blasting on a daily basis. Something we had little to do with 'til we left Eugene. Ben also had bought two more steamers to add to his Columbia River fleet. He offered to keep me as an employee, but I felt he really was being kind so we parted with a good relationship."

We noticed my sea chest and saddle were on the dock now so we pulled the buckboard over, picked them up and headed for Edwin's home. It was close to the city of San Francisco but not in walking distance.

Heading away from the dock, Edwin seemed lost in thought. He started speaking with some hesitation, "Jack, before we get to the house I have to tell you something." Then quickly burst out, "Rose and I are married. I hope this doesn't go against your grain."

Being totally surprised by his manner, I responded just as quickly. "What are you talking about? I think that is great. You and Rose were meant for each other. I think she's a wonderful person. Oh, you mean because she's an Indian. You know I look at people like Father does. We are all equal regardless of our skin color though others may not feel the same. Is this marriage a problem for you in some circles?"

"Yes and no. Rose being a lawyer as well as an Indian woman is something this day's society has to become more accepting of as a woman's role is expanded beyond being a homemaker. Some people give it no thought, but we have had a couple of uncomfortable situations so we have been limiting our social life to those who are not offended. Rose and an Umpqua from Oregon have a partnership firm that is doing well. They keep busy with local Indian affairs and also have a few Negros that like their style better than some white lawyers. Rose has even argued cases in front of some judges in Sacramento and came out well. I am very proud of her."

"Well, you can be rest assured that I am proud to have Rose for my sister-in-law."

"Thanks, Jack. Rose said I shouldn't worry about you. She sure read you right. Something else you should know. We have an Indian girl for our housekeeper and cook. Her name is Little Bird, but we call her Jane. She is Shoshone and came to California from Fort Bridger. She had a club foot, and a Priest that saw her knew of a surgeon here in San Francisco that could help her. He brought her here three years ago when she was just seventeen. When we advertised for a housekeeper, the Priest called and asked if we would be interested in talking with her. She is 100% healthy now and has had three years of school at a mission just down the road from us. Watch out, Jack. She is very pretty and we don't need to find another cook for several years."

"Not to worry. I have too many trails to walk on before I'm ready to get tied down. Just like some of my friends that come to mind. One friend, Cody, has received the Medal of Honor. Art and Carl are still roaming the wagon trails that are left, and a lot of the country around Denver is still waiting to be developed. I have several options and none of them include a wife so you can rest easy."

As we arrived at Edwin's home, Rose was turning into the walk. She had heard the buckboard approaching and turned her head to see us heading for the barn. She ran across the yard and leaped over the front wheel into Edwin's lap like a little kid. She kissed him quickly and lightly on the lips and after a look into his eyes that says he was the love of her life she finally showed me some attention by exclaiming, "Hi Jack, glad you are here."

Settling into the seat between us, she turned toward me bubbling out. "Wait 'til you hear what Edwin has put together for you."

Edwin laughed and told Rose to settle down. "Rose, that can wait until after dinner, and besides, Jack has a few ideas of his own we need to hear about. I think he wants to go roam around for a little while."

Rose jumped down remarking as she went toward the house, "Okay, but I still think he'll want to hear what you've been talking to me about. You two wash up after you take care of the horses and buckboard so you'll be ready for dinner."

After putting the mare in the stall and feeding her fresh hay, we pulled my trunk and luggage off the buckboard and carried them in the house. Edwin left to wash up while I took a look at the bedroom I had used three years ago. As my eyes swept the room, a sensation of returning home filled my senses. Everything was just the same as the day I had left. A comfortable feeling of familiarity made me even more relaxed while emptying my luggage and closing the door behind me to join Edwin on his way to the dining room.

Entering the dining room, Rose greeted us with an air of excitement while presenting a 5 foot 2 inch beautiful, olive skinned girl standing beside her with, "Jack, this is Little Bird but she likes to be called Jane. Jane, this is Jack, Edwin's wandering brother."

Trying not to stare, I tried to casually carry the conversation while Edwin was pulling back a chair from the table for Rose. "Jane, I'm happy to meet you. I think you have a friend we both know. Jim Bridger was one of my most favorite and valued friends."

"Sir, Jim Bridger scratched my arm many years ago to stop the fever. I remember the day you and him left Fort Bridger with his wife and little girl along with Taw."

Looking at Jane questioningly across the table, Rose remarked, "You never told us about that. So you have seen Jack before today?"

"Yes, you cannot forget the red hair, and he used to have a whip. He would show us young children tricks using the bullwhip. You had big black dog too. You look much older now but then that was several years ago."

"Father McDougall came to the fort shortly after the blanket chief left, and I came to California with him to have my foot fixed. I spoke a little English but the nun's helped me to get more learning with much study. I plan to remain in California now and call it my home."

Edwin felt it was time to make his position clear by chiming in with, "And, Jane, this is your home as long as you want it to be."

CHAPTER 2

After dinner, Edwin and I had coffee in his home office. Pulling a couple of letters from a desk drawer, he began reading one of them to me:

My friend, Edwin,

I am now the President of the Colt Manufacturing Company in Hartford, Connecticut. You did some asset adjustments for me when you were in Kansas City, and I have always remembered your attention to detail and honest answers to all my questions. I wrote to you at Abbot & Bunch in Kansas City, and they wrote me that you had moved to San Francisco as their managing partner in that city.

What I am contacting you about is my search for an agency or person that you could put me in contact with that could handle distribution of an item we manufacture at our Baxter Steam Engine Company. We produce 2 hp. to 10 hp. steam engines and have no representation west of the Mississippi River.

If you can be of service to me in this matter I wait your return correspondence.

And it's signed Mr. Richard Jarvis."

"So why are you reading that letter to me, Edwin? I am not an agency nor do I know anything about steam engines or the distribution of anything."

"Come on, Jack, you will be what . . . 24 next month? You have a mechanical background with your gunsmith trade, and you could sell buffalo hides to an Indian. You would be a natural at this. You also have the air of self confidence it takes to do it."

"Anyway, I wrote Mr. Jarvis back and told him I had a prospect in mind and would get back to him shortly. This other letter is his answer to me. He said he would take my recommendation but would like to meet the person before writing a contract. All you need to do is go to Hartford, meet with Mr. Jarvis and with your charm put this plan into action. You have plenty of net worth to establish an agency and I can put that together before you leave. By the way, I have a financial report for you on your assets. You are worth more than twenty thousand dollars with all your investments. I have been lucky with the money you have sent to me to invest for you. The market is slowing, and I am going to turn a lot of yours and my investments to cash and gold as the prospects for next year look iffy to me. Too many of my banker contacts are very negative about the next year and beyond."

"Edwin, you are trying to turn me into something I am not. Do I look like a business man to you? I wear boots and a Stetson hat. My hands are soft now because of the last three years of no hard labor. My skin is wind damaged not smooth and clear like yours. Mr. Jarvis will look at me and laugh at the thought of my representing his company."

"You sell your self short, Jack. By the way, when did you loose that finger? I noticed it at dinner and forgot to say something. And, by the way, you look very stylish with your boots and big white hat. I'm sure Richard Jarvis would approve most heartily since he wants the western influence to accept his product. You don't change anything for him, Jack."

"A good story could be made up about my finger but it was a foolish mishap when two rails came together, and I ended up short one finger. So what is involved with this agency we might put together?"

"Well, you should set up a corporation so we file the paper work as a California corporation. Now you need a name. Your name is James Alburn Knight so we could call it JAK Sales Co. for a start. You need three people for a corporation so we make you President, Rose, Vice President, and list me as Secretary. You issue stock to yourself along with one share each to Rose and me. Rose and I have to pay at least one dollar for a share. You can make your corporation solvent by you buying say 2,500 shares at one dollar each. We have to hold a meeting, write the minutes of that meeting and certify the minutes with all three signatures, and you have a legal entity to work from. You can write contracts, receive contracts, employ sales people and handle all your business through the company."

"Sounds like I'll end up getting tied down and losing my freedom to roam as I please. I need to sleep on this, Edwin. I'm sure we don't have to make a decision tonight."

"Jack, this enterprise can take you places you have never been and never heard of. Don't be too quick to turn your back on what we have talked about this evening. Just imagine where a steam engine of that size could be used and what it could be used for. If you think you need a product line to make you look successful to Mr. Jarvis, I have a company that makes leather belts for industry that needs a distributor. Industrial belts go with the steam engine so you would have two products needed at some of the same locations."

Big brother has left me with a lot to think about. As the west grows and small industry moves in to support the expanding population there will be use for small steam engines all over the country. Edwin has introduced me to the cattle business and railroading. His advice has been good so far. Maybe I should listen to his proposal. I knew with his participation in the corporation he wouldn't let it fail and would continue to advise me if I took a wrong turn. Okay, I'm thinking. I might as well take the gamble and see what is ahead for me.

The next morning, I told Edwin to go ahead with the plan. He was more excited than I had ever seen him in my lifetime.

"Great, Jack, in time you'll find you have made a good decision. I don't think you will ever regret this, and I believe you'll have an enjoyable ride to boot."

CHAPTER 3

On Friday, November 15, 1872, I became President of JAK Sales Company. We had our first meeting and the minutes would be registered making us a legal corporation. My first task would be to make the trip to Hartford, Connecticut to meet with Mr. Jarvis and hope he is willing to accept my young agency to represent his company in the west. Edwin wanted to see my wardrobe to see if it fits my new position. As he looked at the ten suits that were made by Ben Holladay's personal tailor, he remarked that his tailor could use some pointers and wanted to take one of the suits to show him the quality.

"Jack, you can wear these anywhere you go. I'm not sure how your tailor gives them a western style cut, but people back east will probably ask where you have such fine clothes made."

"I had him make the jackets about three inches longer than you wear yours, Edwin, so I can carry my bullwhip and it not be seen easily. Anything else he said was his personal touch to fit my personality. Ben had a lot of parties, and he expected me to show up. I have no idea what these suits cost as Ben would not let me pay the tailor."

"First class, Jack. I told you Ben knew how to live the high life. Looks like he carried you with him. With the black boots and that white Stetson hat you will be noticed back East, although, you might want to leave the bullwhip in your room while you're in Hartford.

On Monday, Edwin had me travel with him about ten miles south of town to a large factory that belonged to Robert Peterson. This was to be my anchor for the sales company. Mr. Peterson had been in business for a year and did the selling of industrial belting himself. He was planning to expand and would be needed at the shop daily with no time for personally representing his product. This was where JAK Sales came in. With expansion, he agreed he needed a larger sales territory. When we left, JAK Sales had its first contract to represent a real business, P&P Leather Company.

During the ride back to Edwin's home, he asked if I knew anyone I would hire for my first salesman? I answered that I thought I was the salesman.

"You're going to be too busy covering all your territory, Jack. You will need help. P&P Leather Company needs someone to call on their existing customers and someone to start spreading the belt business into new areas."

"Well, I know you, Rose, and Jane. I don't think I have a prospect in that group. I guess the company is going to have to have its Secretary ride to the rescue."

"Ok. I do know a fellow that I buy my shirts from," Edwin said as he slowed the horses to a walk. He seemed to be in deep thought as to how to approach this but decided to go ahead as he continued, "He is over qualified to work in that clothing store and has some industrial back-ground. I'll bet we can get him for one hundred and twenty-five dollars a month to start and he would be getting a raise at that."

"You need some shirts so tomorrow we go shirt shopping. You will like Ray Anderson. He is about your age and could sell ice to an Eskimo in Alaska."

Boy, the farther down this road I went, the more boxed in I was getting. Now I was going to have an employee that would depend on me to make all the right decisions for his welfare and the companies to sustain his job. I might end up with wrinkles in my forehead like Harvey at H C and A Freighters.

The next morning while I was paying for the shirts I decided to buy, Edwin started his dialog with Ray. Before he finished the details, Ray said, "Give me the rest of the week with old skinflint here, and I'm ready.

I appreciate the opportunity you're giving me, and I don't believe you'll be disappointed with the results. By the way, where is your office? I'll be there Monday morning by seven ready to start."

"For now, Jack's office is in my barn tack room. Just come to the house, and we can start from there. The address is on the back of my card. Would you like to know what the starting pay is? Jack said we had to pay you if you work for him."

"My salary is twenty dollars a week here. If you give me $20.25 you got me. I know I can sell industrial belting and be a lot happier than in this store. You still want these shirts Jack? I can put them back if you don't need them."

"No. I need them. I have a trip to make, and Edwin wants me to be well dressed so I can impress another client for more business for both of us. We can tell you all about it Monday."

As we rode back to the house, Edwin explained that I needed to get back with P&P tomorrow and get their client list so Ray would have a starting point and could be sent out after he spent a day at Robert's factory. "You might need to make that tour with Ray to learn something about what you're representing."

"Let's see, Jack. Today is the 18th of November. What about planning to spend the whole day in that plant with Ray Monday? Monday is the 25th. After that, we need to see if you can get an audience with Richard Jarvis the second week in December. Tomorrow, I will send a telegram to Mr. Jarvis and try to set a meeting. I imagine we can get you to Hartford in ten days. We need to check with the railroad and set it up for you to leave no later than Wednesday the 27th, if possible."

Edwin received a telegram from Mr. Jarvis on Wednesday stating he would be in Chicago the week of December15th thru the 20th. The telegram also stated that he and I should meet in Chicago to sign our contract and that he would have all the information necessary for me to proceed. A second telegram arrived informing us that he was staying at the Pacific Grand Hotel and would be happy to have dinner on any night but Wednesday the 18th.

That was good news. Now I had time to learn about our belt business and would be better prepared to meet with Richard Jarvis. Leaving the 9th of December, I would be arriving in Chicago in plenty of time. Since

Mr. Jarvis had plans to stay at the Pacific Grand Hotel that would be my first destination with time to spare before our getting together.

I sure hoped Ray could teach me something about sales in two weeks.

CHAPTER 4

On Monday the 25th, Ray arrived at the front door and was ready to work at 7:00 a.m. I had spent two days last week at P&P Leather's plant and arranged for Ray to spend today with the floor personnel and also time with Robert Peterson on costs and what kind of margins he expected from us when dealing with all of his products.

We got into the buckboard for the two hour ride to the plant. On the way, I told Ray about the possibility of adding the Baxter Steam Engine to our line. He grinned and said he knew something about steam as he had worked for the railroad on engine repair for a little while after he left school.

That should be a plus for me with Mr. Jarvis, being able to have a salesman that was very familiar with his product.

"Ray, we didn't get to your pay when we talked. I would like to start you at 30 dollars a week and later put something like a percentage of sales to give you incentive. Can you live with this type of arrangement?"

"That's fine with me. I live with my mother. She is in good shape money wise so I help with our expenses and we live well. I can travel and not have to return because of family so trips out of town are not a problem. I love to sell and think I am good at it. People seem receptive to the easy way I present things. When we leave this belt company, I should be able to have a good story ready for our clients."

"Jack, with a steam engine and the drive belts, people will be looking for us more than we will be chasing them. Company's that need power will look us up, you watch."

Robert Peterson and Ray hit it off right from the start. They both had that swing in their step and confidence in their way of talking that made you want to listen and believe everything they say. Guess that was the appearance of a good salesman.

Robert was looking excited as he said, "Jack, that man will make me have to expand more than I was thinking would be needed last week."

"Just to inform you of our plans, another product we expect to have available is a small steam engine. If that happens, you'll surely be busy. Ray can't wait to have both products to sell."

"With that combination your agency should be very successful. You're getting me excited just thinking about it. California is going to grow, and power will be the thing that makes it happen. You're on a good course, Jack."

By 5:00 in the afternoon, Ray and I made ready to head for home. We fed our horse some oats before heading for the barn. It was getting dark when we arrived at Edwin's, feeling tired; however, after a little supper and a good night's sleep, we would put all we've learned to use starting fresh tomorrow morning.

Tuesday morning Ray was back at seven a.m. We had to buy Ray a horse and saddle today so he could travel around close to San Francisco. Edwin had plenty of room in his barn for another animal so we would keep it there. Ray's mother lived only three blocks from Edwin's so he said he would keep in better shape if he walked it every day.

By Friday, Ray had seen all of Robert's clients in the areas he could make with a horse. He suggested making a trip south for next week to call on some new business. Edwin agreed and suggested we move into the Sacramento area and north into the lumber mills. Wait 'til we have the Baxter engine to head south.

With all in agreement, Ray felt a good decision was made. Sacramento was the center of industry in northern California, and the lumber mills were growing to feed all of the expansion.

Ray planned a trip of two weeks to cover the territory, and I explained I was leaving for Chicago and would return the last week of December.

"Well, we should have the steam engine for the first week of 1873. We are going to have a good year in 1873. No, we are going to have a great year," Edwin said, and we decided our business was over for the day.

On Monday, December 9th, I left on a Pullman car much improved from three years ago and really enjoyed the trip to Omaha, Nebraska. Friday afternoon, I boarded a Chicago Central train for Chicago. After a restless night, Sam, my porter delivered the Chicago Tribune to me early the next morning before going to the dining car for breakfast.

. On the second page I found out what was going on in Chicago next week. The story was about Ned Buntline, the author of the dime novels. He told the reporter he had put together a play to be presented at Nixon's Amphitheater. The article continued by stating the show would feature Buffalo Bill Cody and Texas Jack Omohundro. This I had to see. I wondered if this is why Richard Jarvis was in town.

Sunday noon the train arrived in Chicago. I found a buggy ride to the Pacific Grand Hotel and checked in. Mr. Jarvis had not registered yet so I walked around the block to get the kinks out of my legs. I had heard the wind blew in Chicago, and now I could confirm it blows very cold. My bones felt the cold after a short walk so I hurried back inside, and after having an early dinner in the hotel restaurant, retired to my room.

Monday morning while I was walking into the hotel breakfast room, I was stopped by a server who asked if I was Jack Knight. He directed me to a table where a big man stood up and began with, "Jack, I'm Richard Jarvis. Sorry I missed you last night, but it was late when I got here so I thought it better to let you sleep and get a fresh start this morning. We have lots of time to talk. I'm looking forward to hearing what you can tell me about yourself, but let's order first since our server is right here."

The server standing by hurried away once she was told we would both have steak and eggs with biscuits and hot coffee. Then I felt it was time to give Mr. Jarvis an idea of who I was as we began to have our first cup of coffee while waiting on the rest of our breakfast.

"To start with, Mr. Jarvis, I have been on my own since I turned seventeen. I began as a bullwhacker for the H C & A Freighter outfit, then ran cattle on the Chisholm Trail for Colonel O. W. Wheeler out of Texas and lastly worked for Ben Holladay helping to build a railroad in Oregon.

I'm told I can sell buffalo hides to Indians but have only spent the last month in the sales game. My agency represents a large leather belting company and has had success so far. We have a good salesman with us now, and he is waiting to hear if we have a steam engine to represent along with the drive belts."

"Tell me, Jack, have you ever killed an Indian?"

A little astonished by this statement wondering what it had to do with my work back-ground, I answered, "Yes, I have been in eight shootouts with Indians, and a couple of times I hit what I was aiming at. But I have a hard time relating sales of your product with my ability to fight Indians."

"Just my own curiosity. You know our main line is guns, and I wonder if you carry one of our colts when in the west."

"You bet. I have a friend that used to sell your colt Navy .36 caliber. I was taught to be a gunsmith by him. Right now I carry the Navy .36 caliber when I feel the need of a gun. My favorite weapon is the bullwhip. I find it works well in cases when a gun is not needed."

"May I ask who your friend is? I know most of my larger customers."

"Sure. His name is Diego DeLacruse. He trained me for five years in his craft."

"He's in Denver, Colorado presently," Jarvis relates. "He sells a lot of hardware for the Colt Manufacturing Co. He also helped set up his brother-in-law as a dealer in Santa Fe, New Mexico. His brother-in-law has done well also."

"Back in 1863, when my family moved to Denver, my father, Richard Knight, talked with Diego about making the move with us since he thought Diego could further my education in learning to be a gunsmith along with giving me a greater knowledge of the world across the ocean. We all benefitted from his decision to move with us at the same time. He helped Denver grow and was a great asset to the town."

"Well, Jack, tomorrow night I will have the contract ready for our signatures, and we can finish our business and relax for a day or two."

"You mean you have confidence that I can represent your product from what we have talked about during breakfast."

"I go on gut feelings and haven't been led wrong so far. Your background is to never give up, and it shows. I'm sure your agency even as young as it is will be very prosperous. We might as well be a part of it."

Feeling good about the meeting, we shook hands as I left Richard Jarvis with a final remark, "I'm sure you have details we need to talk about, but let's read your contract tomorrow and see if we have a deal we can both live with."

CHAPTER 5

Tuesday afternoon, a packet of paper work was delivered to my room. I opened it and read the contract. Along with the four page document, Mr. Jarvis included pictures and specifications on all of the steam engines in their line. I wished Edwin could read this contract. To me it sounded like Colt Manufacturing had covered a lot of protection for their company. But as I read on, there was some protection for our agency and several incentives to go along with other legal stuff.

I had looked over our contract that Edwin and Robert had written and saw some of the same language in the Colt contract. Edwin said I would have to make the decision so I read the contract again and saw nothing that could hurt us as long as we performed to a minimal standard.

Tuesday evening, Richard Jarvis and I had dinner served in his room and had an hour discussion on the merits of the contract. After dinner, we both signed four copies; one for me, one for Colt's attorneys, and one for Richard's office, and finally, one for William D. Russell of the Baxter Steam Company.

"Now that our business is concluded, can I interest you in being my guest tomorrow night at a play being presented at the Nixon Amphitheater? Col. E. Z. C. Judson, better known as Ned Buntline, invited General Phil Sheridan and myself to his . . . what he calls a grand display. Bill Cody and Texas Jack are to be the stars. I have two extra tickets and would enjoy your company."

Pleasantly surprised by the invitation, I told Mr. Jarvis it would be my pleasure to accompany him stating, "Bill is a great friend of mine and I have met Jack."

"What a small world it is. How long have you known Buffalo Bill Cody?

"I have known Bill way before he added buffalo to his name. I guess I was twelve or thirteen when I first met him. He has been a family friend for many years. My father used to keep his horses shod for him. Texas Jack, I met three years ago on my train ride to the west coast just before my trip to Oregon to work with Ben Holladay."

"Wait a minute. I know Ben Holladay. Are you the wonder boy that took charge of his construction crew on the Oregon & California railroad? We were in New York City a couple of years ago, and he told me about this young fellow he hired to run his crew. Said you carried a bullwhip and knew how to use it too. I think he told me you carried your gun in the cross draw position so your whip could be at you right hand."

"Yes, that's me."

"Ben said he had never seen anyone so quick to learn. He said he was unable to get that project going, and you came in and had it humming along in less than three months. What kind of an education do you have?"

"I had formal school until I was fourteen. My mother and father taught me after we went to Denver, Colorado. I guess Diego DeLacruse taught me history and geography. The rest is just being blessed with common sense from a loving family I think."

"I must say you are one of the most unforgettable characters I have met up to now, young fellow. Sure would enjoy knowing your whole family. Your brother, Edwin, is a remarkable man also. He saved me a lot of money with his advice and put me on the path I follow now."

Slowly rising from the table, I reached my hand out for a parting handshake and said, "Sir, it's getting late. I know you have more business to deal with tomorrow so I will see you about six in the lobby tomorrow evening. Have a pleasant evening and thank you for the enjoyable dinner."

Wednesday morning, I sent Edwin a telegram telling him I signed the contract with Mr. Jarvis, and we could start business on January 1, 1873 as the western representatives for Baxter Steam Engine Company. Also included in the telegram, I was leaving Chicago Friday morning. I would be traveling on my twenty-fourth birthday next Tuesday and would probably be in Cheyenne on Christmas day.

Wednesday evening, as we were walking into the Nixon Amphitheater with General Phil Sheridan, Richard suggested we go back stage and see Bill before the show. Fortunately, General Sheridan talked him out of it by saying, "we don't want to pass some bad luck their way, now do we?" General Sheridan knew Bill as he had hunted with him. Richard Jarvis had not met Bill so he was a little anxious to meet his hero.

We were lucky enough to be seated in the second row center giving us a total view of the whole stage. A girl came out with a sign with print in large letters stating we were going to see "The Scouts of The Prairie" written by Mr. Ned Buntline.

The curtain opened and there was an old trapper sitting on a stump smoking a pipe. In a minute or two, Bill and Jack walked on stage and the trapper asked, "What detained you?" Bill looked around for a second and said, "I-I have been on a hunt with Milligan." The trapper asked him to tell him about the hunt. As Bill told his story of the hunt with much humor added, the audience broke into laughter several times. As Bill finished the story, the Trapper yelled "Here come the Indians," and Bill and Jack shot and killed all six of them. The curtain closed and the crowd of three thousand or so patrons went wild with applause.

The second act was entertaining but a little amateurish according to the morning *Tribune*. They heard Ned Buntline say he wrote the play in four hours and commented they wondered what he did the last three.

After the last curtain call and as the patrons were leaving, the General, Richard and I headed for backstage. Bill recognized the General and came to get us out of the crowd. He looked at me and said, "Jack? I didn't recognize you for a minute. Those clothes . . . and no bullwhip . . . it just didn't register at first, but the red hair gave you away.

General Sheridan, you have amazing friends. I recognize Richard Jarvis from his pictures. Nice to meet you, sir."

Bill guided us to a small room, and Texas Jack was cleaning make up off his face. Bill introduced Mr. Jarvis to Texas Jack and turned to me. Before he could speak, Jack said, "Bill, I met Jack Knight three years ago. I told you about our train ride together. Good to see you, Jack. You sure look prosperous."

Mr. Jarvis chimed in, "Buffalo Bill Cody and Texas Jack Omohundro in the same night. You guys are my heroes. I always wanted to be like both of you. The generals that I meet and deal with because of Colt Manufacturing keep me informed of your exploits. I really do dream of being your age and living the life you do. Jack Knight gets my attention also, and, yes, he is going to be as prosperous as he looks. He is going to represent one of our companies in the West." Richard continued, "Bill, are you and Jack giving up scouting and doing this full time?"

Texas Jack stood and replied, "Mr. Jarvis, we like what we do with the army and this we will do in the winter time if I can talk Buffalo Bill here into doing it."

Bill asked us all to go have drinks so we waited for him to remove his make up and all walked to the bar in the hotel where he had rented a room.

We had another hour of conversation and the General said he needed to get some sleep. Richard and I rose to leave with him as Bill said, "Jack, how long are you going to be in town? If you have time tomorrow, we could have lunch at the Pacific Grand Hotel. I assume you are there with the General?"

"That would be great, Bill. I will see you at noon tomorrow at the hotel."

At twelve o'clock sharp, Bill walked through the front door of the Pacific Grand Hotel. Several people ran to him for autographs and Bill obliged them. He saw me and we headed for the restaurant without further interruption.

"Sorry about that, Jack, but people expect me to do that. It used to bother me, but when they pinned Buffalo to my name I kind of got used to it. How have you been and what have you found to do that I don't see you anymore?"

"Well I punched cattle out of Texas for a time, went to Oregon and helped Ben Holladay put a railroad together. Now I have this sales agency in California and will be selling steam engines and leather drive belting for a start."

"Sounds confining to me, but then you lived a lot in your younger years and need to find something a little tamer as you age."

"Come on, Bill. I will only be twenty-four next week. I think I have a few more productive years left and I might find some more excitement someplace."

"What ever happened to that big black dog? What did you call him? Thor, as I remember. He was one fine animal."

"The last I heard, he is still alive and well with my sister, Mary Alice, in Kansas. She agreed that Thor was getting older and needed to be in one place. She also was beginning to be more possessive. Like Thor was hers instead of mine."

We ate our lunch and talked for two more hours. Bill said the play last night was a disaster. He forgot his lines, and the crowd made him feel uneasy. But he knew he could pull the act off now that he felt they liked him as an actor.

He and Texas Jack were going back to Nebraska in the spring and work for the army because the theater would be too dull year round for him.

Noticing it was about 2:30, Bill got up and said, "Jack it has been great seeing you and spending this time catching up, but I know Ned wants Texas Jack and me to walk through our parts again before tonight's presentation."

"I read the reviews in the *Tribune* this morning and saw the critics weren't very kind in their remarks of last night's performance. I wish there was time for me to see it again, but I'll look at the reviews tomorrow and take the paper with me for Edwin to read," Jack told him as they began walking toward the door.

"Thank General Sheridan and Mr. Jarvis for their attention last night, Jack. It has been great seeing you. Tell the folks hello for me and let's try to get together in less than five years next time."

CHAPTER 6

Thursday afternoon, I went to the railroad station to check on my ticket for Friday morning. Walking in, I saw an advertisement for the Kansas Pacific Railroad. It had a route to Denver from Kansas City in thirty hours. I knew the Kansas Pacific went thru Abilene making it possible to be at the horse farm by my birthday. Edwin and JAK Sales won't need me till the first of next year so I decided to go that way to see the family.

Two days later and four railroads traveled, I arrived in Abilene, Kansas. I took my bullwhip and gun from my case and put them on. I left my small suit case at the rail station and walked to the south side of town to Joseph McCoy's office located at his cattle pens. It was closed. I had forgotten it was Sunday and started looking for a livery stable. I heard a lot of noise to the south. It sounded like cattle and cowboys whistling. Walking back toward the pens, I saw Mr. McCoy making his way toward one of his gates to open it as his drovers prodded the cattle in that direction. He saw me and watched as I walked toward him, shaking his head and grinning from ear to ear a hearty welcome.

"Jack Knight!" He grabbed my hand, shook it vigorously while spouting out, "You're a sight for sore eyes. You sure don't look like the cowboy that left here, what three years ago?"

"About that. Sure is late in the year to run cattle isn't it, Joe?"

"Brought these up from Wichita, just to get them to a rail and onto Chicago, before the end of this year. What are you doing in Abilene? Oh, that's right . . . . Your family lives up on the Solomon River. You're home for Christmas. Right?"

"Yep, I had in mind to ride up the river. You wouldn't have a horse and saddle I could borrow or rent for a couple of day? I'll be heading back for Denver Thursday so I would need it for five days."

"Not a problem, Jack. There are several nice mares in the barn, and you can borrow my son's saddle. He's in Texas for another two weeks. If you got luggage, I can get you a buckboard."

"Only a small case at the rail station. It'll tie on the saddle easily, but thanks for the offer."

As the cattle started in the gate, Joe and I jumped onto the top rail of the pen. Joe was counting so I remained quiet 'til the last cow was inside.

"Seven hundred thirty-nine." Joe called out to the cowboys as they closed the gate. "I recollect old man Rutherford said there would be seven fifty."

"You're right, Mr. McCoy, but Curtis only sent four of us to run these cows up here, and two days ago nine Indians rushed in during a snow blow and ran off with nine head they'd roped and led away. Didn't seem smart to challenge them at the time and possibly lose the whole herd."

"You did right, Keith. Guess you can't blame 'em. We have run off or killed most of the buffalo they used to survive on in winter. There still is enough beef here to make a train load to Chicago this week."

Joseph, turning, motioned for me to follow. "Well, Jack, let's get over to the barn; get you fixed up with a horse and on your way before dark. I was up to the farm last month and bought six horses for a ranch near Salina. I must say . . . you sure have a nice family. Your aunt made me stay for a lunch that was better than any meal I would have had at a stage house on my way to Salina with the horses."

As we walked toward the barn, I told Joe about the journey I was about to embark on. He looked at me with eyes more like a father than a friend as he remarked, "Jack, you will be fine. You have all the skills needed to succeed. Most of all, your people skills will carry you through."

We picked out a buckskin mare which took the saddle easily, though a little spirited. Shaking Joe's hand, I told him I would be back after Christmas. Next stop the railroad station for my case.

It felt good to be riding again. I hadn't been on a horse since I left Oregon. Trains are fine but the smells of open country are much more appealing from the back of a good horse than in a Pullman car.

I was amazed at the buildings that had sprung up since my last ride to the farm. But a lot had happened over an almost three year period. The growth since the civil war had changed the west. Everywhere I went, I saw people settling new territory. I supposed I'd be a part of that change as my company provided steam engines for producing more items in less time and the railroad would get things to market in a timely manner. So much for dwelling on the economy of the times. That could wait until I got back to San Francisco.

Returning my thoughts to the present, it came to mind that unless Edwin had telegraphed the family, this would be a complete surprise for them. Let me think now. Mary Alice was fifteen last month. She probably looks like a woman now and not a kid.

It was dark when I entered the southern gate of the horse farm. Lights were on in Mother's house so they were probably eating supper. I guessed it best to just walk up and knock on the door.

Father came to the door with an oil lamp and looked past me to the horse at his hitching post. "Nice looking horse for a wondering and lost man to have," he exclaimed.

"Are you going to invite me in or do I have to yell for the woman of the house to welcome me?"

"Well, we don't usually answer the door after dark because of the demons that could get us and take us away to never-never land."

"Father, are we going to stand here and jaw all night or can I come in and have some of that stew I smell?"

"Come on in, son. Mother will be surprised and happy to see you. She's in a very good mood. She received a letter yesterday telling about Ida and Charles' new arrival. And it ain't a horse. It's a boy they named Fredrick William."

I saw Mother and Mary Alice get up at the same time I reached the dining room door. Mary Alice was eight inches taller than mother and filled out like an eighteen year old. Mother and Mary Alice both had their arms around me, and Thor jumped out of nowhere and had his paws on my arm.

As we all proceeded to sit down, Father grabbed my hand saying as he shook it, "Great to have you home, son. We really do miss our boys. Just so you know, Jay Parker is supposed to arrive tomorrow."

"Well, he didn't need to come home just for my birthday."

Mother looked at me a little misty eyed. "James, we are going to have a great week thanks to both of you boys coming home and being here at Christmas time. Now that I am a grandmother, I look forward to having more family around me."

Father finished eating and stood up against a wall and began to ask about Oregon. "Son, my brother James is talking about moving to the McMinnville, Oregon area next year. What does that part of the country have to offer?"

"Father, it seems you can grow anything in that area. That whole part of Oregon grows whatever is put in the ground. Some people say put a stick in the dirt and it will grow. I lived about thirty-five miles north of that area and went fishing on a creek near McMinnville. I noticed they were planting large orchards which were flourishing when I left."

"On the eastside of the Willamette Valley where we ran the railroad, they plant more grains and vegetables than trees. That whole state has people arriving from all parts of the country and if Uncle James wants to farm that would be a great place for him to move before all the good land has been taken."

"Speaking about the railroad. You wrote several times about how well it was going and all of a sudden you are in San Francisco. Did you and Ben Holladay have a falling out? You used to think so highly of him."

"Father, it was nothing like that. We completed rails to Roseburg in southern Oregon. Ben asked me to stay, but he was in no position to keep me. He was having some financial reversals but will come out OK. He put the Oregon and California Railroad into a bankrupt position to protect his timber and shipping holdings and the bank can operate 180 miles of railroad.

"I am very proud of what was accomplished in my time with Ben Holladay, but I felt it was time for me to move on."

CHAPTER 7

On Monday, Jay arrived at the farm before noon. He had a buckboard full of boxes and crates like he was delivering shipped goods to a mercantile store. When he saw me he jumped off the buckboard and hugged me saying, "Jack, it is good to see you're still in one piece. Looks like Oregon agreed with you."

Jay continued, "How is my friend Ben Holladay? He would be shocked to see what a company Wells Fargo has turned into since he sold out. We went through several years of decline but when Lloyd Tevis became President, ousted Fargo and made San Francisco the main office we have been growing leaps and bounds just this year. I now have six men in six different areas doing what I used to do by myself. I report to Tevis directly now but spend little time at the home office. Wells Fargo now has 396 offices and this is the first year in six that a dividend has been paid to investors. The railroad has been the leading gain for Wells Fargo and we are now a recognized bank also."

"Well, big brother, you have done alright considering you just wanted to drive a stagecoach for Ben Holladay when you started on this odyssey in '66. My office is in San Francisco now also. Edwin and I have a sales company and we represent one of Colt Firearms divisions and a leather belting company. Maybe now that I am President of a company Father and Mother will feel I am accomplishing more than just an existence in my life."

"You don't have to worry about that anymore," Jay said with more than a little pride in his voice, "Father and Mother are proud of what you accomplished in Oregon. You might not know it, but Ben wrote Father a letter last year about all you had done for him, and he said he was forever indebted to them for having created a genius at handling men and processes. No one ever has said that about the rest of us boys."

"Don't sell yourself short, Jay. Wells Fargo is one of the most successful companies in the country, and I believe the job you have with them has proven your abilities or you would not be where you are today."

By the time we got all of the boxes and crates unloaded and on Mother's porch, we saw Mary Alice riding up on Powder. Dropping quickly to the ground and laughing gleefully, she jumped on Jay's back for a piggy back ride.

"Look here, girl, you are too old for this horse anymore." Turning suddenly he falls to the ground pinning Allie at the shoulders. "You need to grow up." Before she can get over the surprise of what just happened, he helped her to her feet remarking, "What is this I hear about you and Bill Wheatley . . . the boy from the next farm up?"

"Oh Jay, he is too old for me. He is eighteen and all he talks about is bulls and cows. He could care less about girls."

"Allie, you watch out. If he ever stops to look at you, he will change his mind about girls and won't ever leave you alone."

As all this was going on, Powder walked over to where I was standing and started nipping on my shoulder with his lips like he did years ago. I had almost forgotten about this trick to get my attention. Powder would be fourteen next year. Mary Alice had taken good care of him and he looked very fit for a horse his age. Not to be outdone by a horse, Thor stepped up and started beating his tail on both of my legs while I stroked Powder's neck.

Mother came outside looking for all the commotion in her front yard. She put an arm around Mary Alice. "I want you to ride over to the Wheatley place and invite all three of them to dinner tonight. Tomorrow is Jack's birthday and Christmas is Wednesday. This will be the last day to get together with Tom and Effie until the boys leave. I have baked two big chickens so we have plenty. Tell them everything will be ready by 6 o'clock and we'll all make it a sort of a pre-Christmas celebration. Hurry up, now. Get Powder on the road before Effie starts to make dinner for them."

Mother walked onto the front porch and started looking at the crates we had stacked there. Jay headed her off, "Mother, now you stay out of that stuff. You can see it on Wednesday when I open the crates for your surprise and not until then."

Mother opened her mouth to speak then thinking better of it, went into the house and gave me a chance to ask Jay what was the surprise package he had brought home.

"Mother is one of the best cooks in the country," he explains. "She deserves to have the best cook stove available. I found this Inland Empire stove in Plano, Illinois. It has lots of nickel plate and two large warming closets on top with six stations on the cooking surface with two ovens. It's bigger than the stove she had in the Denver boarding house and it's pretty besides. It has a grate for coal if Father wants to buy coal for her. I'm expecting you to help me set it up Thursday for her."

"OK by me, but now let's get this horse and buckboard over to the barn. Then we can chase Father down and see what's going on in his world. He and I talked for a little while last night but Mother and Mary Alice always had something to add to his comments. You know sometimes it's good just to talk about man things without women folk around"

Even though the sun was shining brightly with no clouds in the sky, it was a cool day in December, although nice weather for Kansas this time of year.

Father was working at his forge when we walked into his small blacksmith shop. He dropped the length of iron into the forge and set his tongs on a bench to greet and hug Jay. "Son, it's great to have you here. There's time to sit down and jaw for a while before washing up for supper. You boys know I'm a grandfather now so I guess that means I can slow down. In the spring, after the snow is gone in the low lands of Colorado, I've been thinking of taking your Mother and making a train trip to Denver. We have never been on a train ride so it should be an adventure for both of us. I want to spend at least a week in Denver. It would take that long to see if our Ute friends are doing well and spend some time with Diego and Harvey, if he's at home. I haven't discussed this with Elisabeth but in a card on Christmas, I am going to invite her to go with me to see her grandson in the spring. What do you boys say to that?"

"She will love that, Father." Jay says.

As we continue our conversations, Father asked, "Jack, how are Edwin and Rose doing in a city like San Francisco? I fear a mixed marriage in a city like that can be troublesome."

"Father, Rose is a professional woman and as such gets some respect from the community that a squaw wouldn't. And if you knew Rose, you would see how anyone in his right mind would not call Rose a squaw. She carries herself with a self assurance you would not believe. She has taken cases to the Capitol and is respected in California as a very competent attorney in Indian and Negro affairs. No, Father, Rose and Edwin are fine and love one another very much. When you have what they have together it is hard to believe they cannot overcome anything. Edwin has confided in me that there are some places and some people they avoid but he and Rose don't let that effect them at all. You and Mother will love Rose when you meet her."

"Well I know what Jay does for a living but since you left Oregon what are you doing to stay out of trouble?"

"How do I start? Edwin and I have a sales company. He felt I should be the President besides being a salesman and expanding the sales territory. We sell leather belting for a company in San Francisco and the reason I am here in Kansas is because I have been in Chicago negotiating a contract with Colt Firearms to represent one of their divisions in the West. I have one salesman working now and with the Colt Division will probably have to have at least one more. As of January 1st we will have two to ten horse power steam engines to offer our customers in the West."

Putting his hand on my shoulder, Father ended our little group time with, "Son, for someone that never wanted to be tied down to an area or something, you seem to have put yourself and life in reverse. I wish you good luck. Be happy."

CHAPTER 8

At supper that night, Jay and I met William Wheatley. He reminded me of Jay and me when we were his age. One difference being he was settled with the land but had big plans that he and his father Tom were going to accomplish with the 640 acres they call Wheatland Farms.

William was curious about the cattle ranches in Texas and about the large drives that come up the Chisholm Trail to meet the railroad. He told me they have been raising about 300 cows a year but expected around 500 for next year's fall market. He informed me that they sold to Joseph McCoy in Abilene and he shipped all their beef to Kansas City, Kansas.

I noticed that William watches Mary Alice but always turns his head when her gaze is on him. This could work into something if I stayed around, but guess all I could do is tell William to work at it. I sure don't know what to tell him to say to her. I have had a hard time myself talking to a girl I might get a hankering to know.

Tom and Effie were much younger than Father and Mother, but they were close neighbors and got along quite well. Uncle John and Aunt Ann along with Tom and Effie Wheatley were Mother and Father's closest circle of adult friends. The next close farm house was over three miles away.

As the men migrated to the living room for coffee and Mother and Effie attacked the dishes in the kitchen, I noticed that William and

Mary Alice had walked out to the front porch. They seemed in serious conversation so I stayed with the other men. Tom spoke as I entered the living room. "Jack, I understand you helped Jim Bridger move from his fort in the Territory to his farm in Missouri back in '67."

"Yes, that was a great trip. A month after his household goods were sent by wagon, Jim, his wife and two children rode in the stagecoach of which I was lead driver. His son, Taw, would spell me when ever we found Jim asleep."

Tom stood to pour himself another cup of coffee and continues, "Back in 1862, I helped him reassemble that home. He bought that home in Pennsylvania took it apart and transported it to Westport by wagons. We spent ten months putting it back together. The money Jim paid me made the down payment on Wheatland Farm. I went by to see him last year when I was in City of Kansas, Missouri. He has quite a farm there. With all those kids, he has turned the whole farm into a vegetable farmer's dream. They grow everything from corn to radishes. He told me between both Kansas cities he sells everything he grows and sometimes he has to buy some back because his boys get over zealous and take too much to market. His health is holding up but has problems with his eyes. Says he can see alright but has given up reading because the printing looks like a black line on the paper even with glasses. His youngest son, Taw, is the only kid that has nothing to do with the farm. He is going to be a lawyer and wants to go back and help his people. I think Jim said he was half Shoshone."

"That's right. As I said Taw helped drive the stage when we came across Kansas out of Colorado. He would ride shotgun in flat country and I would give him the reins if I thought Jim and Mary were sleeping. Probably the youngest stage driver in this country. You would have liked the man he was named after. His real name was Walks Tall but everyone called him Taw. One day he out ran my horse on a fifteen mile run. He was one of the best runners I have ever seen. Jim said there was not a horse at the fort could out run him on any day. I wonder if he's still running that fast today."

Father got Tom's attention with a chat about some trees that needed to come down close to the river. His concern was if it flooded next spring, the trees would cause a problem on Wheatland Farm acreage or cattle pens. Not being interested with that conversation, I gazed out the window to see what Allie might be up to.

Watching the porch, I saw William has gotten Mary Alice to hold hands. Well, Jack, I was thinking, you can forget trying to help that situation. William has it all together for now.

Effie came in from the kitchen and says, "Tom, we need to head home its getting too late to keep these people up. Find your bashful son and let's go."

William heard his mother and both young people came in the front door.

As Father headed for the front door, Effie said, "Elisabeth, when your boys have left next week, I will have you and Richard for supper before the New Year. Ann and John said we were to all come to their house for a New Year's Day early supper to start the New Year right. Oh yes, Mary Alice, you be sure to come too."

William had already helped his mother to her seat while Tom took the feed bag from the horse pulling the buckboard they came in and lit the lantern mounted on the front of the buckboard.

When we were all back in the house, I just had to play the part of a big brother and got something started, "Mary Alice, I thought you said William was too old for you. It sure didn't look that way on the porch."

Allie turned red clear down to her neckline, "Jack, you mind your own business. William can be sweet sometimes but most of the time all he talks about is cattle."

Mother eased the tension by explaining, "Mary Alice is at a disadvantage out here on the farm. The town boys don't get this far out and her school is so small, it has no social life for the kids. We like William, but we sure aren't going to push the two of them together. Although, he is probably a good catch 'cause he works hard and he's not hard to look at."

"Tom would like the boy to become a horse doctor." Father said, "But he already knows more about cattle and horses than the fellow they used to have come to their farm to help with the animals. Tom says William reads every book and paper on animals and their nutrition that is available today and school would possibly be boring to him. Anyway he says he only is building the farm so William will have it later. He'd be a fine son-in-law any father-in-law would be proud to introduce as part of his family."

CHAPTER 9

Jay and I saddled up on Tuesday morning and rode the trails of the horse farm. It felt good to be on Powder. So good Jay agreed with me to ride over onto the Wheatland Farm and chase a few head of cattle around just for fun. Tom and William have done a good job with their herd. They segregated the young with their mothers and had the older cattle in large fenced off areas. We saw water was available in all areas, and around six windmills were pumping the water to the water troughs. This farm would make some ranches I had worked for in Texas look sad if you were to compare them.

We rode toward the large barn and William came out when we approached close enough for him to hear our horses. "What do think of our place? It takes a lot of hard work to keep it looking like a big time working cattle farm but it gives us a lot of satisfaction."

"William, you have what a lot of Texas ranchers would like to have; good grass, plenty of water and healthy livestock. I can understand the pride you and your father show in what you've accomplished with this land."

"Thanks, Jack. That means a lot to me coming from you. I love this piece of land and Father and I learn something every day about how to better work it and to keep improving our herds. Have you been up on the north end to see how we grow winter wheat? We have 150 acres of bottom land planted in winter wheat. That gives us enough grain to fatten our herd before driving them to Abilene."

Jay dismounted asking us to join him as he walked inside the barn. He noticed some grain sacks the right height on which to sit. He took one and motioned for us to do the same. We barely had gotten seated when Jay touched William's arm to get his full attention and said, "Bill, you don't mind my calling you Bill do you?"

William shook his head as he sat on a stack across from Jay. "We need to talk about our sister, Mary Alice. Now don't get the wrong idea. We're all for you two getting together so I would like to suggest your trying a more romantic way of speaking than always talking about cows and land. She's at the age when she wants to be treated like a woman and is a romantic at heart. I realize she was just fifteen a few weeks ago, but she's way ahead of most girls her age. She has worked like an adult since she was eight not because she was forced but her and mother were best friends. Mary Alice just wanted to be with her and worked beside her because she wanted to. Having read *Little Women*, and *Good Wives* more than once and daydreamed of the life of Jo, one of Louise May Alcott's main characters, you can understand why she's so romantic minded."

William has listened quietly but now spoke up before more could be said. "Jay, I hear what you say, and believe me, I want to be the only man in her life. We have talked about the future but both feel she should finish one more year in school. We even talked about marriage on her 16th birthday. I know how she talks she enjoys the land and would stay with me right here at Wheatland and be happy. So you see, I feel in this situation, there is more than you are aware of going for this guy."

Getting up quickly, he continued, "I want to show you boys something. Give me a minute to saddle a horse so we can take a ride over to the east."

As we rode straight into the sun for about ten minutes and climbed up on a plateau 300 feet above the land that slopes slowly to the Solomon River almost a mile west, William stopped his horse, dismounted and ran a square pattern while spouting out, "Mary Alice likes this area for a home for us and our family. See? Look south and you can see her mother and father's home and over there a half mile west of us is my folk's place. From up here, you can see all of Wheatland property clear to the north and all of your uncle's land to boot."

I had let Jay do all the talking up to now, but decided it was time to add my two bits worth. "Looks like we might be pushing something that needs no help from us, Jay, Bill seems to be way ahead of us on this courting thing."

William mounted up and said, "I guess I need to read up on how to be romantic, but I'm not sure that would seem like me to Mary Alice. On the other hand, if I move slowly she might not even know what is happening."

As our three horses headed north, I think two brothers felt a little foolish for being involved in something that was none of their business.

After another forty-five minute ride over Wheatland Farms, we returned to the large barn where we started. Thanking Bill for the tour, we headed for Mother's home. A porch full of crates and boxes were waiting for us with the kitchen stove to be assembled and set so she could cook our Christmas dinner tomorrow. The plan was to get it finished early enough today so that she can have the evening to see how it works.

"Jay, I sure hope you told mother to not build up the fire in her kitchen after she made coffee this morning."

"Yes, Jack, she had such a problem using the parlor stove for your coffee, I had to tell her what we were going to do this afternoon in her kitchen. She is just sure we won't put her kitchen back in order and says if we don't, we'll have to carry our food up to Aunt Ann's to cook it."

"Then we better get going so she doesn't have a hissy fit on my birthday."

The two of us were surprised when we got to the house and found Father had the old stove out of the kitchen and the floor mopped and ready for the new one to be set up.

Working with Jay to assemble and install the Inland Empire cook stove for Mother brought back a lot of memories of our time together building our livery and stables when growing up in Denver, Colorado. We worked together well and had always been able to know what both of our next moves should be. We finished in early afternoon, and Mother

41

just had to build the first fire in her new stove. The back door had to be opened to let the new smell of the stove escape to the winter winds. But then she was comfortable she would have Christmas dinner on her table with little difficulty and the family would have a fine day. Mother was careful to give the credit for the stove to Jay and was passive with Father's and my part in helping to assemble her new stove.

Mother seated herself at the table and excitedly said to father, "Richard, do you realize how much a stove like this would have helped Mary Alice and me if we could have had it in Denver when we had our boarding house? You can cook a whole dinner and keep it warm and ready to serve until it is mealtime. This can do the work that both stoves did at the kitchen in Booker's hotel. When Effie sees this, she will have to have one just like it. She was telling me that Tom is building a bunk house for a couple of men to stay in during their peak work months and Tom has suggested she cook evening meals for them."

"Well, it's about time the family gets some help with that farm," Father finally got a word in. "Tom and William work too many hours and as many acres and animals as they have they need two more men to help year round. It sure would be nice if you and I were younger, Mother. We could sure have a great time with a farm like Wheatland."

Mother raised her eyebrows while expressing her feelings on that subject, "Dream on, Richard, dream on, I have done my time with your dreams, and I like this one here just fine."

CHAPTER 10

Christmas morning had gotten here sooner than I had wished. My time here in Kansas was getting short, and I needed to start thinking about my trip back to San Francisco, besides learning about steam engines and industrial drive belts. My Uncle John surprised me when he and father took me for a ride in the buckboard and showed me a five horse power steam engine that they had installed by the river. The engine would be paired with a pump to move water to an area they wanted to keep grass growing year round. A particular spot they were planning to use to show horses to prospective customers.

Uncle John said, "Tom and William Wheatley are setting up a larger steam setup to transfer river water to a large pond they are going to dig in the middle of Wheatland Farms."

Father was grinning as we walk back to the horse barn. "Jack, I'll bet you didn't think us old farm boys were up on your new fangled machines. We might even get one of those new steam tractors we heard about. Saw one in Salina a few weeks ago. Maybe in a year or so they should have one with most of the kinks gone."

"From what I saw back there, Father, I guess JAK Sales needs to find a pump manufacture to represent also. The farmers in California are going to have to move water for their crops and orchards to have a profitable farm."

Father moved toward a bale of hay and sat down with a motion for me to have a seat next to him as Uncle John busied himself just outside.

"Son, we haven't sat alone and talked for several years. If you have time, I would like to just sit and talk about you and me."

"As a father, I feel I have had some success at raising four of the greatest sons a man could want. All four are successful in their chosen field and will add to the growth of our proud nation. You have accomplished more than most men have at twice your age. People, in time, will forget your name but not some of what you have done."

"My parents migrated to this country when I was thirteen years old. They were very poor Irish but one of my father's brothers killed his commanding officer in the English Brigade by running a sword through him accidentally and felt he would be persecuted and prosecuted if he were to stay in England. He literally ran home back to Ireland, and the whole family felt a move to the United States was something they should all do."

"The whole family came together and settled in Schoolcraft, Michigan. Godfrey, my father bound me out to a blacksmith for my board and room to make sure I would eat regularly and have a trade taught that I could use for the rest of my life. That was a practice poor families used to help raise their young."

"I feel I missed a lot of love and interaction with my family, and that is the reason your mother and I tried to take as much time and effort to raise our family as we did. From what we see now, we see it paid off well and we are very proud of what you all have done in your young lives."

"Father, believe me when I say, all of us are proud to be from your stock and all of us are as happy to have had the love and upbringing you and Mother gave us. Rest assured, we are all proud of the family name you graced us with. We both needed to say what was said here today but I think we knew how we felt before it was said."

"Well, son, that's enough of the mushy stuff for the rest of our lives. I just thought I should let you know how Mother and I feel about our boys."

Mother was ringing the dinner bell, so we summoned Uncle John and climbed back on the buckboard and headed for the house.

I drove the buckboard into Father's small barn and let the old timers go to the house while I put the horse away and fed her. As I started to leave the barn, Mary Alice grabbed me and wanted to talk.

"Jack, what do you think of Bill Wheatley for a brother-in-law? I know I am only fifteen but look at me,. I'm already grown up and feel like an adult in this body."

"Easy, little sister. You're talking about stuff way over my head. You see, I like girls and enjoy their company but have never found one I wanted to settle down with. You're talking about a total commitment for the rest of your life. I know how Bill feels about you. We took a ride with him up on the mesa to the east, and he told us about your dreams of a home over looking all this area. Nice dreams for young people to start a life together. Yes, I like Bill and think he'd make a fine brother-in-law. I understand you have lived a life ahead of your years just as I have and that is an advantage for the two of you. But remember, nothing I can say has any effect. It is your heart that tells you what to do."

"Anyway, Jack, in the books I've read, they tell about how you get a giddy feeling in your stomach and below that when you are in love. Sometimes I feel like that just being around Bill and when we kiss my body goes wild with the desires Mother has told me of. She says that she still has those feelings for Father even after more than twenty-five years. So I guess I really am in love with Bill because no other boy I've known has affected me like this." Looking pleading into my eyes, Mary Alice said, "Please Jack, can we keep this talk just between us? Other people might think I'm silly."

"Sure, but people that watch you two know something is going on. Hey . . . Let's go eat."

CHAPTER 11

At Christmas dinner, Mother's dining room was full. She had added two more leaves for the dinner table to accommodate all the fixings and nine people There would be Uncle John, Aunt Ann, their daughter, Mary Louise, son, John Jr., Jay Parker, Mary Alice, Mother, Father, and me. With all nine of us trying to talk at once it was quite loud. Mother served baked chicken, smoked ham, and roast beef. She sure put the new stove Jay got her to good use. On the side board, Mother had three different fruit pies and two kinds of cake for dessert. Looked like she had raided the root cellar for all the vegetable dishes she had cooked. I took a moment to relish the happiness and gratefulness of being among family for this Christmas celebration.

As everyone finished with the bounty in front of us, Mary Alice and Mother got up to serve the pie and cake. The shy one, Mary Louise, tapped on her water glass and stood up.

"Now that I have all of my family with me, I think it's time to tell you of my plans for the coming year. If I recall correctly, all of you have met Lloyd Applegate. He has been to the farm several times since I went off to Kansas State College four years ago and we have communicated even while I was away. Well, anyway, I will be twenty one, January 12th next, and Lloyd has asked me to marry him and move to New Jersey where his people have a very large potato farm. He will receive his degree in agriculture in May and is looking forward to returning to the farm to better help it prosper with the skills he has learned the last four years."

"Anyway, you have John Jr. to take over the horse farm and he will do great without any help from me. I know . . . I know . . . New Jersey sounds like a long way from Kansas but the rail road goes both ways now so it really isn't that far anymore."

Mary Louise gazed wistfully but determinedly at Uncle John. "Father, I'm sure by the way you are looking at me that this is a surprise for you as Lloyd has not formally asked you for my hand in marriage, but the next time he is here at the farm he plans to discuss with you this plan of ours and ask for your blessing."

Uncle John grinned like a cat with a mouse cornered before he allowed Mary Louise the knowledge that he knew more than she thought. "You think Lloyd comes down here for a couple of days from Manhattan and we don't talk about you? We have gotten fairly close and I'm of the opinion he's a good catch for you. Mother and I wish New Jersey was closer but women are supposed to follow their husbands, and his destiny is that farm in New Jersey. He has made sure I knew what he has planned. How you and he talked about what lies ahead in his future. Mother and I will be more than happy to welcome him into our family."

"Mommy, does that mean when Mary Louise gets married, Lloyd, I mean Mr. Applegate, won't get to sleep with me when he comes to visit?" asked John Jr.

Aunt Ann responded with "Son, that's the way the world works. I'm sure Lloyd would prefer to sleep with his wife if given the choice of you or her."

Jay pushed his chair from the table, winked at me and said, "Jack, it's time we plan our escape from this home for wayward lovers and get back to reality. I need to get to Sacramento, and we could ride together if you could go through Denver and stay overnight. You can ride back to Abilene, return the horse to McCoy, catch the train and meet me in Salina. After I return the buggy and horse I rented, I'll catch your train, and we can be on our way to Denver."

"Sounds reasonable and would give a little more time for catching up. Hope you have a train schedule because I forgot to pick one up when I left Abilene."

As we walk out of the dining room, he half guided, half pushed me to the back door and out onto the porch. "Jack, I didn't want to say anything at dinner but you need to hear this. The telegram I received last night was more than a schedule change for me. It also told me that the Modoc Indians and the Army are at odds up in southern Oregon and northern California. Some Indian named Captain Jack has got his band of Modoc on a rampage of some kind. I need to get to Sacramento and on up north to see what's going on with our stations in the area."

"Well, big brother I guess that's why Wells Fargo pays you so many pieces of gold. Let's get that train schedule and see when it's best to get out of here. You still have some business to take care of in Denver?"

"Yes, I need to lay over and check a couple of things out. That can give you some time to see Diego and Charles, if you like. I won't have any spare time but you can represent me for both of them. Charles and I did some fishing a couple of months ago so we are up to date on most things in our lives. You remember the Christmas Diego and Margo gave me the gun and holster? We talked about fishing sometime then as you should remember. He and I have had several trips up to the high lakes and we got to know one another a lot better. Now I understand why you treasured your time with him."

As we started to go back into the house, Father came out on the porch. "I'm sorry you boys have to leave so soon. Your mother is going to miss you. She is so happy when any of her boys are around. Can't be helped though. Tell everyone hello for us in Denver and you can give them fair warning your Mother and I will be by in the summer."

Jay headed for his room to get the train schedule and returned so quickly it seemed he hadn't left informing Jack, "You need to be at the train station in Abilene by 9:50 a.m., and the train should be in Salina to pick me up around 11:05 a.m. You think you can ride to Abilene in two hours? That means you need to leave here by 6:00 in the morning."

When I really thought of all I had to do, I realized I needed to ride out no later than 5 o'clock in the morning to get there, return the horse to McCoy and get to the station.

"No, Jay, I have to leave the farm at least an hour sooner. That will be no problem. I usually am an early riser and the road should be easy to follow in the dark with all the stars out. I should be on the train when it gets to Salina bright eyed and bushy-tailed."

We both returned to Mother's dining room and headed for the sideboard for a couple of pieces of fruit and berry pie. "Folks, it has been a wonderful birthday and Christmas for me but Jay and I have to leave early tomorrow and head for Denver. With any luck at all, I should be in San Francisco by Tuesday and ready to start my march as a salesman for leather belts and steam engines. Mother, thank you for the pounds I have gained while here and all of you know I love you and wish you all the health and wealth you can handle until we meet again."

Thursday, I woke up early, well before dawn, shaved and dressed for the trip. As I packed my small case with my clothes and gear, I started to put my gun and whip in the case but stopped for a second and slipped the belt with the holster and whip attached around my waist. It felt good so I left it on. Blowing out the lamp, I woke Jay and let him know I'm leaving as I trip over the chamber pot in the dark. Good . . . it's dry since neither Jay nor I had to use it last night.

While I tried to slip out of the house without a sound, passing through the kitchen to the rear door, Mother lit a match for the lamp startling me, "Thought you could get away without a kiss for your Mother did you?"

"Good morning, pretty lady! You should be in bed but nice of you to see me off." `

Kissing Mother and giving her a big hug, I explain that I gotta go. "See you later in the year when we both have more time." I ran for the barn and saddled the horse for my ride into Abilene and the train, trying not to allow the empty feeling that comes so often when leaving a loving home to engulf me.

CHAPTER 12

The three hour ride to Abilene was a cold one even though I wore the oil cloth slicker that was tied to the saddle. It was early but I figured Joseph McCoy would be in his office because yesterday being Christmas, I figured he'd spent time with his family. Getting closer, I could see smoke coming out of his chimney and two horses tied to the hitching post in front of his office. I tied the buckskin at the hitching post and walked to the office door. Loud arguing and angry voices came from inside the office. I lifted the oil cloth slicker's long tail around to get under my coat to get hold of the bullwhip on my right hip. Quietly opening the door and stepping into the room, I saw one man had his gun drawn and the other man had no gun so I instinctively looped the whip around the wrist of the man with the gun, jerking his hand; making the piece hit the wall. McCoy reacted just as fast by pulling a gun out of a drawer, commanding and holding both men still where they stood.

Not taking his eyes off the two, he greeted me in the casual manner of a man who has handled more than one difficult situation. "Howdy, Jack. Nice of you to drop in just now. Ben and Oliver here feel I shorted them on three horses I bought from them last week and want me to give them double the price. Now that we can calmly talk about it, possibly we can come to an agreement that satisfies all of us. How about it, Ben? I agree they are fine stock, but you both were a bit drunk when I bought them from you and you really wanted the one hundred and fifty dollars

I offered for all three of them last Friday. Tell you what. I can go 25 dollars more for each, but believe me, that's about what I can sell them for. How about it, men? Does that sound fair enough?"

"Okay, Mr. McCoy that will help. Oliver and I apologize for our hasty action, but we both felt you took advantage of us in our condition."

"You boys are lucky that was Jack that walked in. Other people might have used a gun instead of a bullwhip, and you would be on the floor. Here is your seventy-five dollars. Now be on your way, and let's just forget this ever happened."

Ben picked up the money off the desk, bent down, got his gun off the floor and both men sheepishly walked out of the office.

"Thanks for the help," McCoy commented as he took a deep breath. "I'm not sure the outcome would have been so good if you had not intervened." He explained that Ben and Oliver worked on a farm down the Solomon River and only came to town to drink and what ever. "Guess they are not bad people," he said thoughtfully, "but I sure won't do anymore business with them."

Not sure of the time, I felt I should be getting on my way "Thanks for the ride and use of the saddle, Joseph, but I need to get your buckskin back to the barn and myself on up to the train station. You go ahead with whatever you have to do. I'll take the horse to the barn and put the saddle where you keep it." Striding toward the door, I turned for a final farewell. "Not sure when I'll be back in this part of the country, but it has been good seeing you. Good day."

By the time I walked to the train station, I discovered there was still time for some breakfast and a cup of coffee. The little diner next to the station was warm and had several people also eating and drinking coffee while waiting for the train to arrive.

The train was a half hour late but I assumed this was not abnormal from the grumbling I heard from some of the passengers loading onto the cars. My mind wandered to my brother who was expecting to join me at the next stop which was Salina. The train being late should allow for Jay Parker to have time for an extra cup of coffee and to relax a little after his buckboard ride from the farm.

The hour and fifteen minute ride to Salina was uneventful and cold. As the train arrived at the station, peering through the window, I could see Jay, and he had what looked like a couple of blankets under his arm.

After he boarded and found me in the second car, he threw me a blanket. "Jack, I brought these 'cause I ride these trains a lot and have come to know a blanket helps to keep warm. Figured you weren't used to the necessities so took two of Mother's just in case."

"While I was having my third cup of coffee waiting on the train to arrive, I caught up on the Indian struggle up in northern California. Jack, it seems this guy, Captain Jack, is reported to be a little on the crazy side. The army was sent to an area called Lost River up in southern Oregon to move him and his band of Modoc Indians to a reservation where the Klamath Indians are settled. The Klamath and Modoc tribes have never been friendly but Captain Jack agreed to the move late in November. I hear tell this feud between the Klamath and Modoc tribes goes back several years to the '60's when they were on the same reservation around Fort Klamath. Sounded like everything was going well on the transfer until Captain James Jackson with a detail of forty troopers came to move the Modoc and asked them to disarm. Captain Jack had never fought with the army and was alarmed at this command. One of the Modoc sub-chiefs, Scarfaced Charley, pulled a pistol and shot at a Lieutenant. He missed but a short battle erupted and a soldier and two Modoc Indians were killed. Captain Jack and a lot of the Modoc tribe retreated and headed for an area around Tule Lake in northern California called lava beds. Besides that, early this month, a militia group from Linkville, Oregon was ambushed by the Modoc Indians on the outskirts of the lava bed Stronghold and all 23 men of the militia were killed. This could go on for a long time. But sounds like the trouble will be confined to the Tule Lake area. Having a station in Linkville, Oregon, and one in a town near Tule Lake, California is making it necessary for me to go up there to be sure there is protection provided if needed."

"Well good luck, brother. Let's hope that will be the last Indian trouble in California as far as uprisings. Edwin's wife, Rose, feels the Indians in California will start using the courts more to settle their disputes against the whites because they're finding out they can't fight the over whelming surge and advancement of the white man."

The train was now moving along at a reasonable pace and as the day progressed, the car warmed from the chilly beginning we had had at the start of our day. It was almost 100 miles to Hays, Kansas, a town large enough to have a short stop for something to eat. With the blanket for a pillow, I found myself able to get some more sleep, and it felt good even from a sitting position with my boots on the bench seat facing me. I opened one eye to see Jay Parker had fallen asleep also. I guessed the last couple of days of fast living did us both in but it was a great visit with the family and the loss of sleep was worth it.

I awoke with Jay pushing on my shoulder. "Wake up, Jack, I think we can get something to eat here in Hays. Last time I was here they had hot cakes all day with several kinds of jam and jelly to put on 'em. Not as good as Mother's but when you can't have hers they're the best I've found so far."

"That sounds good. Sure did sleep for a while. Must of caught up to me."

After two stacks of pancakes and three cups of coffee, we boarded the train for our final leg to Denver. Early Friday morning was when we expected to reach Denver so the boring part of this trip was just beginning. Not really complaining though. This was really the best way to travel for stagecoaches and horseback are just too slow anymore.

"How was Cody doing when you saw him in Chicago?" Jay asked after we re-boarded the train and got settled in our seats. "I haven't seen him myself for around three years. We ended up in a saloon in Cheyenne one night and we got into a friendly poker game with some locals. We ended up walking away with a couple of double eagles more than we started with. Jack, the attitude of the guys in our poker game was totally amazing. They all lost something but were real gentlemen about it. Bill told me all games like that don't end as well as that one did in his recollection. We talked 'til midnight with a bottle and after retiring for the night, I haven't seen him since."

"Well he's looking at a new career. He and Jack Omahondra are play acting with the fellow that writes those dime novels you see around about the West. Says they will do that in the winter and scout for the Army in the summer. I saw the first display. It had some problems but was entertaining and the crowd liked it. The next day I had lunch with

Bill and spent about two hours together catching up on both our lives before he had to get back to practice his new craft. He and Jack are planning to go back to Nebraska in the spring to some Army post to do some scouting for them."

The clacking of the iron wheels as they hit the seams of the metal track put a rhythm in my head that almost lulled me to sleep, but Jay continued to want to talk about my new business and where I expected it to take me.

I give him a little overview of our plans. "Edwin and I think the best way to market our products is through hardware and machine brokers. My first trip next year is to Sacramento to see Huntington, Hopkins and Company. They seem to have a good handle on the market and have stores in Weaver Creek and Mud Springs. If I can get steam engines in that store, they have salesmen all over the Sacramento valley both north and south. The amount of growth in small industries in that state should make small steam packages a real boom. I'm thinking the transfer of water with steam driven pumps will boost the farms and orchards in the central valleys south of Sacramento also. Right now, we have one salesman besides me, and he is a real professional and knows about steam engines." I noticed Jay's eyes were beginning to droop a little.

"Sounds like a good start to me. Jack, this train is putting me to sleep. Think we can sleep all the way to Denver?"

"If we did not stop, I think I would. But I wake up every time the train stops. No matter, after a short time the rhythm of the wheels puts me back to sleep."

CHAPTER 13

We both awoke around daylight and learned from the conductor there were still three more hours of travel 'til we see Denver. Jay looked at me with a twinkle in his eye, reached into a pocket and pulled out a deck of cards, shuffled them on his knee and dealt us both five cards.

"We've got plenty of time to kill. Put a dollar up and see if you can beat me."

"Come on big brother, you play a lot of poker and I have avoided any type of gambling. I still remember you beating me every time you talked me into a game when we were young boys. I figure you showed me back then gambling wasn't something I could make a living doing and it's saved me a lot of silver dollars. Each time the notion strikes me, that memory crops up to change my mind."

"What do you do with your time when you're not working? You don't drink and no gambling. I know you chase a girl once in a while, but that never lasts very long. You're getting too old to play with that bullwhip you still carry on your side. Must be something that makes you tick?"

"In case you haven't noticed, Jay, I read something almost every day. It doesn't have to always be serious. It can be fiction novels, sometime, history and biographies of people that have made our country what it is today. Mother was my guide when it came to books and I find more enjoyment with them than anything else other than exploring some place I have not been. I even read some of those dime novels just to keep up with the times."

"Did you know I have kept a journal, Jack, of some of my travels along with tales I hear about the family? Some day you might like to read them. About our family, it has been a real journey for some of us. If anything happens to me, I want you to have my scribbling."

Listening to his words, it crossed my mind that it was amazing what you find out about a person when you spend time with them. I would never have thought Jay Parker of any of the family to be the one writing a journal of his travels and experiences. One day when he is famous we could trace his life and maybe even write a biography. He must have thought my attention had gone elsewhere since he spoke a little loud as he touched my arm.

"Hey, Jack . . . today is Friday. Charles will be at his shop, let's go down and see if we can stay at his home overnight. If he's agreeable, I can ride back to town and finish my business by early afternoon, and if that works out, we possibly can catch a few fish with Charles in the river that runs in front of his place. You're not going to spend over a couple of hours with Diego, are you?" Without giving me a chance to answer, he said, "I've heard there are some nice trout in that riffle just passed that bridge we helped build several years ago. We can just catch and release if Ida has another idea for dinner."

"Good idea, always nice to have a plan. If you decide you need to go directly to work when we get in, I can ride down and set it up with Charles. The closest place to get a couple of horses will be from that livery down the street from Diego's place. When we rent the horses, to save time, we should make arrangements to return the horses in the morning before it's time for the train to start boarding for Cheyenne. You go get your work done and I'll take care of the rest. Agreed?"

"Agreed," Jay responded as he leaned back trying to relax and I couldn't tell by the look on his face if he was thinking of the fish that didn't get away or of the job he has to do when we get to Denver. I decided to spend some time gazing at the land which seemed to be going by my window faster than earlier.

The train was traveling at a higher speed now that the land was reasonably flat. The mountains on our left were covered with snow and it was a sight I had forgotten about. The Rocky Mountains west of Denver were gorgeous with snow on them and at this time of year they were solidly white and looked so clean and fresh. I loved this country and really had planned to return here to roam those mountains and maybe search for gold or some mining possibilities, but then Edwin, had some power over me and I guess I felt comfortable with his recommendations. I found it hard to believe how the wide open spaces south of Denver were being settled like they are. A little village here and there sprung up to provide miners and farmers with supplies. That would in turn support the growth of Denver as it expanded to help support the west.

The train began slowing down for Strasburg, Colorado, and Comanche Crossing. This was the site in late 1870 that the rails were connected to make a continuous rail from New York to San Francisco. When the connection was made at Promontory Point, it just connected Omaha with Sacramento, California. It was about 35 more miles to Denver. Being so close to our destination, we might as well have stayed awake and enjoy the ride.

Friday morning would be a busy time at the train station in Denver. Our train of five cars had 80% of the seats occupied and I imagined a lot of them would stay in town for at least a day or two even if they don't have a home there. As for me, it had been over three years since I saw Denver. Hope I could recognized some parts of it.

"Jay, where is your office?"

Jay turned away from the window seeming glad for some conversation. "Wells Fargo took over the office Ben Holladay had built . . . added to it for the Express Unit. The Wells Fargo Stage route was sold to Jack Hughes back in late 1869 so we don't run coaches out of Denver any longer. Can you believe that there are 8 stage lines out of the town now? They go east, south, and two lines run west into the mountains and the old gold camps."

He went on to explain, "Wells Fargo Express ships the gold and silver ingots that are processed by Denver Smelting and Refining Works. That outfit is new to you as Judge Hiram Bond, Joseph Miner, and Joe Bates set it up and all assaying, weighing, and stamping of the products are done by the Denver Mint. Remember Hershel, Harvey's brother that went to work at the mint? Just so you know, he's a big wig there now and I see him about any details for all shipping we do by rail or coach."

"Freeman, Hershel's youngest boy works for Wells Fargo Express and seems to have a great future carved out with us. He is a hustler and never seems to stay in one place very long."

Changing the subject to get Jay back to the here and now, "Jay, I think after I set up our fishing escape with Charles, I'm going to ride on out and try to see Harvey and possibly one of the boys. I sure miss that family. They were good to me when I was getting started. Betsy made some good meals for me when I worked for that outfit and I remember she always cooked for Thor too if we were in the bunkhouse."

"Jack, I couldn't help watching Thor back at the farm. He appears to be slowing down and lays around a lot more than he used to. Would you say he's close to fifteen years old now? Sure has been a good dog for a long time. I expect you're going to get a lump in your throat when he goes?"

"I know it has to happen sometime, but I think he has had a good life for a dog. And he brought a lot of happiness to me and to Mary Alice. You know he was one of the best cattle working dogs any of the cattlemen in Texas had ever seen. Yep, he was a natural when it came to cattle and people. Never told you the story about Thor when we lost Able up in the Territory. Thor never left Josh for two days or nights. It was like he knew the heartache he was going through and wanted to help him wash it away. Animals have a process they go through just like people I guess."

The train whistle was blowing and slowing down as it got close to our destination. Jay was right. I could see Denver had grown and the station was located out of town when I was last here. Our enthusiasm was welling up when we stepped down from the train ready to get this show on the road and get us both a horse to ride. For late December, the weather was cool but fair and in our favor of our getting done everything we talked about.

After locating the new livery stable across the street from the train station, we discovered the owners and operators were the two oldest boys of Hershel Bendickson, Harry and Lewis. They had grown into big men and sure are different than when we came across the country to Denver. Lewis must have learned more than we thought during the time he worked for Jay and me at the old livery on Cherry Creek. The design of this livery was almost the same as what Jay and I had put together only larger. These boys were good.

Both saddled a horse and Lewis said. "Hope this place looks familiar to you guys because we tried to copy what we knew had done well and we were right. It has worked alright for us and we think it was because of you and what you tried to teach us that made us what you see today. Many thanks to you both."

Turning toward me, Jay said, "Jack I think we just were complimented on something that came natural to us. I'll bet your whole family is as proud of you as we are. Probably more."

I checked my saddle chinch and mounted up. "Jay, meet me at Charles' home when you finish what you have to do. I'm going over to Diego's, if I can still find my way around. I'll only stay for a short visit then ride on up river to the blacksmith shop."

I found Diego's shop and looped the reins on his hitching post. He was working on something that needed a lot of light and was at the front window looking out as I rode up. A big wide smile came over his face making his mustache spread across his whole face. He ran to the door and as he opened it I heard him yell, "Amigo, what a great surprise. Come in and sit for a spell and tell me about the family."

"They are all fine and enjoying life with all the horses they can stand. Mother is as happy as I have ever seen her, Father is still shoeing horses everyday, and Mary Alice, has grown into a beautiful young lady. Jay is here in town today doing some work for Wells Fargo, and I'm headed up river to see Charles and his new son, Fredrick. Might ride on up and try to see Harvey Bendickson if I have time. That about brings us to now. How is Margo doing?"

"She is fine and not working but Monday and Tuesday's anymore. We have a Black that does most of the leather work now except for the bridles. Margo still thinks she is the only person that knows how to make a bridle. A lot of the customers think she is right so she continues working at least two days a week."

"Jack, do you remember Richard Jarvis? I got a letter just yesterday from him from the Colt Arms Company. He told me you are doing some business with him next year. You know I have never met Mr. Jarvis but we exchanged several letters when I was trying to get Margo's brother set up with the Colt brand. He must be one of the good ones to have searched you out and I can say he has been a great benefactor to me and my brother-in-law. Most of the big companies have reservations working with the Spanish and Mexican businessmen, but not Mr. Jarvis. He treats everyone the same. Must be a heck of a good man."

"Tell me, Jack, ever work on any guns? Don't let your talent go to waste. You need to keep up with what is going on with the gun industry. Mr. Jarvis tells me he will be getting back to me early next year with news about a new piece they are coming out with that will change the handgun forever. Don't let yourself get behind on this stuff."

"Well Diego, right now, Richard Jarvis has got me saddled down with the steam engine. Edwin and I have formed a company to represent manufacturers that need sales expansion to build their base and expand the business. We have a leather belt company and the steam engine so far. Lately, I've begun to see we need a water pump manufacturer. Then we will have complete packages for the farms and orchards that are cropping up all over the west. I have one salesman beside myself but it looks like we'll need another when we get off the ground."

Feeling my time for visiting with Diego had been longer than intended, I mounted my horse to leave, "I need to ride on. It has been great seeing you and wish I had more time to spend with you and Margo, but Jay and I have to leave on the train in the morning. Maybe I will have time for a cup of your coffee before the train leaves though. What time do you come in here Saturday?"

"I open at 7:00 so come on by. The pot will be hot and the coffee's strong as you remember."

CHAPTER 14

The ride through town and up the South Platte River was eye opening. Denver had spread out farther in all directions than when I was last here. A bridge had been built over the river just south of Cherry Creek so there would be no more splashing to get across the water and up onto the old compound and the road to the new blacksmith shop. The brick building that Terrance Grant developed for Charles was impressive. Columns had been added at the corners to stay in character with the other buildings of the area. They were mainly brick and also had columns added. Made for a nice looking addition to South Denver as Mr. Grant liked to call this place.

Another change that was quickly apparent in South Denver was no hitching posts. They had installed rings on the walls of the building to tie your reins on. Some of the people living here seem to want a San Francisco looking city. At least, it looked like they were trying.

As I opened the door at what I thought was a blacksmith shop, I found myself in an office having a lady sitting at a desk writing in some books just like you see in a legal office.

"Excuse me, I thought this was the Knight Blacksmith shop."

"It is sir. How may I help you?"

"I'm looking for my brother, Charles. My name is Jack, his wayward little brother from California."

"Oh yes, you look just like he said except you seem very well dressed for a drifter. He said you didn't stay in one place very long, but the red hair and bullwhip gave you away. I am Georgene and I take care of all Mr. Knight's books and paperwork. His business has grown this last year giving him little time for this kind of work so I answered his add for a secretary bookkeeper and he graciously hired me." Raising her arm and pointing to a door in the corner, she stated, "You can go through that door and find him in the shop area or I will go and find him and let him know you are here if you think you might get your clothes soiled looking for him."

"Georgene, thanks, but I think I can find him alright."

I guess I should have told her that I was the president of JAK Sales Company of California but why burst the little bubble she had formed of me.

Walking through the door, the old smells of the shops my Father had overwhelmed me bringing back memories of home. The coal fired forge and the hot iron smells were always the same in any blacksmith shop. I headed for the back of the shop and the forge area and saw Charles working on an iron wheel cover. He was so intent on the hot iron in front of him that he had no idea I was watching him work.

Finally, I yelled between the blows of the hammer, "Charles lets go fishing."

Recognizing my voice, Charles whirled around and yelled back, "Well, if it looks like a Jack it must be a Jack. How you doing boy? You're a sight for sore eyes. Let me put this iron in the oil pan over there and we can talk. Noisy in here, let's go out back and have a seat where it's more comfortable."

We walked through a door and entered a small patio I guessed was made for lunch time for the workers.

"Charles, I must see five other blacksmith's in here. What's going on? These guys all work for you?"

"You ain't seen nothing yet. Wait 'til I get my machine shop operating next door. I'm getting two lathes, two milling machines along with a couple of large drill presses. South Denver is growing so fast a large machine shop is needed, and it might as well be me that has it. That building next door has seven thousand five hundred square feet, and

I just put a down payment on it. Mr. Grant sold it to me because he wanted money to develop the other side of the river. After I get the machine shop running I'll try to buy this building from him too. What do think of the idea of the machine shop?"

"Why ask me? Sounds to me like you have the whole thing lined out in your mind and you know I am for progress. Hey, Jay is in town doing some work and will be out here later. I had time to see if you have room at the house for both of us? And we would like to take you fishing this afternoon. By the way what are you going to use for power in the machine shop?"

"First things first, Okay? We have lots of room at the house for the both of you. Ida has been putting together a guest room and let me know just this morning that it is finished. She heard that Father and Mother might be coming in this summer so she wanted to be ready for them. When you leave from here are you going to ride up the river and see Harvey? If you are, stop and let Ida know you guys are in town and need a place to stay. Tell her we plan to catch fish for supper and I will be home about 3 o'clock this afternoon."

"Now as for my power, I hear you can buy steam engines in the 10 horse power range and feed them with coal or wood. Got a couple of catalogs at the house to look at if you're interested. Figure if I get two of them and set them up on opposite sides of the shop I would have all the power needed and have my overhead drives divided so only use one engine as needed."

Charles and I both sensed it was time for me to leave and for him to get back to work so he walked me back around to the front of the shop. While mounting my horse, I told him, "I'm going to ride up the river for a little while and will see you at your house around 3 o'clock. Don't order those steam engines today. We need to talk."

The ride to Ida's home was pleasant. Sure would have been nice to have Thor with me to chase a couple of rabbits. The river was running about right for fishing . . . clear and cold. Several nice homes had been built since my last trip up here. Charles picked a great area to build his house. Cold memories come back as I crossed the bridge Jay and I helped build. Not much of a bridge next to the ones Artimas York had to construct for the railroad but a fine bridge anyway.

I saw Charles had two white boy jockeys with rings in their head for his hitching posts so I looped the reins in one and walked up his rock path to the front door and knocked. Ida greeted me with a big kiss on the cheek and dragged me into the house.

"Jack, you look mighty prosperous. To what do we owe this long overdue visit?"

"I just happened to be passing through on my way back to California; I have been in Chicago, Illinois on business and met up with Jay at the horse farm so we're traveling together to San Francisco. We thought we might talk you out of a bed to lie on if we begged a little."

"I got a notion Charles already told you about the spare bedroom I've been fixing up. But we'd find a place for you and Jay even if I hadn't."

"Thanks, Ida for being such a great sister-n-law. Anyway, Charles said he would be home around 3o'clock and take us fishing to catch yours and our supper if that is agreeable with you." Looking around and listening for sounds of a youngster I realized how quiet the house seemed. "Where is that little one? Fredrick, I heard you call him. Mother can't wait to get a hold of him."

"He's asleep, but he will be up in all his glory this afternoon. He is like his Father, an early riser and takes a nap this time of the day. You going to ride up the river to see the Bendickson crowd before you leave? They won't forgive you if you fail to go by."

"Yep, I'm headed up there now. Just needed to stop and give you our plans since you have to cook for us. Hope all this is not going to interrupt any plans you had?"

"No, Jack, just glad you boys take time for the family. Jay gets by every now and then but we don't see Edwin and you enough. Now ride up and see Harvey and Betsy. They are both home. Not sure about the boys. They keep those wagons rolling whenever they get the chance. I think they still run six wagons around close."

The country south of town is beautiful with the South Platte River and low hills to the east. Harvey was lucky to have bought Ben Holladay's spread. There is lots of grass for feed and 20 acres of timber and flat land with twenty-five hundred feet of river front. I saw two new homes up the river. Carl and Art must have built their own places. I didn't think Harvey would break up his acreage for anyone else. Well look at this. A bridge to cross the river. We used to ford the river and get wet sometimes. Riding toward the office, two men walked out and I could see they were Carl and Harvey. They were looking but had no idea who it was. It had been six years since we were together. The closer I got, Harvey started to smile and took his hat off as if he could see better that way.

"Jack Knight. Look at you all grown up and dressed like a city slicker. Still wear the bullwhip under your coat. Get off that horse and let's jaw awhile."

Carl grabbed and hugged me like a long lost brother saying. "We sure miss having you with us. Art is out for a couple of days. How long can you hang around? I think Josh is over in the bunkhouse. I saw him at breakfast anyway. Everybody else is new around here except Burt Culy. Come on over to the house Mother will want to see you."

As I walked through the door, Betsy looked up from her sewing machine. She looked stunned for a moment then I thought I saw a tear in her eye as she stood up and reached out to give me a welcoming hug. "Jack, you are still alive. We have not heard from you or had a letter since you left here. What a wonderful surprise for you to show up today."

"I'm sorry, I never gave it a thought that you would like to hear from me."

Harvey retorted, "Come on, Jack, you grew up with our boys and we look at you as one of our own. We think about you all the time. Carl and Art are always telling stories about your adventures when you worked with us. You going to come back to Denver and settle down?"

"No guys, I'm just passing through on my way back to San Francisco and have to get back to work. I have a sales company that represents manufacturers to distribute their wares. I have two companies at present. One is a leather manufacturer that makes industrial belting and just signed a contract to represent Baxter Steam engines. They are a division of the Colt Arms Company in Hartford, Connecticut. We are just getting off the ground but it sure looks good for a wondering roughneck like me."

Carl pushed a chair under me and said. "Last we heard of you was when you were in Oregon with Ben Holladay building a railroad."

"Yep, we built over 200 miles of rails across Oregon. Ben got over extended so a bank is running the railroad now. But he will come back after this financial hiccup is over. Edwin says he believes in another year things will start rolling again."

"Bet you didn't know that Art and me are both married now." Carl chimed in. "Come on down to the house and meet Louise, my wife, and probably Phyllis, Art's wife. She and Louise are close and when one or the other of us is gone they seem to migrate together."

I explained to Harvey and Betsy my time was short so I must say so long for now but would be back this summer when Father and Mother come to visit Charles and his new boy.

Betsy said. "Oh? They're coming to Denver? That's great, We can turn that into a party. I'm glad I got advance notice on that news."

"I'm going to get out of here now and let you get back to your sewing. Come on, Carl, let's go meet your wife then I got to ride back down the river."

Sure enough, both Louise and Phyllis are at the kitchen table having coffee. I hugged them both, grabbed a cup off the counter and poured myself a cup of black coffee.

"You girls are very lucky to have trapped two of Denver's most notorious members of the never get married society."

Louise replied saucily, "We had them figured out from the start. We kept running just fast enough to out run them and one day they never knew what hit them when we stopped. We both got married at the same ceremony so they couldn't get away. Phyllis has a sister that is waiting for you to move back to Denver so she can catch you. These boys think it would be a good match."

"Tell you what. Soon as I finish this coffee, I better get on my horse and start running. I have a couple of things to tend to before getting caught. I'm glad you four are happy though and hope you stay that way forever. Carl and Art are on the top of my list and I mean that. The whole Bendickson family is top drawer people."

The ride back down the river was bitter sweet. I could have spent another whole day with those people, but my mind told me Ida would be looking for fish to fry pretty soon.

CHAPTER 15

Ida sent me to the tack room on the north side of their barn to find three poles and an insulated box that Charles keeps crickets and grasshoppers in for bait. I rounded up two dozen of the critters and put them in a bait box. It's almost 3 o'clock and I'm ready for both brothers to show up for some riffle action.

Fredrick was awake so I got a chance to hold the only nephew I have in the world. Never had much to do with little ones so he was a marvel to watch and carry around the room. Couldn't tell yet if he had the big Knight nose, but then, I think he favors Ida more than Charles.

I heard horses on the drive up from the river and went out to meet them. Jay dismounted and took Charles' horse reins and picked mine off the ring and headed for the barn to put them away for the day.

Charles brushed past me, entered the house and patted Fredrick on the head in passing. "While you finish getting acquainted with your nephew, I need to change clothes. These smell like the shop and fish seem to have a sensitive sense of smell in this clear river. See you got our gear out and ready. Be back before Jay gets the horses taken care of."

We made the short hike to the bank of the river and lost no time baiting our hooks. I thought we all had our bait in the river at the same time. With in a minute, we all three had hooked our first fish. We pulled out three nice fourteen or so inch fish. Within the hour Charles counted our catch and saw there were 12 fish and knowing that was more than enough for supper reluctantly headed us for the barn to clean our catch.

Ida was waiting in the kitchen preparing vegetables when we came in. Charles handed her the catch with a peck on the cheek then invited Jay and me into his large living room with the huge White Buffalo hide hanging over the fireplace.

"Jack, remember when Chief Walking Bear gave me the big robe for my wedding? Looks quite impressive up on the wall, don't you think?" I nodded in agreement and he continued. "If I remember right, Chief White Feather was with him. Sorry to say White Feather has gone to the big Elk hunting ground wherever that is. He was a great chief for many years. As for Walking Bear, he's getting old but is in good health. He says no young buck can out ride him still, but I feel the young ones have too much respect for him and make sure he continues to out ride them. He asked about you the last time I saw him. Fredrick and one of his grandsons, Tall Bear, are blood brothers. Tall Bear's father, Walks With Claws, is the real Chief now of that small band of Utes and is getting the tribe ready to move farther southwest with a larger tribe on the other side of the mountains. They have a small reservation down in the southwest corner of Colorado, and the weather is a little kinder so I feel it is a good move for everyone involved."

"Charles, I am sorry I have no time to go see Walking Bear. If they are still in the area this summer, I will make it a point to go to their village for a visit. Sorry to hear about White Feather. He was a great hunter and kept a lot of meat available for his tribe during the cold winter months."

"Enough local news, little brother. What are you doing with yourself now that you are no longer with Ben Holladay up in Oregon? A letter came from Father telling us you were in California but had no idea what you were doing. Don't hear from Edwin that much but Father wrote he is doing quite well."

"To make a long story short, I'm in a sales company that handles leather belting and other leather products produced by P&P Leather Company, and we represent a steam engine company. Baxter Steam Engines are manufactured by a division of the Colt Arms company. The largest engine we represent right now is 10 horsepower. That was the reason I said don't order your steam power 'til we talk. I can have two of those engines in Denver within twenty-one days from Tuesday of next week when I get to my office in San Francisco. After you get your layout for all your overhead drives designed, let me know what your needs are. We should have no trouble shipping within 10 days. That is better service than you can get out of Chicago, or St. Louise, I will wager. By the way, this company called JAK Sales is mine. I am the President, and controlling partner. Brother Edwin and his wife are also part of the company. I have the particulars and pictures of the engines in my travel bag so after supper if you're interested, I will get them out for you to look at."

Charles responded with, "I'm not in that big of a hurry; I just got the building situation in hand last week. I have hired an experienced machinist to start next week on the layout and whatever else is needed to get this thing rolling. I am as excited for you as you seem to be about this new business of yours but it sounds like you won't have time to roam around like you used to like to do. In a manner of speaking, you will be tied down. How do you feel about that?"

"I guess I learned a lot from Ben while I was with him. The responsibility has little effect because I learned to grab on to that a long time ago. I learned that with structure, you can complete any task so I am enjoying the experience up to now. I have one salesman and with the steam engine to represent now, Edwin and I both feel we will need one more to cover all the territory we have. As far as travel, I think the schedule I will have will satisfy my wondering needs and keep me content. Our friend, Bill Cody, had lunch with me in Chicago a couple of weeks ago and gave me a piece of advice that sounded pretty good. He said, 'Jack, just remember to take a deep breath and enjoy the ride.' He said that is what gets him by. By the way I saw his acting debut, and it was a sight to see."

Jay, who had been listening now interrupted, "I think we got our boy on the right track. He really does have a good outlook on things now. I used to wonder if he would ever find his niche in life but he seems to have it all together now. Hey, can't you boys smell our supper? My nose tells me you found a great cook in Ida."

Charles had Fredrick in his arms in a familiar rocking chair. The boy had fallen asleep. I thought I remembered Father in that same rocking chair with Mary Alice when we lived in City of Kansas, Missouri. Almost the same scene with a smaller man. Might be Charles looked more comfortable than Father had. He got up slowly to take Fredrick to his bed while Jay and I walked into the dining room.

As we sat down for supper, I saw Ida had put a glass of sarsaparilla at the place set for me. What a memory she has. Although she must keep it in the house because she had no idea I was coming for a visit. The trout had been fried perfectly and Charles had taught her the heads were to remain on the fish to serve them. Her vegetable dish of green beans were as good as Mother's, and the hot bread with fresh butter and her peach preserves topped it off.

After supper, we men retired to the living room for coffee. Jay and Charles have a sip of Brandy, but I just had coffee. We talked about plans for Charles' machine shop. Of course, what would round out an evening better than each of us sharing our opinion on what it would take to help President Grant bring the financial stability back to the banks and the nation?

With that, Jay stood up, stretched while stifling a yawn. "Jack, we need to get some sleep so we can get up around 5:30 in the morning. I have offered your services to help me guard a gold shipment to the mint in San Francisco. Wells Fargo Express had a large shipment of silver to ship yesterday, and they put three guards on the train for that trip to the mint. Now Box Park Mining needs to ship over forty-nine thousand dollars worth of gold ingots tomorrow to San Francisco. Because we don't have any more guards available for this shipment, I said we would do it. I will get you a voucher for pay when we get to San Francisco. I thought you would say yes to the idea so went ahead and volunteered your service. Was I right?"

"Sure, why not? Might as well have something to do besides read and gaze out a window. What are the chances for trouble? The last train hold up I remember hearing about was somewhere around Reno, Nevada."

"That was a Wells Fargo Express shipment also. Caught the boys the next day and recovered all the gold. I'm afraid the news got out on this shipment tomorrow due to some body leaking the time and place and people are talking about it in town. Probably no problem but Wells Fargo wants good protection on this one so we get to work as guards. Only place I have reservations about is the area between the Colorado Territory line and Cheyenne. Got some hills and valleys to travel, and trains have to slow down at times. Always thought if I was going to hold up a train, that would be my choice for a good spot to do it. Anyway, Jack, we are going through there during day light, so I wouldn't give it much thought."

Charles was grinning as he took another sip of his Brandy. "Jack, looks like you're looking forward to this little escapade Jay has roped you into. You two boys always seem to find something exciting to be involved in. Look at me. I just plod along with life in the safety of a shop that nobody would want to rob or even possibly try to steal anything. Just hooking a fighting fish for excitement, I must have chosen the wrong way to live."

"Now, Charles, you know I envy you and the life you have made. Look at you. A nice home, a beautiful wife, and the little boy. You have a good trade and are respected by everyone you know. Don't think what Jay and I do or have done even can compare with what you have accomplished in your short life. And yes, I'm looking forward to this trip. It has been a while since I have had time to spend with Jay Parker and am looking forward to a couple of checker games in the express car to stay alert."

"Thanks for the bed and taking the time you spent with us at the old fishing hole. You and Ida are great hosts, and with that and a trip to the kitchen to thank your wife for the wonderful supper, I think I will retire for the evening. By the way, I will send you prices and delivery costs for the steam engines as soon as I return to my office. Good night. Oh and if you're up for coffee I will see you in the morning."

I knew Jay wanted some time with Charles, so I headed for the kitchen and a short visit with Ida and a hug before bedtime.

Five thirty came fast and even though I slept well in the feather bed the Knights have for their guests, I was a little stiff from the horseback ride I had yesterday. Jay was up. I heard him and Charles moving about and clinking coffee cups in the kitchen.

"Good morning, gentlemen. Are we ready for this day? What do I need to do for Wells Fargo this morning besides getting to the train on time? If that is all, I told Diego I would stop by and have coffee with him."

"Jack, ride with me to the Express office and take my horse back to the livery stable for me. I will have two fellows from the mint ride with me in a buckboard with the shipment to deliver it to the train when it arrives around 9 o'clock. Please be at the station when we get there so we can load the shipment and send the other fellows on their way. There is a large safe in the express car to load the shipment into. Once that is done all we need to do is stay close to the safe all the way to San Francisco. We have biscuits, bacon, and some cheese in the express car to eat since you can't let your guard down to go to a restaurant. When we stop in Cheyenne; we will transfer to the train headed on the line to the coast."

"Wells Fargo will have people there to help with the transfer so we will have no problems in there. Remember Jack, we do this all the time so there won't be any foul-ups. I have never been used for a guard before but have been involved with many transfers."

"All right, Jay, I got the schedule. Whenever you're ready, we can head for your office."

The ride into town was cold and damp. The moon was out and almost full so it was easy to see the way. Jay dismounted at his office and untied his small case from the saddle and motioned me on. It was still early for Diego to be at his shop so I stopped at Booker's Hotel, and headed into the kitchen. Ho Sing, the cook that worked for Booker was still there and was preparing for the day.

Ho Sing said, "You the Knight kid that your momma used to bring for breakfast some-time. You grow up but still carry the whip. You look same only older and wiser. What you doing in my kitchen this early in morning?"

"Ho Sing, I came to see you. Thought you might remember how to cook some bacon and eggs for me. It is good to see you. You used to say you would go back to San Francisco, but I never see you there."

"You live San Francisco? Me never get chance. Mr. Booker too good to Ho Sing to leave him and go San Francisco. He even give me Tuesday off to spend time with family. No work for anybody else. You want some breakfast? I make for you."

He fried me eggs, and some ham he was working with to make bean soup. The smell was out of this world. I guess Booker knew a good thing when he had it. After finishing my food, I hugged Ho Sing, and I thought I saw a tear in his eye as I walked out the door.

I picked up both horses and headed for Diego's shop. The moon was gone and the eastern sky was showing some light as I tied the horses in front of Diego's. He had the lanterns on in his show room and in the shop also. Walking in the door, I could tell he had banked the fire last night before leaving to go home because it was nice and warm inside.

"Diego, I have about an hour before meeting Jay at the train station. Well, my friend, I told you what I was doing with my time when I saw you yesterday. Tell me about yourself and Margo. Is she as sweet as she used to be? I can tell she doesn't beat you too bad. By the way, Father and Mother are coming out to see you guys this summer and told me to tell you both hello from them."

"We received a letter from them a couple of days ago giving us a heads up on their visit which would please us anytime."

"I see you are carrying the 1871 Springfield, .50 caliber. I had one of those up in Oregon for my hunting rifle. Shot a nice Bull Elk from over 150 yards. Dropped him where he stood. That rifle has power. You sell many of them?"

"Yep, around 50 of them so far. Everyone that has one likes the feel and the fire power it has. Two fellows that hunt way up north said they both knocked a Grizzly down with one shot apiece. You know Charles bought one for Chief Walking Bear. I think the old man gave it to his son Chief Walks With Claws because he is getting too old to hunt anymore. Did Charles tell you that the tribe's possibly moving? I hear they have a small reservation down on the Utah border that has better weather year round. Hey, what ever happened to your dog, Thor? Is he still alive?"

"Yep, he's still around. Getting old but seems to enjoy being with Mary Alice. She blames me for his gray hair but I think he had fun when we were together. I rode Powder when I was back at the horse farm. He is Mary Alice's favorite stud so you know he is happy. Well Diego, I need to get going. Jay and I are guarding a load of gold to San Francisco for

Wells Fargo and Jay said not to be late getting to the station to help load the shipment. Goodbye my friend. I hope life continues to be kind to you and Margo."

I rode to the livery stable and turned the horses in. Lewis was on duty this morning and was in a talkative mood for a fellow that used to be so quiet and subdued in his younger years. He wanted to know about Mary Alice and the folks. What had I been doing the last three years and what had happened to Thor?

I related as much news as I could 'til I heard the train approaching the station.

"Lewis, I gotta go now and be at the station when Jay gets there. You boys have a great business here. Keep up the good work."

CHAPTER 16

As I walked to the station, Jay and three men rode up in a wagon pulled by two horses and backed up to the first express car behind the coal tender. There was one more express car and five passenger cars making up the train this morning. George Acker, the conductor opened the express car door as the wagon was backed up to it. Jay introduced me to the three guards and the gentlemen in the car as I lifted myself onto the wagon. Peering inside the car, I saw the safe that was bolted to the wall and floor was being opened by Jay.

The three guards hauled the heavy strong box into the car and drug it over to the safe. One of them had a key and opened the box. The ingot bars in the box were not very large and it amazed me how small an amount of gold it takes to make up 49,000 dollars. I made a remark about the amount and Jay informed me that what I was looking at was about 150 pounds or so of the bright yellow stuff.

About the same time George said, "You fellows look like you have this all under control for now so I'll get back to my passengers. I'll check on you two a couple of times before we get to Cheyenne, but you be sure to lock the doors before we pull out."

The three guards picked up the strong box and loaded it on the wagon. Since they need no help from us, I checked out the car we would be occupying the next few hours. In the meantime, Jay was shutting the door and locking it.

Taking a seat across from me, he took a deep breath and slowly let it out. "Well little brother, it's you and me against them all now. For what it's worth, I sure am glad you decided to come on this trip."

"I'm only doing this for the money. I haven't had a payday since I left Oregon. By the way, what am I getting paid for this trip? I don't remember any discussion about that."

"Wells Fargo Express pays its guards well, Jack. Three dollars and fifty cents a day and also pays for your meals when traveling on a job such as this."

"Jay, I pay my salesman more than that, and he has little chance of being shot at unless it would be some gal's husband chasing him for making love to his wife. Wow, I could make fourteen dollars on this trip." Trying not to sound like I was bragging, "You know Ben was paying me 500.00 dollars a month when I was in Oregon and furnished me a butler and a handy man to boot." Sighing deeply for emphasis, and with a hang dog expression, I said, "Well, that's over now and I probably will never make that kind of money again in my life."

"Sounded to me like he got his money's worth from what you accomplished. Maybe some day, I'll be in that class if I make it to the head office as a Vice President or something of that sort. The car lurched forward as the train began moving and after regaining a comfortable position, Jay said, "How about some checkers for a while? These chairs are better padded than the seats in the coaches so we might be more comfortable up here than in the back. You might want to take your coat off. The stove will warm it up quickly now that the doors are closed."

We played checkers for over two hours and one stop somewhere north of Denver.

Jay stood up and said as the train slowed for the second time, "We are coming into Greeley. You would remember this area as it was called Fort Latham for years. It has grown rapidly since the railroad came through. I remember you stopped a hold up at the old stage depot. I was driving stages back then for Ben Holladay. Yep, country is sure different now. People all over the place building farms and ranches. I left here one morning with a strong box for Julesburg, Colorado with a grizzly old man riding shotgun. Think his name was Gordon something. Anyway, we were letting the team have their head and moving along pretty fast and came upon a sweeping turn. Right in the middle of the road these three guys had felled a big old cottonwood tree. I tried to stop the team but they plowed into the tree and two of the fellows headed for the coach. Gordon let each have a barrel of shot from his shotgun. and I got the other in the neck with that piece Diego and Margo gave me. First time I ever shot and killed a white man. We backed the team up and got down to check on the two men Gordon shot. One was dead and the other one was ready to meet the big man upstairs. Gordon said there was nothing anyone could do for him so we laid them all three together, chopped the tree away from the road and drove on to the next station. You know, Jack, that killing bothered me for a time 'til I got into a scrap up in Nebraska with a bunch of Sioux and had to kill again. Doesn't seem to bother me anymore."

The train spent about fifteen minutes changing passengers and taking on water. My stomach was letting me know it's time to check the box of biscuits and bacon for a snack as we pulled out from Greeley. It had begun to rain hard enough that you could hear it hitting the roof of our car. Hail was hitting the car roof now so I peeked out the small window in the car door and could see it was starting to build up on the ground. This northeast corner of Colorado was famous for its heavy doses of hail and freezing rain any time of the year.

Two hours out of Greeley, the rain and hail had stopped and the train was slowing. I heard foot traffic on the roof of the Express car and all of a sudden, the sound of rushing air filled the brake system. I could hear the cars behind us piling up on the couplings. The train has stopped and immediately started forward as the doors at both end of the car were hit with something very heavy, opening them, allowing two men to rush into the car.

Jay was standing close to the safe as the guy that came in the back door headed for it. I saw the flash of gun fire and the man fell backward, tripping another man coming through the door. As the fellow that had come in the front entrance raised his gun to shoot at Jay, my bullwhip caught him around his head, and he was blinded as the whip covered his eyes. His gun fired but the bullets hit the floor with the two rounds he shot. The third man had aim on Jay but I managed to drop the whip and pulled my gun and shot him before he got a round off.

The train was slowing now and coming to a stop. I jumped over a box and hit the man that was trying to unwind the whip from his head with a hard blow from the butt of my gun. At the same time, Jay was opening the side door and said, "There must be more or the train would not have stopped. Watch the front door. They might come over the coal tender."

Jay got the door open enough to see out and there was a fellow on a horse holding the reins of four more horses close to the train.

Looking out the front of the car, I saw the fourth man coming over the top of the coal tender and he spied me waiting for him. He filled his hand with a gun shooting at me with three shots but missed every time. Even if I had my bullwhip there was not room enough to use it so my gun blasted off a shot hitting him in the right shoulder causing his gun to fall all the way to the grade below and he landed on the floor in front of me.

I heard Jay telling the rider to dismount but could hear him riding off leaving the four horses where they stood.

Jay said, "I could shoot that boy, but I'll bet he was no more than fourteen years old. One of these guys might be his Pa. Maybe this might turn him around to stay on the side of the law."

"Maybe," I yelled while jumping down and heading for the engine to see if the two railroad fellows were alright. Both were still a little shaken, but not hurt.

The Engineer shakily filled me in, "That fellow made me stop the train and his partner unhooked the rest of the cars and had me run away from the other cars. Did you get them all? Heard some shooting but stayed down like the fellow told us. Better back up and get the rest of my cars so we can get into Cheyenne as soon as possible."

Returning to the Express car before the train reversed to retrieve the other cars I could see big brother had all four in a row against the other side door.

He got out that two were dead and the other two were handcuffed to the floor ring before asking, "Everybody OK in the cab up front?"

"Yes, they're headed back to get the rest of the train and will be fine soon as they get their minds straight enough to stop shaking. You need to explain to Wells Fargo the need to reinforce those end doors on the

Express cars. Those fellows should have to work harder to get in and give the guards more warning."

Hearing one of the injured men groaning, I asked, "You know anything about doctoring for those two? We are still an hour or more from Cheyenne."

"No. I just protect the cargo. Don't do no doctoring. That is way above my pay grade and those wounds will hold for couple of hours as cold as it is in here now that we have no doors to keep the wind out. Sure glad you were fast on the one behind the guy I shot. I had turned around to help you and never saw him."

Trying to ease the tension, I said, "Jay, I think he was pointing at your other ear to make both sides of your head even where the Indian shot you along time ago. I wasn't too sure of his aim so I stepped in to make sure he missed his shot. Hey man, I got to put my coat on. That stove is of no account with out the doors."

Calming down a little, Jay also tried to lighten the situation by asking, "Did you really have a butler when you were in Oregon?"

"Yep, James was good. He cooked and cleaned the house and had my clothes ready in the morning when I let him know the night before what the next day's dress would be. Also had Benny for my stable boy. He had my horse or a buckboard ready in the morning and took care of my livestock and gear like saddles and bridles and the rigging for the buckboard I used. Benny also took care of the yard work and any repairs to the barn and fences on the place."

"Ben sure did spoil you. Think you can come down and live like the rest of us after all of that high living?"

"I'm back, Jay. I enjoyed living that way at the time but I worked hard for it. It gave me lots of time for fishing and hunting in some of the best lakes and streams the West has to offer. I will miss that more than all the comforts Holladay provided me. I wished sometimes you were there to enjoy those trips with me."

The train was back together and we're headed for Cheyenne again. The fellow I had hit on the head was coming around and was asking about the boy with the horses. Come to find out, it was his son and he was concerned we had shot him and left him to die on the rail grade.

I said, "No sir we let him ride off and hope if you get the chance to see him or his mother you explain the facts of life to them and make him understand this is the wrong way to get ahead and could very well shorten his life"

Jay interrupted so I didn't get into a mini sermon, "Jack, I will get to Nathan Early, the Deputy Marshal, in Cheyenne while you stay with the cargo. Two fellows, Gary Robbins and Dick Huber, from Wells Fargo Express will be at the station to help move the gold to the train headed west to San Francisco later today. Make sure to see some identification if I'm not there. They are familiar with the transfer so it should be no problem for you."

The rest of the trip to Cheyenne was quiet except for the robber with the bullet in his shoulder. He had to be in pain and babbled nonsense now and then. After an hour, the train began slowing down and came to a stop. Jay peeked out the small window in the side door and headed out the rear door of the car.

Shortly after, someone banged on the side door, and looking out the window I saw a buckboard being backed up to the car. Slowly opening the door, two men were showing me Wells Fargo identification badges and name tags. I moved to the side as they lifted a strong box into the car and slid it over to the safe mounted on the wall. The transfer was made and loaded into the buckboard faster than I could gather up our provision box and my hat.

When the buckboard pulled away Jay and two more fellows wearing big silver stars pulled their wagon up next to the door and climbed aboard.

Jay introduced them as Marshal Early and Deputy Goldsmith. "You have lucked out. The fellow you shot in the neck is Ray 'Bad Man' Walsh. There is a hundred dollar reward for him dead or alive so you get paid twice for this job. Give Marshal Early your card so he knows where to send the reward and you can take Edwin and his wife out to supper some night."

We helped the Marshal load his prisoners and the two dead would be robbers in the wagon and shook hands with Nathan Early and his deputy. The wagon pulled away, Jay shut the door to the car and pointed to the rear door for us to get off the train. He told me without giving me a chance to answer, "Let's head over to the Union Pacific station and wait with Gary and Dick for the west bound to show up. It usually is in when the short line from Denver gets here and we should be late with the little misunderstanding we had back there. Union Pacific has a fair record for promptness except for bad weather. No telling what is going on over in Nebraska this time of the year. How about some hot coffee? I'll bet Gary has some with them at the wagon."

It was almost dark and I could see a light way to the east. It had to be the Union Pacific Train. Gary was sitting on the tail gate of the Wells Fargo wagon with his left arm resting on the strong box and his right hand on his Colt Navy .36 caliber pistol.

Dick offered us coffee from a pot in the wagon, "The station manager brought us this coffee and said the train ran into snow at Pine Bluff. He received a telegram from the station at Pine Bluff saying it had been snowing for two hours before the train got to them and was still coming down an hour later when he sent the message. That much snow will slow a train way down with such bad visibility."

As the train rolled to a stop, Dick started backing the wagon up to the Express car and waited for the door to open. Union Pacific Railroad had much more modern cars than the short line. The Express car was clad in metal, and the door was a lot heaver than on the wood car we rode to Cheyenne.

Warm air flooded the wagon as the door opened. It took little time for Gary and Dick to toss the strong box on the floor of the car.

Jay, jumping into the car called to me. "Come on, Jack, this will be our home for a couple of days, we might as well get used to it. Gary, Dick, we sure thank you for the help and I will see you in February unless my schedule changes. Soon as you pull out I will shut and lock the door. Jack we have no safe so let's put the strong box under the desk and cover it up with a blanket from the pile over there. Being a new car we haven't had time to install a safe yet."

The trip to Reno was slow and boring. You could only play so many games of checkers and with the weather the way it was in the high mountains, the train ran slowly in some spots. Fortunately there was one cot to sleep on so one of us got to sleep while one stayed awake to guard the cargo. Gabriel, the conductor, kept us in biscuits and coffee until

Reno but told us we were on our own now because he lived there and would be home for a day and back on the train going east on Tuesday.

The weather from Reno to Sacramento was cold and clear. Thankfully, there was lots of snow on the side of the rails but none on the tracks.

"Jack, I'm going to hold this shipment at my office in Sacramento. We are twelve hours behind schedule and I can have this delivered to the mint in San Francisco Wednesday with other cargo with less hassle than us going on and having to transport by ferry. I have no idea what the ferry schedule is and don't need this box running around in plain sight. Let's end this trip at my office. When we stop at the station we can unload the box, and I will run over to Wells Fargo and bring a buckboard back to carry the cargo to our safe. It's only in the next block from the station."

After we got the strong box to the Wells Fargo office, Jay said, "The railroad runs to Oakland, from here. If you can catch a ride in the morning you can ride a ferry on over to San Francisco in the day light. I have two bedrooms at the house so you can get a good night's sleep before you head for home."

We walked the three blocks to Jay's bungalow as he called it.

Opening the door, I'm surprised. It was warm and cozy as we walked into a lighted room just off the kitchen.

Jay rushed over to a chair with a red haired girl sitting in it that looked to be twenty or so years old and pulled her up and hugged and kissed her as I stand there with my mouth open.

Composing himself, he explained, "Jack, this is Mandy. She was a Harvey Girl at the "La Fonda" in Santa Fe, New Mexico. We met about a year ago when I made a trip to Santa Fe. Had to go there two more times and saw her both of those trips. She couldn't leave her boarding house to see me so we could only talk at the hotel. She wanted to come to California, so I found her a job here in Sacramento. When her contract with Harvey House ended she came here and we became very close. What could I do Jack? You can't leave an Irish lass in a place she is not happy."

"Well Jay, it looks like you got the best end of the deal. Mandy is a beautiful girl and you need someone to keep you straight." Looking at

Mandy, I went on, "He sure was tight mouthed about you. We have been together for almost two weeks and not a peep from him."

"Jack, her folks moved to Stockton in November." Turning from me and looking into her eyes with complete adoration, Jay said, "And Mandy, I wasn't sure you would be here when I got back from this trip. I sure am glad you wanted to stay with me."

CHAPTER 17

The ferry ride home was cold and wet. I found a wagon belonging to a dry goods store located a couple of blocks from Edwin's home and hitched a ride after helping the driver load his cargo off the ferry. I had been gone for four weeks and was glad to be getting home to my own bed even though it belonged to Edwin. It was nice to see and visit with all the people, but I thought I needed to do some work besides guarding a gold shipment from Denver.

It had been a week since I left Abilene and for goodness sake, today was the first of January 1873. We could start selling Baxter Steam Engines tomorrow. It would be a good idea to find a water pump to add to our products to give us a full line to move into the farming and orchard communities.

Butch, the wagon driver, delivered me right to Edwin's door. It was difficult to express how much I appreciated the ride to my front door in this heavy rain.

Rose answered almost immediately when she heard my knocking on the door. She exclaimed, "Jack, I heard the wagon from the dining room and figured it had to be you. We expected you would be in yesterday but glad you made it safely whenever. Did you enjoy your stay at the horse farm and Christmas with the family?"

"Absolutely! It was all great, but I'm glad to be here where I can relax and catch up on some reading and do some real work. Edwin must have gone to work today. The town seemed awful busy for a New Years day. I saw the banks were closed but most everything else looked normal for a rainy day in San Francisco. By the way, where is Little Bird?"

"She'll be back tomorrow. Father McDougall came up before Christmas and asked if Jane would come to the Mission to help with the girls living there for the holiday season. Remembering how much the Mission had been a part of her life, she was ready to help in any way she could. Edwin said he would be home early probably around 3 o'clock. I'm home today because Elk Horn, my partner, has traveled to Lake Tahoe to see his family for the day so we decided to just close up shop for a couple of days. We have nothing pressing as far as clients go so felt the office could close with no effect on anyone."

I went to my room and peeled off my coat and gun belt and just lay on the bed. I looked toward the window and saw a small desk had been added to the furnishings and also a pile of paperwork on the top shelf of the desk. Curiosity overcame my need to relax so I got up to see what was in the paper work. It was a statement for December 1872 for JAK Sales Company. We sold over 7,500.00 dollars worth of leather goods for P&P Leather Company and the 6% JAK received was 450.00 dollars. After all expenses, including my trip to Chicago and Ray Anderson's wages and expenses, we lost 237 dollars and 46 cents for the month. This made me feel as a business man, I had come up short for the month but, on the other hand, I sure had enjoyed myself. Guess it was good I had made 14.50 working for Wells Fargo Express and would be collecting 100.00 dollars for the reward on Ray 'Bad Man' Walsh.

On the desk, I also found a sketch and letter from the Gould Pump Company of Seneca Falls, New York. With it was a note from Ray Anderson stating he had found this company and had heard they needed some representation in the West. This could be just the thing I had been thinking about to give us a complete line to sell to the farms and orchards all over California.

Rose called from the kitchen and asked if I would like a cup of coffee.

"Be right there, Rose. Sounds like a good idea." Looking through some papers I saw a new bank book on my desk. Edwin must be feeling the time is short for the market to fall on its face. Jay, our brother that works for Wells Fargo, told me his company was not doing any expansion either as long as the financial climate stays as it is today."

While Rose was pouring coffee into a cup she had set before me, she let me know about Edwin's ideas for them, "I think Edwin wants us all to look at buying gold ingots to protect most of our savings and investments for the next year or so. He plans talking to you about it when he gets home this afternoon. He said a lot of the banks in the east are getting shaky and has gotten him worried."

Rose made great coffee and I was not letting it get cold. "Rose, he is probably right, but you know I think the growth and prosperity we see here in California will continue to a greater degree than on the east coast. I just hope the banks out here don't make the mistake of not loaning the money it takes to keep this part of the country prosperous. There is something else I'm curious about. Have you got any newspapers with news from up north concerning the Indian troubles with the Modoc Tribe? I heard they went on the warpath late last month when I was in Kansas."

"I know a little about the problem," Rose replied. "Seems the Indian agent has orders from President Grant to put the Klamath Tribe and the Modoc on the same reservation. This fellow, Captain Jack of the Modoc Tribe, says the Klamath Indians treat his tribe as if they are slaves and his people are not going to put up with that kind of treatment. He has taken most of his tribe into the lava beds in northern California and told some he would fight to the last Modoc. Recently, he and his band attacked an army wagon train and killed all of the solders in the train. I also heard a treaty talk is scheduled, but nothing else has come up since that was announced."

We heard the front door open and a wet Edwin stomped his feet on the hall rug to clean his shoes of the wet and grim of the rain soaked walkway, removed his rain slicker and seeing us enjoying some coffee said. "Hey Jack, you made it home. We have a lot to talk about before supper. Soon as I get some coffee and kiss my wife, the three of us should have a board meeting and get you caught up on everything that's been going on. We're moving at a rapid pace but need another product to continue the prosperity. Ray and I have been exploring the chances of getting the Gould Pump Company to join our efforts to civilize the

West. Just imagine, irrigation with the steam engine and a water pump getting water to the farms in the valleys south of Sacramento out of the streams and rivers that run year around. Jack, I believe the possibilities are unlimited."

"Edwin, I saw that being done at the horse farm in Kansas. Uncle John has a pump driven by a steam engine that he uses to water an area for showing his stock to prospective buyers. I have been thinking about all the possibilities since then. I saw the Gould Pump letter on my new desk. See there, great minds work in the same direction when an idea is needed. Have you put the pump situation into action?"

"Not yet. We needed to talk to you about it first. I have sent a telegram to Seabury Gould, the owner and inventor, in Seneca Falls, New York for more information. We should hear from him by the end of next week if he's interested in us. We received a lot of literature and pricing express mail from the Baxter Company. Ray has been given the impression that he has Huntington, Hopkins & Company Hardware on board for the Sacramento area dealers for the steam engine. They have a couple of more stores around the area. Makes me think Sacramento and the surrounding area is well covered. Bet we can sell pumps to them also along with belting for package deals."

"Okay, I guess the first thing needed is a deal put together with Huntington, Hopkins, and Co. this week then Ray and I can to go to Sacramento to try and finalize the deal. I talked with Albert Gallatin and another partner, Horace H. Seaton. We should have little resistance with that group. I sold Charles on two 10 horse power units for his new machine shop in Denver. That should come up in February. We need to find a dealer for that area or how about his company being a dealer for the steam engines? On second thought, probably not a good idea."

Rose asked Edwin to repeat parts of Ray's trip north to Shasta, California with which he continued our discussion.

"Yes, Jack. Ray made a trip two weeks ago as far north as Shasta. It is the last large trading area before reaching the Oregon border. He talked to a hardware and dry goods owner who showed interest in the steam engine and decided to start with a 5 horse power version. He says he would also need a pump for the miners to use up in the Trinity Alps area for water washing sides of hills. They use wooden pumps now but they fail rapidly, and he heard that cast iron pumps are now available. It's called placer mining and has been used since the 1850's, but the need for better pumps and hoses to carry the water can improve the method. There is a lot of mining going on in that region so we need to explore the possibilities. Ray tells me Huntington, Hopkins and Co. has a line of fire hoses that sell well. Rubber lined with cotton webbing for strength. Ray thinks it is manufactured in Boston."

"Here all this time I thought our market would be farms and mills. Sounds like power will be needed in every phase of building this country. Let's get enough dealers together to get a shipment of steam engines headed this way. Richard Jarvis let me know Baxter and company had stock on hand and delivery would be no problem. We need to get some information fast about the Gould Pump Company. Edwin, can we send a telegram and maybe speed their response to us?"

"Let me fill you in, Jack. The Baxter situation is this. Their offices are in New York so I have a credit line set up for twenty thousand dollars with Anthony Smith of the Brooklyn, New York branch of his New Bank. William D. Russell of the Baxter Company has had contact with New Bank so you can make up an order whenever you feel comfortable you have the order sold within a month. Your credit line is month to month and in New York, you pay 7% interest only on the total money used. That was the best rate I could get. I hear some are paying close to 10% so you're in good hands with Anthony. We might want to make other arrangements later because I hear the bank rates are going to escalate later this year. All part of the financial problems looming on the horizon being talk about."

Rose who had been taking notes, stopped writing and got up saying, "I need to leave this meeting and put something together for supper. You guys go ahead off the record. We can finish later."

"Jack, we need a dealer here in San Francisco. Shouldn't you concentrate on that and let Ray set up the Sacramento thing? He can do the paper work. If the partners have a problem with anything you can go over and straighten it out. Ray knows the pricing and all of the discounts for belting and the steam products so let him put that together. There are some big hardware dealers down close to the water front and cold calls will have to be made 'til you find some interest."

By Friday, Charles G. Hooker, of Hooker & Company Hardware and I have had lunch and he agreed to have his company represent the Baxter Company. I've also gotten a verbal commitment on the Gould Pumps if we attain the rights to sell their pumps. They seem to be the largest store that has a full line and also sells coal to stoke the steam engines.

Over the next year, our little company hired another salesman. Keith Robbins came to us as an expert on pumps, and he was that. He found sales for the Gould pump line that even amazed the inventor. Our company expanded north to Seattle, Washington Territory and as far south as San Diego, California. We had dealers in Salt Lake City, Portland, and Eugene in Oregon. Any town serving agriculture, mining, or manufacturing became outlets for our products. With three of us covering the West, we divided the territory with Ray covering southern California and Arizona territory, Keith taking care of Washington, Oregon, and Northern California and with myself serving the other territories and states that we felt could use our products. I traveled by railroad, stagecoaches, and horse back when necessary. By November, 1873, I had seen more of the West than I had ever imagined was out there.

The business grew so much, we had to move out of Edwin's home and get an office on California Street next to our hardware dealer, Hooker and Company. An accountant and an office girl would also have to be hired to take care of all the paper work.

A letter came to my office in late November from Richard Jarvis of the Colt Firearms Company. I was out of town in New Mexico so it remained unopened for two weeks since he had addressed it to me. When I returned from my trip I read the following words:

Jack, I have an opportunity to offer you. As you know we developed the .45 caliber single action, six shot Colt for the Army. We now have this in a .44 caliber piece to offer to the public for around seventeen dollars. We need some representation out there and you came to mind.

I have not discussed this with William D. Russell of the Baxter division and will not until I hear from you. I hear your company is keeping them busy and they are very happy with what you have accomplished for them. I don't feel a gun line would be a good addition to what you have going with JAK Sales, and should be a separate endeavor. This is probably selfish on my part, but I feel you could do an exceptional job with this product. Let me know your thoughts on this matter. Signed Richard"

My trip to the southwest during the late fall months included the eastern Arizona and New Mexico Territories and over to El Peso, Texas. I picked the late fall and early winter to miss the heat that I had experienced at an earlier time when in that country. The fact that I was exhausted from my trip and tired of travel gave me reason to avoid the letter even though it was from Mr. Jarvis.

On my desk also was a week old newspaper. I had been so busy for the last month I had failed to keep current with the news. The front page caught my eye. The headline contained the words *MODOC WARS* drawing me into reading the story.

Earlier in the year, I remembered reading about Captain Jack killing General Canby at a peace conference but had heard little about the wars continued effect on northern California.

I had the opportunity to meet General Canby since he was a close friend of Ben Holladay. We had spent several days at different times walking barefoot on the sandy beaches at Ben's home at New Port, Oregon.

Now they announced the hanging of Captain Jack and Boston Charlie on October 3, 1873 at Fort Klamath for the crimes committed by the Modoc tribe. It went on to say that the Army had moved what was left of the tribe to Oklahoma Territory and a reservation in the northeastern part of that territory.

The rest of the front page was filled with articles about the ensuing depression. The collapse of Jay Cooke & Company's banking firm in September and the projection that the default of many banks would cause several thousand businesses too fail in the next two years. Looks like Edwin was right; the financial world was falling apart.

CHAPTER 18

It was Monday, December 8ᵗʰ, and a misty rain had followed me from the ferry to the office and now all I wanted was to find a trolley to take me home to Edwin's.

In the last year, living with Rose and Edwin, I have been home possibly 30 nights. And the longest time I remember was five days with a sprained ankle from jumping from a moving cable car when it started running the Clay Street route back in early September. That was a stupid move on my part since the car was going to stop anyway and I got anxious to get off to make a stop at my bank.

Little Bird, or Jane, spent more time nursing me than paying attention to her housework and Rose actually had to cook supper twice because Jane was helping me soak my ankle to make it well enough to make a trip to Salt Lake City.

It was still early in the day when I reached home and only Jane was there. She must have been watching the street. She opened the door as soon as I walked onto the porch.

"Hi Jack, I'm glad you're home. There's some hot water on the stove. Can I make you a cup of tea? Edwin brought some new Black Leaf home and I like it. I think you will too."

"That sounds good to these tired bones. It has been a long trip and I must be getting too old for these month long excursions. I can just hear

Father laughing if he heard me say that. Wait till you see what I got for you in Santa Fe."

She started forward in anticipation but I moved away to keep her in suspense. "Let me take my case to my room, put down my bag, shed this damp coat and I'll bring it to you."

Jane had our tea steeping in the dining room looking puzzled as I walked in with my prize behind my back. "Close your eyes, Little Bird. This is a Navaho design, but it will look beautiful on you with your dark skin and long neck."

As Jane closed her eyes like a little child, I placed a turquoise and silver squash blossom necklace around her neck and tied it in the back. It was very heavy so she knew it was in place and opened her eyes.

"Oh, Jack," She squealed as she looked in the mirror over the sideboard. "This is the most beautiful thing I have ever seen. I've seen these in pictures, and one of the older Indian women at the Mission has one but none have been so large or had so much silver on them. Jack. You sure you want me to have this?"

"Yes, Jane, it is for you. You can call it pay for helping with my ankle or just a present to a wonderful person that means a lot to me."

Jane ran around the table and put her arms around me and planted a kiss on my lips. A tingling sensation spun through my being even with the quickness of her touch causing me to envelop her in my arms, and we held on to each other reluctant to part. Now I have been with some nice ladies but Jane's body clung to mine like no body had touched me before. I felt heat around my neck and reluctantly pulled away.

Jane whispered, "I'm sorry Jack, but that feels so normal with you. I have adored you from the first day I saw you clear back at Fort Bridger, I think. I have to say this, Jack, and if you have a problem with me because of it I am truly sorry. The necklace is a dream to hold on too, and I will wear it proudly. As for anything else, it is up to you."

"I have to think about this, Little Bird. Rose warned me not to get too close because they need you. But I guess you would have a say in your future if it came right down to it. I do have feelings for you but always put them on a back burner because I have never given any thought to settling down."

"Wait a minute, Jack. I would not want to hold you down and have no illusions of wanting you to marry me. I just want a relationship with you. If it lasts for a lifetime or just when we can be together it would be fine with me. I have confided these feelings with Rose and I think she understands. Anyway she says she does."

Realizing the tea was getting cold, I sat down and added some sugar to my cup and pored tea into both cups.

"Jack, you spoil the taste of the tea with sugar. You drink coffee without sugar you should try tea the same way. Well, now look at that. Here I go trying to change the way you do things and you don't need that. Forget what I just said, but you might like tea without sugar if you try it. I remember Mr. Bridger telling us children about how sugar was not good for our teeth."

Jane got up and started getting things out of the cupboard. "I have to start supper. Edwin brought home a salmon at midday and asked me to bake it for your expected return today. I have some squash and some green beans to have with the fish. And I made a cherry pie yesterday when Edwin and Rose were gone to breakfast at the hotel for their usual four cups of coffee and sweet rolls. I can make sweet rolls as good as the hotel but I guess when you have been going there as long as they have it is the only time they feel special."

I picked up the cups and tea pot to take them to the kitchen. I needed some time alone in the barn tack room to think about the afternoon and also the letter in my office. I have had a thinking chair made of old leather out there and seemed to be able to put things in the right perspective when relaxing in it. I started a small fire in the pot belly stove more for smell than heat. Sitting down with my feet elevated on a table I closed my eyes and all I saw was Jane. What's going on Knight? You don't need to have confusion in your life now. I wondered if the fellows that sold and kept the books for JAK Sales would be able to buy the company. There was plenty of money available to buy Rose and Edwin out. They could pay my share over the next two or three years. If I took the Colt job, I would have to be in California sometime and could still see Jane during those trips to the far west.

Wow, what are you doing? Planning your life around a woman? That's not Jack Knight. You better get your head on straight, boy, before you take this situation to Edwin. The fire was warming the tack room nicely and without realizing it, I fell asleep.

My boot heels hit the plank floor of the tack room at the same time I awoke out of a sound sleep. Edwin had swiped my feet from the table. It's dark outside and I had been asleep and dreaming for well over an hour.

"Hey, little brother it's time to rise and shine. Supper is on the table, and you need to tell me what you said to her to make Jane dance and sing an old Shoshone song while setting the table. I don't know the words, but have heard her sing the same song when she was happy about something. She's been dragging around since you left last month and this is the most excitement she has shown lately."

Still in a daze, I said, "Must be the squash blossom necklace I brought her from New Mexico. She liked the thing, I guess. Let's go have some salmon for supper. Jane said that was what we were going to have when she was starting to cook."

"Not so fast, partner. Are you sure nothing is going on between you and Jane."

"Well . . . since you brought it up, I can tell you I really don't know. We find we have feelings for each other, but right now I have no idea where this is going. We talked about our feelings a little this afternoon but nothing was resolved. And I can tell you one thing. Neither one of us is looking at marriage if that is crossing your mind."

"Jack, we need to talk more about this later. The girls are waiting for us to come in to supper so hold the thought 'til after we eat"

Rose gave me a big hug and we all had a seat at the table. Rose started with, "Was your trip a success, Jack? We have heard of several orders being wired to the office. One of your hardware companies in Albuquerque, I think that is the way you say it, ordered three Baxter Steam Engines and several different Gould Pumps to go with them."

"Oh yes, worked on that for a couple of days. Some rancher south of there wants to pump water out of the Rio Grande River to irrigate and water stock. Big, wide open ranch but the guy seems to know what he is doing."

Edwin spoke up, "Dennis, our bookkeeper, reported that your trip has generated over twenty-five thousand dollars already. What are you doing to charm those southwestern entrepreneurs?"

"Has to be the red hair, I guess. Then most of the wives get a kick out of my trick of cutting a cigar in half while in the husband's mouth with the bullwhip."

"You don't really do that! Do you?" Rose exclaimed.

"I have offered and if I should miss I tell them they don't need to buy; but if I cut the cigar the order is mine. I have done that a couple of times and have never failed to cut the cigar."

"Well." Edwin says. "Whatever you do, it works, so keep it up."

"Since you brought up work at the table, let me throw a thought out for discussion at the board meeting. What do you guys think about selling our company? The financial community looks like it is going into a stall for a couple of years and I have an idea that would relieve your work load as far as the company and show you both a good gain. Just an idea roaming around in my mind so can we talk about it?"

Talk about quiet. The room all of a sudden seemed to get cold and everyone was staring at me speechless.

Edwin cleared his throat before speaking, "Jack I know you're tired from the trip and have a lot on your mind, but we need some serious thought put into this proposal. Let's sleep on this and talk about it tomorrow. You have spent a year putting this company together, and believe me; compared to many companies this one is having great success. I'm not sure about the numbers, but I think only forty percent of businesses started are successful the first year. As far as the burden on Rose and me, it is nothing now that we have the office downtown. Dennis is more than capable of scheduling the salesmen and does all of the banking and bookkeeping that Rose and I used to do. The company is solid and will make you a wealthy man. Even with the current depression that is forming, JAK Sales will still have a market as the country continues to grow. The banks will inhibit the growth but can't stop it."

"Edwin, you have led me into more than one adventure in my life. I am grateful for all of that. I would in no way choose to make light of your contribution to my success, what ever it is; but I have an opportunity to represent the new Colt Manufacturing Company's peacemaker .44 caliber pistols. They want to introduce them to the public at large. It's the same gun the Army has had for over a year now only not in the .45 caliber used by them. Richard Jarvis feels it needs exclusive representation with no other line of product. I haven't responded to his letter since I only read it this morning when I was in the office."

Slowly as though not willingly to make any rash statement, Edwin replied, "It's your life, but we need to have a board meeting tomorrow to discuss the possibilities."

CHAPTER 19

It was Tuesday morning and nobody was talking at breakfast. Jane had made pancakes and fried bacon to go with our coffee.

Edwin finally broke the silence, "I have to go to the office for at least an hour. What is your schedule looking like this morning, Rose? If you're open, we could meet here at 9:30 and discuss Jack's proposal. Jack, you'll need to be sure of what you want because I don't have much time for this nonsense and would like to get it figured out today. I will bring the November statements from the company when I come home."

"Wait a minute, Edwin. The letter from Jarvis is over two weeks old. I haven't had any contact with him about content or contract for a job. Do we need to re-act this quickly? I might have jumped too fast on this, and, anyway, I don't remember having said we had to make any decisions immediately."

"Okay, no decisions, but let's have a board meeting and see where we are anyway. I might have overreacted, but yes I am upset. I thought we all had a good thing going here."

Jane cleared the table and stayed in the kitchen. Rose left her chair with her coffee in hand, walked around the table and pulled a chair up next to mine. Edwin headed out the door for his office.

Rose said, "Jack, I thought what we had put together was just what you wanted. You get to travel all over the west and see new people every day. You have had great success with the people you've hired and really have had no set backs that a lot of businesses are experiencing. Edwin isn't upset for us but only has trouble trying to figure out what you really want out of life for yourself. To him you have it all. Yes, you have responsibilities, but we both don't see you as tied down and unable to follow your original dream. The fellows that work for you are doing very well, and you could take some time off and just take a trip to Oregon to fish some of the rivers you talk about. The company will go on and when you're refreshed we can continue as we always have."

"I understand where you're coming from, Rose. I guess I see a life with the gun more adventurous than a life selling leather belts and water pumps. So far, I've not lasted very long at one thing. Maybe it must be born into me to be always looking for the next big deal. I don't want you and Edwin thinking I'm not appreciative of what you've done for me but I just have to explore this offer. First of all, I need to telegraph Mr. Jarvis, before going off half cocked. I might not even like his deal after I see the whole offer."

We left the kitchen with a sense that the matter wasn't really settled. I dressed for the day and rode to the telegraph office and sent an answer and some questions looking for more information on the proposal.

Edwin was home when I returned to the house and had paper work spread on the dining room table. He had removed his coat and vest to be comfortable but I could see his jaw was a little more firmly set for his expected confrontation.

Rose had coffee and three cups on a tray as she entered the room. She set the tray on a side table, filled the cups for each of us and took a seat for the meeting to begin.

"Jack," Edwin was speaking in a somewhat controlled tone, "let me start this meeting by bringing us up to date on the company as of the end of November, 1873. We have $19,451.00 in cash and reserves in banks. We have outstanding payables at just fewer than 8,500 dollars. This includes any loans to banks and any invoices not paid to date. With the petty cash in the office, we have around 11,000 dollars in liquid assets. We own livestock and wagons along with the office equipment of about 4,250 dollars. The company presently has four employees. Your company today is worth just over $15,000.00 on paper. Let's see now, you invested 2,500 dollars and Rose and I another 2.00 dollars about one year ago. Not a bad return if you also realize you were paid 2,400 dollars in wages, and Rose and I have received 200.00 dollars for our participation in the company. And don't forget, the bulk of your expenses were paid for your travels all over the west."

Sounding a little exasperated, he continued, "Jack, I participate in the affairs of many companies and can tell you that any of them would like to have the success that you have had. I know you have put some brutal hours in traveling and talked yourself hoarse at times to make this thing work, so I don't take lightly your hard work and time involved. I wish Father was here to help me persuade you to keep this endeavor going. No that's wrong, he might see it your way."

"Ok . . . OK . . . Edwin, I haven't taken the new job. But let's say I do. What about the company buying you and Rose out for say 500 dollars each and I sell my 2,500 shares to Ray Anderson, Keith Robbins, and Dennis Erickson for say three dollars a share? They pay me over the next five years at five percent simple interest and they own the company. That would be less than 50 dollars a month each and the company should generate that level of extra income in any market. If you have a better idea, tell me now. I'm listening."

"You're a fool. But then, little brother, you always have gotten your way so why should this time be any different. Let me do the negotiations with your crew, and I will let you know where you stand after that."

The next day, I received an answer to my message to Mr. Jarvis.

Hello Jack, Have sent by post the particulars of job offer. Enclosed also are two copies of a one page contract that if you sign, you become an employee of Colt Firearms Company. After your receipt of same let me know your decision. Richard.

Good! That would take 10 days or so. Hoped I could get everyone speaking to me again and try for a normal household 'til I can make my decision.

By early evening Edwin and Rose were both home and Edwin asked me to have a seat at the table.

"Jack, whatever you decide on we can all live with. Dennis feels we can make a deal with the three of them, and Rose and I want what you want. So it is up to you how this thing ends up. Now let's talk about you and Jane. I know something is going on between you and she and both

Rose and myself only want to protect Jane in this matter. If you hurt her or her feelings in any way you will answer to me. I feel responsible since she is like a daughter. If there is something between you two, please keep it discreet and don't flaunt it in front of Rose and myself or anywhere else in this town. If you take this other job, you are welcome in this house anytime you are in this area if it is to see us or Jane. Now, if I missed anything, please tell me because we need to return this to a home of peace and happiness. By the way, I still think you're a spoiled brat but love you anyway."

"Thank you, big brother, for your attitude in the whole thing. Mr. Jarvis has a package on the way for my consideration. In the meantime, I have a trip to Reno, Wells, and Salt Lake City scheduled and by the time I return the package should be here. As for Jane, I brought her a silver squash blossom necklace home from my last trip and because of that we have started a relationship that we have no idea where it will lead. Yes, we have feelings for one another but not anything that is permanent or need for your concern that she is going anywhere. Did I get that to come out right, Jane?"

"I think so Jack, but I must add that I liked Jack for more than the necklace he brought me. He is comfort when in this house."

Rose said, "Jane, we worry about you. The only life you have away from this house is your two to four day trips to the Mission every couple of months and that is the extent of your social life at present. If you and Jack find something in common, I am happy for you."

"Alright, we will discuss the company situation when you return from Salt Lake, For now, let's get back to normal living." Edwin said to wind up the meeting.

Jane had supper ready to serve and went about her work of setting the table and presenting a beef pot roast for our approval.

Late that evening after everyone has gone to bed, my door quietly opened and Jane glided over to my bed. She whispered in my ear, "Jack, I need you to hold me."

She lay next to me, raised her head to look into my eyes before continuing, "I know you're leaving tomorrow and did not want you to leave not knowing how I really feel about you. I have never had a lover but was raped when I was very young so I know a little about what lovers do. Love is a white man's word, but I like the sound of that word better than the Shoshone word for two people coming together."

My skill as a lover was limited, but I had been taught by some women well versed in the art of softness and tender actions that seemed fit for the occasion. Jane responded and we were as one for one of my most unforgettable nights yet. We fell asleep for some time and as the sun started to lighten my window, Jane, kissed me lightly on the lips and said, "I need to get to my own room and get dressed for the day. I love you, Jack. Never forget that." I stayed in the bed a little longer not wanting to give up this strange sweet sense of togetherness of being with another person who seems to have touched the inner heart. I came back to earth as noises of a waking household infiltrated the walls, jumped up and splashed water on my face to get me started for the busy day ahead.

Breakfast was wonderful with ham and eggs, fresh baked biscuits with fresh butter and extra jams, and everyone seemed normal again except Jane. She was singing in her native language and had a perpetual smile on her face.

Rose said. "Jane, how can you be so happy. Jack is leaving for ten days or so, and you seem to be walking on a cloud."

"That's alright. While he is gone, you're going to help me sew a dress to go with my new necklace then Jack can take me up town when he returns for coffee and talk like you and Edwin do sometime."

CHAPTER 20

The ride to Reno was quiet and I had a lot of time to read. As the train rolled to a stop in Reno, it started to snow. All I can hope was that it was only something local and not over the whole state of Nevada. I needed one day here in town and should spend at least two days in Wells. My plans were to ride up to a mine in the Humboldt Mountains to check about some pumps for their water transfer abilities. If that area got this snow I might as well head on into Salt Lake City.

It was Wednesday and had not stopped snowing. The railroad announced the road to Sacramento was closed in the Truckee area because of it but open to Salt Lake City. Can't go back. So on to Wells and just one day in that town. The hardware store there handled mining and farm equipment and has had some success with all our products it stocks. I was sure it was the time of the year, but since they have not had an order in for over two months, I needed to spend some time with Cal Jenkins. I wanted to make sure he remembered us in the future.

The going was tough for our train. The snow was so dry it blew with the wind and made seeing ahead very difficult. We were traveling at possibly twenty miles an hour. Trying to read was difficult while the conditions outside kept my eyes wandering to the window instead of concentrating on the printed page. At this rate, it would take eighteen hours to make a regular nine hour trip.

As our train pulled into Winnemucca, the snow seemed to be letting up. The last one hundred miles had been brutal due to the storm.

After hot coffee in the station, I asked for information on conditions ahead.

I was told the telegraph lines to Reno were down but working to Salt Lake City. If the snow continued to recede, we should make Wells seven hours behind schedule or so was overheard from someone listening to the conductor in his conversation.

My concern was heightened as the snow was now coming down harder than before as we began pulling away from the station. I remembered the area east of Winnemucca was mountainous and we would be going higher in elevation. Not good for less snow.

An hour later, we came to an instant stop. It was starting to get dark and looking out the window I saw about twenty Indians headed for the rail cars. As they get closer, I could see they were women and children with a couple of old men in the group. They looked like they were in trouble. I saw, behind them, a pack of eight wolves following and gaining on them.

The conductor came through the car and announced we had hit an avalanche and couldn't continue forward. He had not seen the movement outside so I directed his attention to it.

He hurriedly said to me and another passenger, "Help me at the rear door and see if we can get those people inside before the wolves get to them."

As he opened the door, I jumped out into the snow and helped the first woman carrying a small child up to the waiting hands of the conductor. I reached for the next person and saw the animals were about to attack two of the old men at the rear of the group. The old men were in the way to shoot the front running animals so I ran to the open area and pulled my .36 caliber pistol and fired at the front running wolf. Missed him as the bullet hit in front of his front feet. He halted from the shot and gave me time to aim at his body. The second shot caught him in the shoulder and he was dead before he hit the snow. The next two animals fell over the dead one in an attempt to run the old men down. I was lucky with the third shot, and one of the wolves caught a bullet in the neck.

By now, I was in the middle of the pack and they turned to me because I was the closest person in their way. I had six angry animals at bay and waited for all to get set to charge together. The passenger that came with me to help with the Indians was on the snow with a gun and shot two of the closer animals, and the other four started retreating. I shot one more round but missed as they kept running away.

We turned our attention back to the people still trying to make it to the train and helped them on board. The conductor placed half of the group in the car behind us and the rest in our car.

I began using sign conversation with one of the women, but she said she spoke English. She explained that the avalanche had roared through their camp and overran the tee-pees and all of the village was under snow now. She thought everyone that was in the village made it out but they have lost everything and had no where to go.

"Where are the men of the village?" I asked.

The same woman replied. "The men left to hunt early this morning and we do not expect them back today. We are a small band of Paiutes and live here in the mountains as we are of one family."

Turning my attention to our situation, it is apparent that we were in a mess. The conductor said the engine was still on the tracks but was over half buried in the snow from the avalanche and unable to go forward or backward. We had wood for the stove in the car to last through the night, but after that, we might be looking at a cold car to stay in.

The conductor came into the car from the express car and had his arms full of wool blankets saying, "We have a lot of these blankets up front. They were being shipped to Salt Lake City, but I think we need them more right here."

He saw to it that each Indian child got one and headed back for more to distribute in the rear cars.

I walked through the express car and crawled over the tender car to the engine. The fireman and engineer were eating from a lunch box on the floor of the cab.

The engineer watching my approach said, "Soon as we get done eating we are going to try and shovel the snow away from the engine and back us up. You look young and strong; want to give us a hand? It has quit snowing and the moon is out so we can see what we are doing.

I did this once before but never thought I would let the same thing happen again. I saw the avalanche coming but could only slow down before it hit. Good thing we were not 200 yards farther up the hill. The snow would have turned the whole train on its side or worse. Was that you shooting back there? What happened? As you can see, we still can't see behind us."

"Just a pack of wolves trying to catch some Paiute Indians for their supper. If we start now how long you think it will take to move enough snow to back this thing up and get back to Winnemucca?"

"Well, son, probably all night with the three of us. You need to shovel for say an hour and come back in the cab for ten minutes to warm up if you want to go all night. Sweeny will keep the firebox hot and ready while we work. He only needs to stoke the box every hour so he will work on the snow as much as we do. What's your name son?"

"Jack Knight from San Francisco. Taking a trip to Salt Lake City. Or I was before this."

By daylight the three of us had the left side of the tender and engine cleared of snow to the iron wheels. Two more hours and the engineer said it was time to see if he could move the train.

The boiler was at maximum pressure as Sweeny had kept the fire box stoked since the train had hit the avalanche. At the same time the engineer mounted the cab to move the train in reverse, ten horses with eight riders moved toward the train. It was the men of the small tribe we had saved from the wolves the night before. They stopped and were looking at the four frozen wolves. By the time two of them had dismounted, myself and a couple of the women from the tribe were within the circle of riders. One of the women was the one I was able to talk with last night.

She started dialog in Paiute, but changed to English when she realized I was at her side. The man was tall for an Indian and spoke good English. The group of eight men had two other horses with them and they had two Elk and three Antelope tied to the two pack horses.

The tall Indian put his hand out to me and said, "I am Chief Sand Hill. This is my wife, Small Fawn. I thank you for what you have done for my people. We came to the place our village was and saw the destruction. We were very worried until we started tracking to the west of the village and followed the trail. Later we saw the tracks of the lobo's and again the worry set in. Small Fawn say we lost no one and for that we thank you and the railroad. We hear the big noise but stay away from it because we know it is for white men not Indians."

"Chief, I am Jack Knight. What will you do now that your village is gone? The conductor has wrapped all your people in wool blankets and that kept the cold out in the railroad car but out here in the snow they are not much help."

"You see those trees on that hill just beyond the little valley in front of us? There is shelter in the trees, and we will be fine. In a few days the snow will go and we can recover the skins and other trappings from the old village. We have plenty to eat with our kill and if we can have the blankets you covered my people with we will get by."

All the Indians were off the train and standing close to a horse for warmth. Some had taken the blankets off and try to hand them back to the conductor. He held his hand up and would not take it from them.

I asked if there were any blankets left in the express car, and the conductor said there was one more bundle of about twelve.

I told the conductor to get the bundle and give it to the Indians and let me know who I needed to pay for all of the blankets. Also, to please collect the other blankets he passed out and give them to the Indians.

Carl, the conductor said. "Knight, you sure you want to do that? Those are Hudson Bay "Point Blankets," they are 4 and one ½ points. That is a very expensive wool blanket and there was four dozen of them in the pile."

"Just get me the delivery address and don't worry about what it will cost."

After the blankets were given to the Indians, Chief Sand Hill walked over to me and shook my hand and gave me a bear hug.

"Jack Knight, you are friend. Come see us again. We stay in this area all year round so easy to find."

As the Chief mounted his horse, I heard the engineer engage some gears, and he spun the wheels of the steam engine. The train moved about a foot in reverse and stopped.

The tribe of Indians headed for the tree area the Chief had pointed out and I boarded the car before the train started its run back to

Winnemucca. As I headed for my seat, Carl brought me an envelope with the paper work for the blankets.

Carl told me, "We could have folded the blankets that were left and the railroad would have to take the loss for the few the Indians had on."

"You're right, Carl, and some of those Indians would probably freeze to death tonight without the warmth of those blankets. No, Carl, we did right. Just thank the Lord we were able to be where we were to help at this time of their hardship.

CHAPTER 21

I had become very hungry by the time we arrived back in Winnemucca. No wonder. I realized I had not eaten since yesterday when we were in the Winnemucca station and had worked for over ten hours shoveling snow before the two hour ride back here.

The agent was asked when the line would be open for travel and he said it would probably be tomorrow at the earliest. The avalanche had taken the telegraph line down leaving me with no communication with Wells to learn the true damage to the rail line.

Nothing left to do but find the hotel and a seat in their dining room and enjoy a good breakfast.

Since we had no representation in Winnemucca, after breakfast I went exploring for an agent. I found a hardware store in the middle of town and walked in.

I had made a lot of cold calls in my short experience as a salesman but never had a greeting like this one.

"And jes' wha' the hell do ya want walkin' in here with that big white hat and that whip a hangen' in your sid," retorted a light haired girl that looked to still be of school age.

"I—I'm Jack Knight of JAK Sales out of San Francisco representing P&P Leather Co., Gould Pumps and the Baxter Steam Engine Company." Then regained my composure and added, "And I would like to see the owner or the manager if possible."

"You're a looking at both of 'em. My pa was killt last month 'bout whure yore standing by a big fella dressed 'bout like you. He didn't have no whip but I saw a long barreled pistol and ifen I ever see it agin I'll know it. Didn't make no sense. He and Pa got into an argment bout whuther the Levi pants we're sellen were the best or worst pants made in the west. My pa handed 'im a pair and askt him to tear the pocket off ifen he could, and the stranger jes' got mad and pulled that pistol of his'n and shot Pa in the chest, grabbed a pair of Levi's and fled out the door. So now there's jes me and Ma, and she ain't well enuff to work in the store. All the folks Pa bought from come by and hep with the orders that I buy, and I ain't goin' to add nutten else 'til I know whut our customers want that we ain't got exceptin' maybe some lumber and winders."

"I'm sorry for your loss and wish I could help you but you're probably right to only buy from the people your father bought from until you understand the business a little better. Mind telling me your name?"

"Dad called me Connie, but my name's Constance Churchill. Ain't no need feeling sorry fur me. Pa showed me how to run the store these las' three years. Ma and I will be jes' fine. Only wish I could go to school but I can read for my larning now." As an after thought, Connie added, "I turned sixteen this year. Lots of girls my age are out of school by now."

I excused myself and headed back to the hotel for a room and a place to take my boots off to let them dry out. I looked around the room, trying to think of something to help me relax while the boots dried. I thought about the Jules Vern book.

I remembered having started reading Around the World in Eighty Days, upon leaving Sacramento. I got it out of my valise, laid on the bed and began again to read but found I could not keep my eyes open even reading about Phileas Fogg's adventures. When I awoke it was the middle of the night. Moving off the bed, I found I had used some muscles I had forgotten I had shoveling the snow from the around the train.

Fumbling around, I found and lit the coal oil lamp on the dresser and checked my boots. They were dry enough to put on but looking at my watch it was only three in the morning and being sure nothing would be open to find food, I picked my book up and read for three hours.

As the gray dawn was peeking into my room, I figured the train depot and telegraph office would be open soon. I pulled my boots on and washed my face in the bowl on the dresser and headed downstairs.

The lobby was empty, but I heard noise from the area of the restaurant. As I walked in, an attractive young lady offered to seat me at a table. She said, "Sir, we open for breakfast in less than an hour, but I have coffee on and can get you a newspaper 'til then. Winnemucca usually is up and moving around but this snow storm has kept most people in their homes where it is warm I guess."

"The coffee and paper will be fine. Thank you."

She served the coffee and left a paper from yesterday on the table and I watched as she disappeared through a door into the kitchen.

On the front page of the Winnemucca Daily Republican was printed the executive order President Ulysses S. Grant executed back in October.

The President of the United States commanded it to be known that all soldiers that had deserted their colors and who shall on or before the 1st day of January, 1874, surrender them-selves at any military station shall receive a full pardon only forfeiting pay and allowances due them at time of desertion and shall be restored to duty without trial or punishment on condition that they faithfully serve through the term of their enlistment.

It was signed by E. D. Townsend, Secretary of War.

This situation had festered during the depression and the President needed to put an end to the problem.

Other news was just normal for the times, continued financial problems with banks and the conditions causing the New York Stock Exchange to continue its decline. Not what people wanted to read about but they needed to be aware of what was going on.

By the time I had finished the local news the girl had returned and asked for a breakfast order. Having seen all the cattle pens at the eastern side of town, I asked for steak and eggs to go with the toast on the menu that was touted as the best west of the Mississippi River.

I had just finished my breakfast when I heard a train whistle to the east of town. It had to be the west bound train and that meant the line was clear to Wells. That was good; I could get out of this cow town and closer to Salt Lake City.

At the train station, I learned the east bound would leave at 9:00 this morning. I headed for the hotel, picked up my valise and put my gun and whip belt on.

Back at the station, I recognized several of the passengers from our ill-fated trip to the avalanche, and some shook my hand and thanked me for giving the wool blankets to the Paiutes for their survival. Glad to be on board, I found my seat and returned to Phileas Fogg and his trip around the world.

The five hour trip to Wells went by fast as I became more interested in the book and read most of the way. Carl, the conductor, told me when we were about five miles from Wells; that my station was coming up shortly.

Wells was a small town with only one hardware store, Pacific Hardware. Due to the mining operations around Spruce Mountain and Cherry Creek, the store had done a good business in pumps and had sold several Baxter Steam engines to power them. I had thought about making a trip out to a couple of the mines with Cal Jenkins, the owner of the hardware store, but with the amount of snow on the ground I decided to forego that trip for now and just made a call at the store.

Entering the station, two fellows with what looked like cut off shovel handles, attacked me with their clubs and yelled, "Indian lover, get the hell out of our town."

My reaction was slow causing me to take a couple of hits from their clubs before ducking behind a post in the middle of the station and getting my bullwhip out of its saddle on my belt. I wrapped the legs of the closest man to me with the whip and set him on his back and his head hit the floor hard. He seemed out of the scuffle so I used the handle of my whip on the jaw of the next man, and he backed up and shook his head and headed into me again. He was big. When he hit me with his club it hurt to the point I got mad and drew my gun to try and stop his advances. He saw the gun but continued his charge so I shot him in the leg. His eyes went wide and he staggered back in disbelief and fell down.

By the time he hit the floor, the passenger that had sat in the seat next to me had the club out of the big fellow's hand and was standing over him ready to use it if he started to get up. The second man was getting up so I wrapped the whip around his body with his arms inside the wrap. Both men were still calling me an Indian lover and cussing about my ancestry.

I said, "Is there any law in this town and where do I find it?"

The fellow guarding the one on the floor said, "We don't have a lawman right now; but there is a judge, and we have a jail that can hold two people at a time. We can put these fellows in the jail and let the judge know what happened. This fellow needs to see a doctor 'cause the bullet is still in his leg."

We got both men to the jail and someone brought the doctor for the one with the bullet in his leg. About that same time, a short, well dressed man walked in and said, "You're under arrest, big fellow, for attempted murder. I hear you beat the hell out of those two fellows and tried to kill one of 'em. I'm Judge Longstreet. Please give me your gun and that bullwhip.

The judge was so short I almost had to get on my knees to talk to him.

"Judge Longstreet, you can arrest me, but I assure you this was all self defense as both men had clubs and attacked me and were yelling about me being an Indian lover just as I entered your train station. I assume this was only due to my giving forty eight blankets to the Paiute Indians that were run out of their village by an avalanche back near Winnemucca."

"Makes no difference. You shot a man from this town, and we don't hold kindly for acts like that. Now we're going to have a trial tomorrow and I need you to surrender to me right now. We will keep these men here in the jail and you can post bail and stay at our hotel tonight. Bail is set at 100 dollars just to make sure you stick around."

I gave up my gun and holster belt and, fortunately, had more than five 20 dollar gold pieces on me. The little man told me where to be in the morning for the trial and we all left the jail and walked toward the center of town and the hotel.

The next morning, I walked to the school house as directed and was surprised to see a lot of the town's people standing around it. I walked in and the judge was sitting at a desk at the front of the room. The two men I had problems with yesterday were next to him in chairs on his left. He pointed to the single chair on his right and said that was mine. After I sat, the room filled with the citizens of Wells.

Judge Longstreet hit his gavel on the desk and said, "Alright, people, let's get this over with so the school marm can ring her bell for the school day." The judge said. "What's your name, son, and where you from?"

"James Alburn Knight and I live in San Francisco, California."

"Okay, you are charged with attempted murder of a citizen of Wells, Nevada and we need to know how you plea."

"Not guilty your honor. I had to shoot the man in the leg for my own protection. And if I had wanted to kill him, I would have shot him in the head."

"Never mind the other stuff; your plea is not guilty, but you claim self defense. Is that what I'm hearing."

"Yes, your honor."

The judge said "Well, let's hear your story, and remember, some of these folks in this room were present and witnessed this crime."

"I walked off the train and attempted to enter the station. As I entered, two men with clubs confronted me yelling,' Indian lover,' and started swinging the clubs at me, hitting me before I had time to say or do anything. I retreated to a column in the station and got my bullwhip out and pinned one of the attackers to the floor and he was knocked out temporarily when his head hit the floor. The other man came at me and hit me several times with his club. I hit him with the butt of my whip, but he kept coming at me so I pulled my pistol and shot him in the leg. The first man was getting up by then and I wrapped his body and arms with my whip as a gentleman from the train stepped on the second man's leg to keep him out of the fracas. That is my total recollection of the crime as you call it. your Honor."

I saw Cal Jenkins from the hardware store stand up and address the judge. Cal said, "Judge Longstreet, I have asked several witnesses about this conflict and from their stories, what Mr. Knight has told you is the truth. I have known Jack for a year now, and I can tell you he is an honorable person and would not try to take another man's life unless it was to protect his own. Vern Logan is lucky it was Jack shooting at him or he could be dead right now. That's all I have to say judge and thank you for the time."

Judge Longstreet hit the gavel on the desk and announced "Not guilty, court adjourned."

CHAPTER 22

After my call on the hardware store and thanking Cal Jenkins for his little speech on my behalf, I headed to the train station to see when the next train to Salt Lake City was leaving, I was relieved to learn my trip could be continued within the hour. My pocket was now one ounce lighter than yesterday because the judge ruled I owed ten percent of my bail for cost of handling. He had no change so the cost was twenty percent or one of my twenty dollar gold pieces. With his attitude, I got the feeling I had gotten off cheap.

The 180 some miles to Salt Lake City took six hours and gave me time to complete my book by Jules Verne. The station was in town so the hotel was in walking distance and also the customer call at the Eagle Emporium Mercantile. Since it was late Saturday, Monday would be the earliest I could make a call on William Jennings at his mercantile. At Union Station, I picked up a newspaper called the *Tribune* for some outside news of the day and to find a possible theater guide.

After having checked in at the Hotel Utah and removed my boots, I sat by the window to read the paper. The front page had a couple of obituaries and news of another New York bank that had succumbed to the pressures of the times. The second page had a sports section with an article describing a British Open. It was a golf game played earlier this year at St. Andrews, Scotland, and was won by a fellow named Tom

Kidd. He had beaten twenty six other players and won by one stroke over the second place player. Kidd had received 11 pounds for the win.

Baseball was getting popular in the east and several teams were listed as the possible top teams to beat next year. This year the Boston Red Stockings won the pennant October, 22nd in Boston, 1873 being the second year in a row they had won the pennant. The names of some of the teams seemed silly but if you were into these sports, I guess you would have liked to identify with your team.

New York City had the Mutuals, Washington, the Blue Legs, and Boston the White Stockings. Some of the players had names like Cherokee Fisher, Lip Pike, and Deacon White.

The theatre listings were on the back page and the only play that I knew anything about was at the Salt Lake Theatre. I had seen **Othello**, by Shakespeare, so I could pass on that. The Aiken Theatre had a musical and I would pass on that also.

Tomorrow was Sunday, and I remembered seeing a Presbyterian Church on my way from Union Station. I would worship in the Presbyterian Church, and be much more comfortable in my choice. I had nothing against the Mormon religion which was prevalent in this town, I just didn't understand it. Father taught us to respect all religions and I had done business with several Mormons. They were great people to deal with but they would really rather work with other Mormons. My company had something they needed so presently they worked with me.

Monday morning, I walked to the Eagle Emporium and asked for William Jennings. I brought the shipping documents for the forty eight wool blankets given to the Paiute Indians. They had been consigned to the Mercantile at the Eagle Emporium, Attention: William Jennings. I knew him as the owner and the person that ordered my product.

The boy on the floor said he would find Mr. Jennings and for me to feel free to look around while he fetched Mr. Jennings. In the area with books for sale, I saw one I had heard about and had a curiosity to read. It was Uncle Toms Cabin, a story about slavery in the south. Someone told me it was first published as a forty one part series in the weekly *National Era* paper. It had been in print since 1852, but this was the first one I had seen outside a library. Having finished Around the World in Eighty Days, it was time to start another novel.

After my purchase, William Jennings walked to the front of the store and greeted me warmly and shook my hand.

"Jack, I was not sure we would see you anymore this year. I do have a list of items we need if you can get it here before spring. I hear we are in for a heavy snow pack. The farmers say the squirrels have picked up every nut available and that's supposed to mean a rough winter for us this year."

"Well if that is true you need to reorder the wool blankets you were expecting this week. I took them off the train and gave them to some Indians that were left homeless by an avalanche back outside of Winnemucca last week. The shipping documents in my hand gave me no idea what they sell for, but I told the railroad people I would pay for them if they gave them up to the Indians."

"Jack, no one else but you would pull a stunt like that. I wouldn't expect less than that from you. Even if I don't hold with Indians 'cause they have murdered some of my people; I guess there has to be some good and some bad just like the whites. Let's go up to the office and see just how much you are into me for. As I remember those were supposed to be very heavy wool and a large cut. I have to order those out of Canada, you know."

"Oh yes, here it is. Those were over four point wool blankets I was told. They were 84 inches by 60 inches and premium wool. Looks like I paid three dollars plus eleven dollars for shipping. I would sell them for 5.25 each so let's say you owe me about $4.00 each or 192 dollars and call it even. Consider that fair, Jack?"

"I wasn't asking for a discount but that seems more than fair under the circumstances. I do appreciate the cut, and I'm sure some of those Paiute's would have frozen to death without the use of those blankets. They'll also be put to good use after they get their tee-pees out of the avalanche and snow that wiped out the village."

With the blanket incident taken care of, William proceeded with the business at hand. "Jack, here is my order. I need 200 feet of 3 inch by ¼ inch leather belting. Send me five of the W-25 gallon series Gould pumps and three 10 horse power Baxter Steam engines. I have a couple of fellows south of here that are planting peach orchards and will need to move water for the irrigation systems."

Thanking him for the generous order since I had not expected that much business this time of the year, I added, "I need to try and catch the train today and head for San Francisco. So let me get out of your hair and on my way. And I will send the money for the blankets as soon as I am back at the office. And again, thank you."

Making the Monday west bound train, I settled in with my new book for the long 500 or so mile trip back to Reno for an overnight stay and to see another customer before continuing on to Truckee, California. Then it's on to home, looking forward to a possible breakfast with Jane at a downtown hotel for conversation and more coffee than I should drink at one sitting.

After reading for what seemed an hour, I looked over at my seat partner sitting opposite me on the isle side of the car. He had been watching me, I noticed out of the corner of my eye. Putting my book aside, I introduced myself to him.

"Hello there, I am Jack Knight, from San Francisco," Having offered my hand to shake his.

As he took my hand, he said, "My name is Frederick C. Zimmermann of Dodge City Kansas traveling to San Francisco on business."

"And just what business are you in, Mr. Zimmermann."

"Hardware and I am also the Dodge City gunsmith. I'm building the hardware store on Front Street which also will handle general merchandise along with lumber for my customers."

"Sounds like you are a very busy man, Mr. Zimmermann."

"Please call me Fred if you would care to. Yes, with my wife, Matilda, we keep busy every daylight hour of the day. And what do you do to keep busy besides reading deep novels like Uncle Toms Cabin?"

"I have an agency that represents three major manufacturing companies to people like you. I was also trained as a gunsmith for five years and became quite efficient at the art of repair and rebuilding of weapons. My teacher was Diego DeLacruse, originally from Spain and a fine teacher he was. He is also a fine knife maker and now lives in Denver."

"DeLacruse . . . I have two knives made by him. I have a friend that knew him in Kansas City, I believe it was. I bought the blades from him last year and he told me of this man and that he was from Spain. The bullwhip you carry, are you proficient with that as a weapon?"

"I like to think so. It has come in handy several times and prevented a couple of deaths from bullets, I feel. Are you on a buying trip to San Francisco for your hardware store, Fred? I have a lot of contacts that might be of service to you if you are inclined."

"No. I have a consigned load of merchandise that was shipped by water via the overland trail in Panama and am picking it up to load on a train returning to Dodge City. The only reason I feel the need to meet that boat is my merchandise is all from London and I want to make sure it is complete and nothing was lost on that long trip. Never having been in San Francisco, you could be of service to me on a place to stay for three days, and as you suggested, I might want to talk to some suppliers about some hardware."

"Well, Fred, I am sure we can help you on all those counts. My company has a wagon and would have no problem loaning it for transport of your merchandise from boat to the rail-road. Finding a good transporter can be a pain at times. We have some very nice hotels, and I can attest that some are as nice as the Pacific Grand Hotel in Chicago, if you are so inclined."

"Thank you in advance for the wagon loan. That is one problem solved. I don't need anything as grand as the hotel you describe. Just a reasonable and clean room with food available and I will do very well. What are the manufacturers you represent?"

"We have a leather company, Gould Pumps, and the Baxter Steam Engine Company. Our business started around a year ago and we have had great success with all three of our clients. I have two other salesmen working territories from Mexico to Canada giving me time to work the southwest. Our office is close to down town with an office manager and girl Friday taking care of local distribution and what ever else comes up."

"Jack, I have a leather company out of Kansas City that I use right now. The line of pumps might be of interest, and I'm not sure about the steam engines. Let me think about it, and we can talk more before I leave town. I heard you ask about arrival times in Reno. Are you planning on staying overnight?"

"I had that in mind but after I found out the time of arrival my mind is changing and will pass on staying overnight. I did see the customer last week on my way east so staying is not that important this trip."

"Tell me Jack, how does the train get to San Francisco from Oakland? I saw on a map the rails seem to stop in Oakland, but my ticket is to San Francisco? There seems to be a large body of water between the two and no bridges to be seen."

"As you'll soon see, they have a barge ferry carrying the rail cars to a terminal on the waterfront in San Francisco. You'll be riding this same car across the water and stepping off in San Francisco. There is talk of a bridge to be built but probably will happen several years from now. A rail runs from Oakland to San Jose and from there you can take train north into San Francisco, also." Looking thoughtfully, Fred said, "Sounds like the far west is well ahead of us Kansas farmers."

CHAPTER 23

The next day we arrived in Sacramento. The weather was typical California. The sun felt warm after all the snow we had encountered east of here. Fred and I both got off the train and walked for a couple of blocks to get the kinks out of our legs.

I walked with Fred over to the Huntington Hopkins Hardware store for a peek at what was considered a premier hardware store in our area.

He was impressed and remarked that his store had along way to go to attain the magnitude of what we saw in front of us. Dodge City had to grow also to support something of this size. He said. "Jack, I was born in Prussia, lived in Paris, France and London, England. It's hard to realize that the West will ever be as civilized as the European countries, but seeing the progress in just Sacramento and the buildings here I believe it can surpass Europe someday. I don't believe Dodge City, Kansas will ever become as large as the cities out here, but that is fine with me. My wife and I love Kansas and hope it grows but not like this area has. We have a farm we are improving on just west of Dodge City, and it has very fertile ground that we have high hopes for. I want to show the people of Ford County that wheat will be a profitable crop and help to feed the incoming families. Rambling on so much has taken so much time; I guess we'd better get back to our train before it leaves us here. Thank you for this little side trip, Jack, and enjoy your company. If you ever get to Dodge City, we would be pleased should you stop by and see us."

Walking back toward the train station, some thoughts came to mind, "That might be sooner than you think, Fred. I haven't discussed this with anyone outside my family as yet, but I possibly will be on the road selling firearms early next year. I have a feeling that Kansas has need for this particular piece. The cow towns will be my main concentration for a start. You have heard of the new Colt .45 caliber for the army, I'm sure. Well, they want to introduce a .44 caliber on the same frame. I am involved with Colt Manufacturing through the Baxter Steam Company which is a division of Colt. Mr. Jarvis, the president of Colt has offered me the position of representing the Colt. I have responded but not accepted the job yet. What would you say to Colt if offered to you?"

"To tell you the truth, if I were single like I was when having a job just like that several years ago I would naturally say yes. You are single, are you not? It sounds exciting, and yes, I know of that single action .44 caliber frame. I heard they want to call it the Peacemaker. Could be a good name for it but probably won't be used by everyone to make peace if I know the average gun totter. We have some ruthless people out here in the west and it's going to take a lot of years to bring the law as we would like to see it. If you do this, make sure I am your target in the Dodge City area. I can sell a lot of that model to the cowboys that end up in our fair city. I heard this particular gun might sell for around seventeen dollars. Back when I sold guns I sure didn't get rich. You sure you can pass on what you have going now for this type of life?"

As we were now boarding the train, my mind was swimming with some of the conversation about money and life style Fred had added to my thought process. He was right. I sure would have to sell a lot of guns at seventeen dollars to make the kind of money I've taken out of JAK Sales the last year. Fred was probably ten or fifteen years my senior and had seen more of the known world than me, but even with his advice and wisdom that word adventure kept passing in front of me and possibly blinded the reality of any possible hardship. Fred bought a book on European history in Reno so I had time to read a little from Reno to Sacramento catching very little sleep. Finally with the bright sun, it was hard to keep my eyes open so I covered my eyes with my hat and fell asleep.

As sleep overtook me, I started the same dream again. Since leaving San Francisco, all my dreams had been of Jane. This was not normal for me as women had never had a lasting place in my thoughts or dreams. My mind tried to concentrate on something other than Jane, but the harder I tried, the less I seemed to succeed at altering my dream pattern. I gave up and just enjoyed the ride we were taking in a buckboard to somewhere. I couldn't see the path with my eyes because of the cloud cover on the trail ahead. The vision was in black and white except for the squash blossom necklace. Its turquoise and silver colors were brightly visible. The horse was white and the buckboard was black, and we were floating on a white cloud so even the ground wasn't visible. The ride was smooth as if gliding but the wheels were turning, seeming to not touch the trail surface. We never spoke but we laughed and smiled when our eyes made contact. The farther we rode, the darker the sky became and soon I found myself riding in the buckboard alone. No clue to what had happened to Little Bird, but I was the only rider and the cloud on the ground was gone. The wheels are now hitting the trail with a vengeance, and I was being thrown side to side, and up and down. I awoke suddenly and my book was still on my lap just as it was when I fell asleep.

Fred noticed I had awaken and jovially remarked, "Hope that was a good sleep? You sure had a great smile on your face. My wife smiles in her sleep just like that, and she says she never has a bad dream and enjoys her sleep when a dream appears. I have dreams, but they always seem to have work related visions. I seem to be clear back in my young life when an inspector for arms for our army in Cologne. That was a happy time. I was single and had enough of an income to be able to sport the ladies around. Never seemed to dream of the ladies. Only something on post about some new advance use of firearms. I do dream about the farm. But then I am planting something or harvesting a crop. Seem always something to do with work."

"Sounds as though you have high hopes for your little city, Fred. I hear there are a dozen or so men buried in a cemetery called "Boot Hill" there. All shot in gun fights of some kind in Dodge City. Do you have any lawmen to keep the peace? Sound like a wide open place for any drifter to me. I remember when Abilene was the first cow town in Kansas but don't remember killings like that happening when I was there. We had fights with other cow hands from other outfits and the brawl might last for several minutes to a half an hour but there were lawmen to break the scuffles up before someone was killed most of the time. I remember other outfits would pick fights with my cow hands just to watch me use the bullwhip to break them up and no one died in those scuffles. I hear they even shoot men in the back in Dodge City."

"There are two factions working against each other in Dodge City, Jack. It has become polarized with the cowboys and cattlemen wanting the open society of gambling, easy women, and lots of whiskey, against the other side of town that want schools, churches, and a respectable place to live. Ford County appointed Charlie Bassett as their Sheriff and things are improving but being just one man with two deputies or under-sheriffs to help it isn't an easy task. It was just last month Charlie was elected to the post and has gained more respect now than he had before the election. We are not incorporated as a city yet but will be early next year, and then a town Marshall will be added for further protection. Dodge City needs the cattlemen to grow so we will have to learn to live together and even though it is divided by the railroad tracks we are one town."

We both went back to our books until we reached the docks where the train cars were to be loaded on the barges for the trip across the water to San Francisco. It was cool outside the cars but we both got off the train and stood at the rail of the barge watching the small waves of the bay lick the sides of our transportation to the big city.

Fred said wistfully as he gazed out across the bay, "This brings back memories of rides across the channel between England and France. The water is smoother and calm next to the sea water of the channel but the smell is close and I had forgotten how much I miss smell of salt water. That large opening to our right is the way to the Pacific Ocean, I assume?"

"Yep, the ships all have to come through that passage to get to San Francisco or any of the several cities docks on the bay. See that island on your right? That is Alcatraz Island, the federal prison for the country's worst offenders."

The trip across the bay had been uneventful, and we were on dry land in less than one hour. We both took our luggage from the iron wheeled cart the railroad uses to transport its passengers' belongings. It was only a two-block walk to JAK Sales office from the ferry building so we walked the short way before summoning a buggy to take Fred to a hotel and me to home. I agreed to meet with Fred in the morning to help him arrange delivery of his goods by JAK Sales' wagon and horses to the rail head for his trip back to Dodge City. Afterwards, Fred and I would join Edwin in his office. Fred wished to gets some banking information from Edwin and we would do most of that discussion over lunch. When he questioned me about some banking processes, I suggested Edwin would be more informative about that than I.

Fred chose the Pacific Railroad House recommended by Ray Anderson who was in the office doing his paper work from a trip to Los Angeles that week. The hotel was just off 4th Street and close for me to pick him up in the morning.

Ray wanted to talk about my leaving the company, but I cut him short because now all I could think about is getting home and seeing Jane before supper time. Again it was like my dreams; I had never been this distracted by a female before in all my life.

CHAPTER 24

The house felt warm after the buggy ride from the office. Jane was cooking something that smelled good as I quietly closed the front door to surprise the cook. Her hearing was better than I expected. She ran into the parlor to meet me before I had walked four steps from the door. Having thrown her arms around me, she kissed me as softly and warmly as though I had been away for a long time, not just nine days.

Pulling slowly away she said excitedly, "We thought you wouldn't be home until tomorrow, but I'm glad you made it home today." Then somewhat sheepishly or teasingly, she continued, "Rose is in Sacramento and won't be home tonight. Edwin told me he would be home for supper early and was going to ride the train this evening to San Bruno for a meeting with some bank examiners and would be staying overnight. You know what that means? We have the house to just us. I hope you have a good book to read to me tonight."

Having taken control of my emotions and trying to sound more normal than the feelings that her touch had stirred, I said, "I don't believe you would enjoy Uncle Tom's Cabin that I have been reading but maybe a story about my brother, Jay and me and one of our escapades would be better listening. We had an adventure last year that is worth repeating."

Reluctantly leaving her so she could go back to the kitchen, I took my luggage to my bedroom. By the time my travel case was unpacked, Edwin was home for supper.

"Well, hello, Jack. I just left your office and they said you had gone home. Ray also told me between his trip to San Diego, your trip to Salt Lake City and the order from Hooker; we have the biggest month on record without even hearing from Keith yet on his trip through Oregon. And it is only the middle of December. I have a question about an article in the *Examiner*. There was a story about you or some other guy named Jack Knight and some Paiute Indians in Winnemucca, Nevada. It stated you took some four dozen Hudson Bay blankets and gave them to the Indians. What the hell is that all about?"

"Well big brother, those Indians would have frozen to death without the blankets and you nor I could not let that happen now could we? I've already made arrangements to pay the person the blankets were consigned to that were being shipped on that train."

"You're right. I probably would have done the same. Made one hell of a story and several of my colleagues had to show me the article. And Rose said, 'see I told you he had a heart too big for his body.' There must be more to the story than was in the newspaper so spill it now and I'll share it with Rose later."

"I did have to kill off some wolves that were chasing the women and young ones, but I had some help with that. The small tribe had their village wiped out by the same avalanche that caused our train to be stopped, and they just appeared and needed some help with the wolves closing in on them."

"Good story. How come you always seem to be the Knight in the right place at the right time? I never get to experience the adventures the rest of my brothers seem to be a magnet for."

"Edwin, you forget the people who look up to you as a hero. I know you have gone out of your way for guys like Joe McCoy in Abilene. He worships you and look at Richard Jarvis. He says he would not be where he is without your help. They're just the ones I know of. It wouldn't surprise me if you've left your mark in so many places you can't count them."

"Okay . . . Okay. You made your point. Let's have some soup and whatever else Jane has made for supper so I can make my train to San Bruno. My firm represents a bank in trouble and I'm not sure I can help them. We became involved too late I'm afraid. These are not the best of times for a bank short on money and heavy into mortgages. By the way, I asked Jane this morning if you came home today should I have Ray Anderson's mother come and stay with her in the house while both Rose and I are away. She assured me she knew how to handle a knife well enough to protect her self. So watch yourself, little brother. I wouldn't want to come home and have your scalp hanging in my kitchen."

Laughing out loud at the thought of Jane raising a knife to control my attentions, I replied, "Don't worry about me, you go do what you have to do and I will survive."

Turning to go down the hall, Edwin asked me to hitch his horse to the buggy while he got his overnight case together and take him to the train station. We caught up on the events of my trip and people I had seen during the short trip.

When I returned, Jane had the barn door open for me to put the horse to his stall and the buggy into its lean-to shed next to the barn. Brr-r-r-r. the later it got the colder the weather, so the warmth of the house felt good to my body.

Little Bird was sitting at the table with a cup of coffee, got up and poured one for me also. She had her hair pulled back with one braid streaming down her back. Looking at this slim silhouette that moved so gracefully about the room, I realized she was more beautiful than I had remembered.

The warmth of the coffee removed the chill from outside and now I was becoming totally absorbed with the presence of this enchanting person I had been dreaming about so much.

Looking at me tentatively, she placed the coffee pot back on the stove. My mind snapped to attention as she spoke, "Jack, it is too early to go to bed so would you please read to me for a while. I found this book of poems in Rose's library and they sound so much like how I feel; I would like to hear how they relate to my thoughts. I love you Jack, and nothing will ever change that but again I say to you I am not wanting you to settle down. I just want to be with you when you are in

San Francisco. My life is to serve Rose and Edwin, and I have no desire to change that."

Having taken the small book from her while trying not to become confused by her words, I opened it and found a group of poems by Emily Dickinson. The first poem was called "Surrender". It sounded appropriate for this occasion.

Doubt me, my dim companion!
Why, God would be content
With but a fraction of the love
Poured thee without a stint
The whole of me, forever,
What more the women can,—
Say quick, that I may dower thee
With last delight I own!
It cannot be my spirit,
For that was thine before;
I ceded all of dust I knew,—
What opulence the more
Had I, a humble maiden,
Whose farthest of degree
Was that she might,
Some distant heaven,
Dwell timidly with thee!

Looking at her, I saw she had closed her eyes and was still as a statue. Opening them, they seemed to be misty when she began speaking in a soft voice, "Oh Jack, I'm not sure I understand everything you said, but the way you let the words tumble from your lips is like what I imagine I will hear in the hereafter. I am sorry but I probably say the wrong things but I hope you understand what I say."

"I think I do. But remember, this is an area I know little about."

As she arose from her chair to leave the room, Jane asked, "Would you come and lay with me now? I would like to have you close to me for a little while to relax from the day."

Before getting ready to retire, I checked both doors and banked the fire for the evening; Jane had removed her dress and had cuddled between the sheets in my bedroom when I returned. Feeling unusually modest, I asked Jane to turn toward the wall while I undressed.

After I covered myself, I put my right arm under her neck and her head ends upon my chest. The warmth of her body against mine was beyond words. She was so beautiful and her body was so soft and smooth. Every nerve of my body became inflamed with desire. We lay in each others arms saying nothing for sometime.

Jane raised her head, looked into my eyes and began speaking softly, "Jack this is that distant heaven you spoke of in the poem. I have put myself to sleep for many months thinking of you and I like this. I have spoken of my feelings to Rose and she said she had spent many nights in my bed before I arrived with the same thoughts about Edwin before he even would acknowledge the attraction he had for her."

Startled by her comment, I replied, "You and Rose talk about our feelings for each other!?"

"Jack, she is a romantic just like me and we can talk of such things in a caring way and do not judge one another in any way. She is happy for us both but is afraid I will be hurt in some way. That will not happen as I expect nothing but love from our being together and want nothing else from you."

Bringing her closer, we kissed and became one. My entire being seemed transformed to making sure she knew my love was total and for her alone. I knew in my heart I had found what most men can only dream of and this gave me the will to make her enjoyment even beyond mine.

Afterwards, lying spent from our efforts, Jane said, "I wish every woman could experience the total joy that you give to me. I want to sleep for a while and try that again. Can we just hug and sleep for a time, my love?"

We both woke at the same time and it was still dark outside. We began once again to touch each other caressingly, restirring passions anew, until we became locked as one for the second time of the night and experience total joy of togetherness.

Later, waking suddenly from a sound sleep, the sun was trying to shine through my window. I got to my feet quickly remembering I had made a commitment to help Frederick Zimmerman retrieve his cargo from the ship that morning and to carry it to the railroad ferry docks to be loaded for his trip back to Dodge City. I looked at my watch and saw it was only 8 o'clock in the morning. I had agreed to have the wagon at Fred's hotel by 9:30 to pick him up. If I didn't shave and hurry, I'd make it to the office, pick up the wagon and arrive at the hotel with a minute or two to spare.

Fred was standing outside when I pulled to the front of his hotel.

"Good morning, Jack," he greeted me as he approached to get onto the wagon. "We have a nice day in the making. I assume you have heavy fog a lot of the days in this part of the country." As an afterthought, he added, "Hope you had breakfast already. I was up early and have already eaten."

"Fred, I've been so busy this morning I haven't even had time to shave yet. I rode my horse to the office bareback this morning 'cause I was afraid I would be late picking you up if I took the time to saddle her. What the heck. I might as well spill the beans. I overslept. My brother and sister-in-law are out of town and the house was too quiet."

Fred pulled himself into the seat beside me in the wagon and we arrived at the ship's dock while the crew was still unloading crates of goods. Fred jumped down and walked over to a pile of crates and waved a signal at me to bring the wagon. There were 8 crates with his name and Dodge City address on the sides and top of each one. Each weighed over one hundred pounds so it took us both to load them into the wagon. After he received the manifest package, we took off for the railroad ferry.

Fred consigned his eight crates to Wells Fargo Express and told them he would be in Dodge City to claim them five days from now.

We swung by Edwin's office for an hour and had lunch served in the office so Fred and Edwin could complete the business that had been on Fred's mind.

That being taken care of, we headed for Fred's hotel. Before entering the door, he called out, "Jack I would like to go to the theater tonight. Would you and your best girl like to accompany me? Tomorrow I leave so this will be my last evening in San Francisco and I would enjoy your company at my expense, of course. If you're agreeable, how about supper here at the hotel and you pick the theater for us?"

With an idea brewing in the back of my mind, I answered, "I think we can make that work."

When Fred entered his hotel, I parked the wagon and entered from the rear entrance to the restaurant and asked for the manager. He was summoned fairly quickly. I must have had a tone of urgency in my voice.

"Yes. I am Aldo, how may I help you sir?"

"My question, Aldo, is do you mind serving Indians in your dining room at night with your regular dining guests?"

"Sir, as long as he or she is properly dressed, we make no differences between Indian or white at this hotel. I would be glad to serve any guest you bring with you tonight or any other night."

"Thank you Aldo, then I'm quite sure we will enjoy the dining experience in this restaurant tonight."

This had to be done for I would not tolerate a scene with Jane as the person being made a spectacle because of her race and that could happen in some of the establishments in this town.

After returning the wagon and checking on this week's paper work, I rode bareback to the house and fed and put my horse away.

Walking into the house, I saw Jane was having something to eat and she invited me to share her plate. Declining being satisfied from lunch, I said, "Jane, I hope you have finished that dress you said Rose was going to help you make because we are going to dinner at a nice hotel and to the theater after with Mr. Zimmerman from Dodge City, Kansas."

Looking both surprised and pleased, she said, "It is finished, but I had no idea I would need it so soon. You will love it. Rose bought several yards of the most beautiful white linen fabric and there was enough for both of us a dress. Mine was made to run five inches below my knees and then Rose slit the skirt two inches above my knees on both sides. She said she saw that on a Chinese girl and knew it would look better on me with my skin color. Let me get it and show you."

"No, let me see it when we are dressed ready to go."

I picked up the *Examiner,* turned to the theater page and found, *Hunchback,* an 1832 comedy I had seen with Saki in its production playing at the American Theater. Saki was not in this play but I was sure both Fred and Jane would enjoy it.

When late afternoon came upon us, Rose arrived home from Sacramento and seemed worn out from her experience.

As she slumped into an easy chair with a despondent look on her face, I asked, "Was the trip successful? You seem weary from either the trip or the case you were working on."

"Jack, it is a sad case. Some Chinese workers were attacked while helping build a tunnel for the railroad up north and six of them were killed with no fault of the railroad. Two men have been caught and identified by the survivors. Because the men that were killed were Chinese, I don't think their wives will see any satisfaction from our state about the killing or any compensation from the railroad. My partner and I took the case for the wives but had no expectation of obtaining anything for them. Because of this, we decided to take the case for no fee."

"I'm sorry to see how hard this is affecting you, Rose. I doubt we will see equal rights for some of our foreign friends in our life time. But some day, I believe, we will all be accepted as equal and skin color will have no bearing on cases like yours. My father brought us all up to believe that someday that would happen."

CHAPTER 25

Walking into the parlor in her white dress with her glistening, black hair streaming over the heavy color of the turquoise squash blossom necklace, I noticed Jane's choice of shoes. They were dress moccasins of white leather with lots of turquoise beads with silver buckles. Her skin color was highlighted by all of the white in her dress and to me she was the most beautiful woman I had ever seen. For a person standing just over five feet tall she filled the room with her presence like a princess.

Rose catching the appreciation of the vision in front of us said, "Jack, what do you think of our creation? That dress turned out great. I had no idea it would show her off like it does. I once saw something like it on a beautiful Chinese girl."

Not taking my eyes off of Jane, I answered, "You did a great job, Rose. Jane tried to tell me about the dress and I wouldn't let her, but I had no idea it would turn her into the most beautiful woman I have ever had the pleasure to look at. I am so proud of her. She will be stared at tonight by men and women at the restaurant we are going to for dinner and at the theater we will be going to afterwards."

While Jane was showing her dress off, Edwin walked in the front door and whistled in a low sound as he grabbed Rose and planted a kiss that lasted too long for my taste, but then he's had more experience than I in that kind of stuff.

"So what is the occasion that warrants my goddaughter getting all dressed up? You look very nice, Jane. I hope Jack is wearing his whip and gun if you're going out like that with him. He might just need the added protection."

Jane bubbling with excitement said, "We are going out for dinner and to the theater with one of Jack's friends from Dodge City."

With that we were on our way. I hitched the four place buggy up with two horses and made sure I had nose bags with oats for them to eat while we had our supper.

Jane was giddy with excitement as we made our way to Fred's hotel, but when we stopped and set the horses for their stay in the street a calmness came over her and she stepped from the buggy like she had done this every day. Entering the restaurant, we could feel the eyes on us, and looking over the crowd, everyone had a comforting smile on their faces. Seeing Fred at a table, I directed Aldo to take us there.

Fred got to his feet. "What a pleasant surprise. You have excellent taste in women Jack."

"Fred, let me introduce you to Jane. She is Shoshone and we have known one another for over a year. This will be Jane's first dinner out, and we are looking forward to the good food and the fine company. For your pleasure, for after dinner, I have chosen the comedy *Hunchback* for the theater tonight. I hope that is agreeable with you?"

"That's fine, Jack. I have read about that play but have not seen it as of yet. Now I don't drink liquor but don't let that stop you or the lady. I spoke with Aldo about the menu before your arrival, and he told me the seafood is the specialty of the house and felt no one does it better in San Francisco."

"As for liquor, we are not hard beverage drinkers either. Just never got a taste for it, but I love Sarsaparilla if they have it."

"Jane would you like a glass also?"

"Yes please, Jack."

Fred asked the waiter to bring three glasses of Sarsaparilla to start with and we had agreed on the Pacific Salmon and baked squash with the butter and molasses sauce for our dinner.

Fred continued, "How about a bowl of your Boston clam chowder for each of us also? That should take care of us, and we will finish with a cup of coffee for our conversation time after we have eaten."

Fred spent more time talking with Jane about her education and her background as a child than conversation with me. She was enjoying herself and seemed very relaxed with the company. She told Fred about her living at Fort Bridger and he related his time spent with Jim Bridger at his farm in Missouri.

After our coffee service, we took the buggy ride to the American Theater and found the only seats left were in a private balcony setting with a great view of the stage. Watching Jane enjoy the play made the rest of the world seem far away and I found myself relaxing and enjoying being together as a couple.

We dropped Fred off and said goodbye with a parting hand shake. He was leaving early in the morning for his trip back home. Jane blushed as he kissed her on her cheek and I was thinking that must be as close as she had been to anyone besides me since her childhood.

Riding home, with eyes sparkling with the wonder you see in a child when it has been filled with much happiness, Jane burst out with, "That is the second best evening I have had in my life, Jack."

I asked what she felt was the best if this was only second best.

She quickly retorted, "The best was the first night you made love to me. That memory will remain with me as long as I breathe, Jack."

The next day a package was delivered to the house from Colt Manufacturing containing an employment agreement with a letter explaining that they would set up a warehouse in Denver at a Wells Fargo Express Office to hold product for shipment. They offered me 150 dollars a month plus expenses for any travel by rail, stagecoach, riverboat, or steamship. My meals and lodging were my responsibility. There would also be 2% additional compensation on my gross sales out of the Denver and Hartford facilities. I could accept this agreement starting January 1, 1874 by telegram to Mr. Jarvis.

In a wooden case, I found a .44 caliber, nickel plated Colt Peacemaker engraved with running cattle and a bullwhip on each side of the 7 ½ inch barrel for an extra incentive to accept the contract. What a beautiful pistol. I would have to get Margo to make me a new holster as my other gun had a shorter barrel. I supposed I would have to make up my mind today so Edwin could finalize the paper work on JAK Sales if I was leaving the company.

Since Richard Jarvis had sent me my present for my 25th birthday, I sure had to follow through and accept his offer. I saddled a horse and rode to the telegraph office and sent a message of acceptance to Hartford, Connecticut.

That evening the meeting in Edwin's office with Rose, Ray Anderson, Keith Robbins, and Dennis Erickson ended very well even though Edwin had increased the sale price by 2,000 dollars more to add to his and Rose's share which was fine by me. Over the next five years I would receive seven thousand, five hundred dollars plus interest for my one year of work and three men would grow with the west they love and not have to answer to anyone but themselves.

As for me, I had decided to make Denver my permanent residence. I knew the area well and the location would be about in the center of the territory that I would be serving. I knew I wouldn't be in Denver very much but everyone should be from someplace.

A letter had come today from my sister, Mary Alice, addressed to Edwin and I. She was married now to William Wheatley and very happy. They had completed the home they wanted to build on the high bluff over looking the two farms, and she wrote they were happy to just stay at home in the evenings and spend time with each other. Father and Mother went to Denver in August and stayed for three weeks. When they got back home, Mother needed to rest for two weeks as she had never stopped moving around when she was in Denver. Both farms were prosperous and everyone was well. Mary Lou, our cousin married the boy from New Jersey and was thrilled with potato farming. Powder and Thor are well. Both William and she sent their love until we see them later.

In a couple of days, I needed to head for Denver so I spent as much time as possible with Jane. We had been going up town for lunch and coffee almost every day. Our nights were filled with passion and we seemed to never tire of one another. I had told Jane I would try to make a swing through San Francisco at least every four months on trips to southern California and when I headed up into Washington and Oregon. She seemed happy with that so I needed to try and make it happen.

I packed my small trunk with a couple of suits and the rest of the clothes accumulated over the year, not forgetting saddle soap for my saddle to soften the leather, because I would be using it again as soon as I could find a horse whose back was worthy of it. Denver should be a good place to find horses bred with lots of stamina due to the altitude.

Since next Wednesday was the 24th of December and also my birthday, I would leave on Thursday, Christmas Day for the trip to Denver. This left me six more days in San Francisco and almost a week with Little Bird.

I asked if there was anything she would like us to do before I left.

She said, "Yes I would like you to take me to the Mission Santa Clara and visit with Father McDougall with me. It has been several months since I have visited him, and I would like to see him before the year is over."

I arranged for two train tickets to Santa Clara for Sunday and we made the round trip with six hours left to spend at the Mission and a two hour lunch with Father McDougall. They set a date in March for her to come to the Mission for a 4 day visit to help with the children as she had done in the past about three times a year. Being very tired when we arrived home, we went to our own beds for a good nights sleep. In the morning, when she got up to start breakfast for everyone she came and kissed me good morning and informed me it was time to get up for the day.

During breakfast Edwin remarked, "Well, Jack, I guess this will be your last week with us for some time. Rose tells me you have decided to travel on Christmas Day. This last year has been good and I guess I will miss having you with us from time to time. If I were only twenty five years old, I would go for the adventure you search for myself. You be careful and travel safe. We want you to come see us every now and then. By the way, JAK Sales still has a Knight as a stockholder. The three partners want me to take stock for Rose's and my buy-out. They feel I have a 20 % position and want me to be a Vice President. So what you started will still remain partly in the family."

"That's great news. You made it all happen so you deserve to remain part of the company. I'm sure that will give some comfort to Richard Jarvis; that he still has a viable agency to represent his Baxter Steam Engine. Speaking of good news, I heard P&P Leather is building a new site and will expand the 30,000 square foot plant to 90,000 square feet by March of next year."

Edwin also filled me in with, "Robert Peterson has added a sales force in Canada and he says that market will double his production but still feels the only reason he's successful as he is has to do with you and your salesmen pushing his product all over the West."

"Alright you guys," Rose interrupted, "That's enough bragging on one another. We need to talk about Jack's birthday. How about we have a leg of lamb roast with all the trimmings on Wednesday afternoon and afterwards open some of the presents we have for each other for Christmas. Jane and I went shopping Saturday and we need to do this Wednesday since Jack is leaving early Thursday."

The next three days passed quickly. With the memory of a wonderful dinner and an evening of tender love making with Jane, I boarded the train to Denver Christmas morning with mixed emotions about the future.

CHAPTER 26

I finished reading Uncle Tom's Cabin before reaching Cheyenne. When boarding the train to Denver, I saw a familiar face walking toward the same car as I. Carl Bendickson saw me and hurried to get into the same car and got seated across from one another.

"Hi, Jack. You on your way to Denver or just passing through?" He said to open the conversation.

"I'm going to make Denver my home for now. I'll be traveling a lot and won't be home very much but will need a place to come home to from wherever I might end up. I represent Colt Firearms Company and plan to use Denver for a distribution point."

"Why don't you consider using part of our bunkhouse for home?" Carl suggested. "We only have two bullwhackers staying in the bunkhouse and can wall off the far end and put a door outside for that part of the building. That would give you a large private room just for yourself when in Denver. No need to rent a house for the short time you'll be in the area. Mom and Harvey would love to have you, and Art would be pleased to have you around sometimes too."

"That could work. Let's see what comes up with the rest of the family first then we can talk about it. What in the world were you doing in Cheyenne without a wagon or a horse?"

"Harvey sold 15 horses to a fellow up here and I drew the straw to deliver them so now I needed the train to get back home. So where do you sell your product?"

"I'll be calling on gunsmiths and general stores that carry firearms anywhere in the West. Colt has another man in Texas and the southwest so my territory will be north of there. I also have all of California. You can see why I said I wouldn't be home very much of the time."

"Sounds like you have taken on a large project which could amount to too much for one man. I wish you luck in the endeavor but glad it's you doing the traveling and not me. I like the short runs we have now and enjoy my time with wife and family close to home. Some of the trips we used to run were great back then, but since getting older, I feel the long trips are made for younger guys. I sure have to take my hat off to Burt Culy. He's much older than me but still likes to take any long runs Harvey has to offer. He's been a great friend and teacher for Art and me. When Harvey bought those wagons and mules up in the territory and Burt came with them, it was one of the best deals my father ever made. Yep, I really enjoy hearing many of his stories again and spending some time with him."

"You know, Carl, the idea of staying at your ranch has a good feel to me and would probably work out fine. I could board my horse with your cousins when taking the train out of Denver and have a way to get back to the ranch when I returned from a trip. Are you sure Harvey will rent a part of the bunkhouse to me?"

"Jack, I assure you it will be no problem and everyone at the ranch will be delighted to have you with us."

The rest of the ride to Denver was pleasant, and I got the story of the romances and eventual marriages of both Art and Carl to their wives and the building of the homes they had close to the river so their wives could catch fish for supper. He said the girls liked to fish as much as both of them and were as good as or better than the boys at it.

I asked Carl if he knew of a place to find a good horse for sale and he says his cousins seem to keep as good a stock of horse flesh as anybody in that part of the country, and their prices are reasonable also. Might as well keep the money circulating in the same family.

Carl walked with me to the Bendickson stable, and I started my search for a mount that could compare with Powder. Forget that. I needed to back off and be reasonable in my thinking. Louis ran a big shiny black stud in front of me that must have been 17 hands high. He said the horse came down from Breckenridge where the altitude of 9600 feet bred stamina into him.

"Well, Louis, I don't know about the stamina part but he looks like a horse with a lot of heart. Was he broke to ride when you got him?"

"Come on, Jack, this fellow has never had a saddle or bridle on. I would not want to sell you a used horse now would I? If you break him yourself, he'll know better what you want and also know who's in charge. First cousin price is one hundred fifty dollars, and the hackamore stays with him till you get him up to Harvey's ranch for the games to begin. Believe me, Jack, this is the best horse flesh available in Denver today."

That was the short story of how I came to have Black Jack as my traveling companion for the next few years for my shorter trips out of Denver. He also learned to ride the rails in some of Wells Fargo Express special transfer cars designed to handle horses and mules. The breaking of Black Jack to ride was not as short of a story as the one when he became mine.

I was right. He had heart. At first, I thought he was a black hearted devil and was set on showing me that he was not a horse ever meant to have a saddle on his back. He learned early to expand his chest so I could not tighten the chinch strap. We had several go rounds with that trick but my knee finally won that battle. Even before that battle he had to learn what a bit was for. Black Jack might have won the war on this part. We ended up with a grazing bit as the only bit I could get him to accept.

I walked Black Jack with and without a saddle. In the beginning, if I reached for the saddle horn he proceeded to buck and kick. I tried blinders to no avail. We walked around the corral, walked in the river and in the woods with me softly talking to him all the time, and he would answer me with a snort. The morning of the third day my patience was wearing thin and I almost thought the horse was going to win. An idea came to me to treat him like I had seen my Indian friends working with mustangs.

After removing the saddle, pulling the bit out of his mouth and putting the hackamore on with four feet of rope, I walked him to the corral fence, climbed to the top rail, and jumped on his back. He stood still and never moved. I started talking in a low voice, pulled his head toward the center of the corral and gently touched him with my boots. He walked to the center of the corral, snorted twice, and stood up on his back legs so fast I slipped off his back onto the ground. Black Jack turned around put his head on my shoulder and never moved until I got to my feet. I immediately grabbed the rope and his mane and mounted him again. He stood on his back legs but I was ready this time, and we rode around the corral for several minutes with a couple of heaving motions and a lot of snorting. He finally settled into a smooth prance that was comfortable to my aching body.

That horse never again balked or tried to be anything but agreeable to any command I gave him. He even pulled a buckboard for me one time when an injured man needed to get to a doctor up in Nebraska.

The noise from the corral was so loud that everyone on the Bendickson ranch came to see how my breaking of Black Jack was progressing.

The corral rail had people all around as I dismounted and walked the horse to the gate where I had taken the bridle and saddle off, slipped the hackamore off and slowly pulled the bridle over Black Jack's ears. He never moved as I placed the blanket smoothly on his back and lifted the saddle in position. Wonder of wonders . . . as I pulled on the chinch he exhaled and let me pull it tight. Picking up the rains and tossing the right one over his shoulder, he still never moved. The crowed was silent as I grabbed the saddle horn, lifted my left foot into the stirrup and with one smooth motion mounted the horse then slowly walked around the corral.

Everyone around the fence rail clapped with approval, and I swore that horse bowed his head to them and went from a walk to gated prance with no help from me.

Burt Culy said. "Jack, when you led that stud onto this ranch I would have bet a silver dollar you would still be trying to break him in February or March. You got yourself a lot of horse there . . . . You think he would let me ride him?"

"You're welcome to try Burt. Let's see what he does."

Burt opened the gate, walked up to Black Jack, and petted him on the neck and worked his hands across his body and on to his rump. The horse turned his head and watched Burt as he walked around him. Burt kept his hands on him and petted him all the way. As Burt reached for the saddle horn Black Jack turned his head and tried to bite Burt. Burt was fast to recoil and the horse missed. Burt tried again to get a hold on the saddle, and the horse moved sideways. Burt handed me the reins and said, "Jack, you have a one man horse there. Not many like him."

That's enough cowboy stuff for one day so I rode Black Jack to the stable and gave him a good brush down for his day's work.

Heading back to the bunkhouse, I heard a saw cutting wood and remembered Burt was building a wall for my office and bedroom in the back of the long room that was once a bunkhouse for about 10 bullwhackers. That was back when H C and A Freighting Company had a bunch of single guys running the teams long distances before the railroads came to the West.

I grabbed a hammer and started installing my outside door at the back of the bunkhouse. The finished room will be 20 feet wide and 20 feet long with a divider part way up for a wall between my bedroom and living office space. For 8, dollars a month it would be my home and office when in Denver. I talked Burt into a door between the remaining bunkhouse and my quarters so I could have heat in the winter time and a way to get to the checker board without going outside. He agreed about the door but suggested a pot belly stove should be put in my quarters also.

Late that afternoon, Freeman Bendickson from the Wells Fargo Agency rode to the ranch to let me know the shipment from Hartford had arrived and with it a letter from Mr. Jarvis wishing me good fortune in my new venture along with a list of existing Colt gun dealers to start with in my territory.

Now that it was midweek of the first week in 1874, I needed to line up my first trip and get the new Peacemaker introduced to the gun toting public. I decided to start in St. Louis, Missouri and work my way west by railroad. It came to mind that would be the most southern railroad available in my territory and would cover a lot of Missouri, Kansas, and Colorado.

Thursday, riding Black Jack into Denver, I ordered a holster for my newly received Colt .44 from Diego and sold Diego a dozen of the Peacemakers in various barrel lengths from 4 3/4 inch, 5 ½ inch, and 7 ½ inch with both bright nickel and standard finishes. He also wanted the standard Colt .44 caliber center fire ammunition manufactured by Colt Firearms Company designed for these pistols.

After an hour of jaw jerking with Diego and a history lesson or two I rode to the train depot to buy tickets for my trip to St. Louis, Missouri. The agent scratched his head as I ordered a ticket to St. Louis with a trip back two days later with a stop over night at O'Fallon, and again overnight in Columbia, and next an overnight in Boonville, and on the next day to Brownsville. He looked up after completing the necessary tickets questioning, "Son, you sure you want this many stops on your way back to Denver?"

"Tell you what. Give me one more ticket to the City of Kansas, Missouri and I will get my tickets through Kansas when I'm ready to leave Kansas City because I don't know where I might stop on my way across the state."

He wrote one more ticket and stamps all of them paid and counted out seven tickets telling me I have two separate tickets to St. Louis since there would be a change of railroads when I got to Missouri.

If I left Saturday, Margo would have finished my holster, and I could be in St. Louis late Monday. Now to the Mercantile to find a new novel for this trip.

I picked up The Gilded Age, written by two authors unknown to me. Mark Twain and Charles Dudley Warner collaborated to write a fictional story about corruption and exploitation at the expense of public welfare in the 1800's. Could hold my interest for 500 or so miles I guess. It is no dime novel but I can afford it at two dollars and .thirty four cents.

CHAPTER 27

Black Jack had no trouble returning to the stable from which I had bought him. Harry and Lewis were very verbal in their praise on how well the stud acted after his transformation to having someone on his back. I told them he probably would not let someone else beside me ride him so don't expect to rent him out while I was gone.

Harry seeming surprised that I would think they would consider such a thing said, "Jack, we wouldn't do that with a horse of yours. We will feed him well and might even brush him down a couple of times if we have slow days."

My sleeping car was comfortable and had plenty of leg room. Every time I rode a train, it seemed they had improved the comfort for the passengers.

Talking with other passengers, the one thing everyone had on their minds was train robbers. Since July of 1873 when the James gang robbed the train at Adair, Iowa people were concerned it would happen again but all wondered what part of the country the gang would strike next. Newspaper articles all over the West talked of the James brothers and Cole Younger's gangs riding together and robbing the rich and giving to the poor but you never heard of the poor getting anything from them.

While traveling and talking with others, some cautiously asked about the gun in my holster and where I got such a piece. This gave me a chance to brag about my new venture and let fellows know the gun would be in the hands of gunsmiths and mercantile stores that handled firearms in the next few weeks and months depending what part of the country they were in.

When I removed it from the holster, I always unloaded it to demonstrate the single action feature and felt safe handing it to them so they could also feel the balance and weight. I guess I had become what people called a drummer since I was always trying to sell my goods to whoever was around.

Their response was not surprising to me as I knew from the first time I had the gun in my hand it was a winner. I had 10 pistols with the 5 ½ barrels with me in a case in the baggage car but was saving them to let prospective customers have a sample before their shipment arrived if they wanted to start taking orders in advance. Diego said he would bet he had to get another dozen before I got back but I refused his bet because he had sold two before I left.

I was not getting much time to read. As soon as one man approached me about the gun and left the seat next to me it seemed another wanted to talk about the piece. I was amazed at the rate of speed the news of my offering was passed around the train. Men got on at a stop and shortly they were waiting for a fellow to leave the seat next to me so he could sit and talk.

In the three days of travel to St Louis, I had talked with thirty some men and two women that would have one of the guns as soon as both found them for sale. Interesting that four of the men were active law enforcement people and all believed this will be the gun of choice for outlaws. I had that thought myself but had tried to pass it off.

My arrival late in the afternoon Monday, gave me time to find a street car and a trip to the Planter's Hotel before dark. The man on duty at the hotel was able to give me directions to the Huffman Hardware Company that I knew handled Colt products and would be my first call on Tuesday morning.

After a good supper at the hotel and also a great nights sleep without the clack, clack of the rail car wheels on iron tracks. I woke to a driving rain outside my window. I stretched my arms and legs with a try at placing my palms on the floor without bending my knees but found that too difficult so I dressed and shaved leaving the stretching to someone else for today.

Being still full from the late supper, I forego breakfast and unpacked my oilcloth slicker and headed downstairs. I had my gun and whip on under my slicker and was carrying a box with a 7 ½ inch Peacemaker and a container of ammunition tucked under the rain coat. Leaving the hotel and heading for the nearest street car I saw a tall man watching me near the corner of the hotel building. The hat looked familiar and as he ran toward me I recognized him as one of the men I had met on the train. He looked straight at me and I realized he was going to try and tackle me right there on the street. I dropped the two packages in my hand and caught him in the groin with my knee and he dropped to the ground but as he turned over I saw a pepper box pistol aimed at me. Not able to get my whip out, I had nothing but a boot to stop his firing at me. Swiftly raising my foot, I caught his wrist and the motion of my leg sent my boot into his face. He was out cold lying still on the sidewalk.

A fellow ran from the hotel lobby and showed me a Pinkerton Badge and asked what was going on. I tried rapidly to let him know I thought the man was trying to rob me of what I was carrying in my holster. At the same time, I was reaching under my slicker and handed him the bright nickel .44 butt first. He handled the piece with the dexterity of a professional and remarked," I guess that would be something someone would try to steal if he wanted it bad enough."

"By the way, I'm Wade Thomas and was about to leave the hotel when I saw you two and thought I was in a dream for a second or two. Let me put some cuffs on this guy and see if we can find the law around here."

As we got the would-be attacker up off the wet sidewalk, a local policeman joined us. Wade knew him and explained the situation. The policeman wanted to know if I was willing to press charges and told me where his station was located.

I let him know I had a stop to make and would come by after finishing with my business.

It had stopped raining but the humidity was so thick it might as well still be coming down cats and dogs.

"You have time for a cup of coffee?" Wade asked. "They serve great coffee in the hotel, and I could sure use one right now."

"Good idea, Wade. My name is Jack Knight from Denver, Colorado. I represent Colt Firearms Company and am going around introducing the Peacemaker you had in your hand a little while ago. You can get that same .44 caliber gun with a 4 ¾ inch barrel which might fit in your shoulder holster if you're inclined."

"I sure will give it some thought. I assume Huffman Hardware will be carrying them since they have the Colt line now."

"Yep, that's my next stop."

After coffee, I shook his hand and took leave of his company and again headed for a street car for the ride to Market Street and Huffman Hardware.

Two cars and thirty minutes later, I walked into a huge store compared to the ones in Denver, and remembering the large stores in San Francisco; my sales smile is on my face immediately. I asked for the proprietor and a lady headed for an office on a mezzanine in the middle of the store. To my amazement, another attractive lady dressed in a tailored suit walked down the stairs to meet me.

With an air of assertiveness, she spoke, "Yes sir, how may I help you? I am Katherine Huffman, co-owner with my husband, Jeffery, who is out of town on a buying trip."

"Madam Huffman. Very nice to meet you . . . I'm Jack Knight with the Colt Firearms Company here to introduce our new line of pistols."

"Please call me Katherine. Good. We have been expecting you. We have had advance notice from Hartford of the new piece. Please, follow me to my office and we can talk more about this new and destructive piece of merchandise available to the public."

Wow, what have I gotten myself into this early in the morning?

"Mr. Knight, I saw a real change in your face with my last statement. I did that for my own curiosity to see your reaction. I was looking for dissatisfaction in your face when you were thrust upon a woman in a man's world but did not see that when we met. Forgive me, I am good at what I do but some men almost refuse to do business with a woman so I scope them out from the start to see if we can work together. For some reason I don't seem to scare you so let's get down to business. I see you have a sample with you besides the one you carry. If you have some bullets let's go to the basement and see how this gun performs."

"OK, lead the way."

I followed Katherine to a large basement that opened to a back street. It was used for warehouse space and a lot of farm equipment and tools. I loaded the Peacemaker while she set a target some forty feet from where we were standing. She pinned a printed target onto a bale of straw, walked back and said to go ahead.

I pulled the hammer back and fired at the target missing the bulls-eye by three inches and reset the single action hammer and fired again. Same result three inches to the left.

"Please reload the two you fired and let me try." She pulled the hammer back and fired then pulled the hammer back immediately five more times firing all six shots into the center rims and the bulls-eye. "I like it. Let's go write up an order and telegraph it to Hartford for immediate delivery so we can start getting these on the street especially for the lawmen. They call this the Peacemaker but you can bet the outlaws will love them just as much if not more."

Back in the office, I was given an order for two dozen of each barrel length and one dozen of the bright nickel, seven and a half inch barrel length, pistols with 100 boxes of ammunition to go with the order. Katherine directed me to the telegraph office and it was only a block from the police station where they were waiting for me to file my complaint from this morning's incident.

I thanked Katherine for the order and told her I hoped to be back within a year and looked forward to meeting her husband, Jeffery, on the next trip.

After sending the order to Hartford, I walked to the police station and found if I pressed charges I would need to stay in town for a hearing. I asked if they could hold the man until I left town and they agreed to hold him until late Wednesday after my train had left town.

Next stop O'Fallon, Missouri. The town consisted of a heavy German population with mostly farmers and livestock handlers. O'Fallon was no metropolis but Colt had a gunsmith, Daniel Westhoff, which stocked their product. He had been a dealer for the Colt brand for six years so I needed to show him the new product available.

I found his small shop was at his home with a sign out front with D. Westhoff Gunsmith written on it. A very tall man answered the door when I knocked. Daniel was well over 6 foot 5 inches tall and stooped to shake my hand and led me inside.

"Hello, I'm Daniel," he introduced himself as he continued to lead me to his kitchen table where he offered me a cup of coffee from a silver serving pot on the table.

"Thank you, Daniel. I'm Jack Knight here representing the Colt Firearms Company. I have a sample to show you of the new .44 caliber single action piece they call the Peacemaker."

As I talked I was removing the sample gun from the box and handed it to him butt first.

Taking the gun from me, he looked at it closely while saying, "Mr. Knight I am familiar with the .45 caliber on the same frame. I will give you an order for six of the 5 ½ inch barrel models and a dozen boxes of ammunition. Just so you know, I don't sell a lot of guns, but this model should sell very well as the news gets around. We have little use for guns here but several men like to have them about."

After finishing the paperwork, I arose to depart and said, "Thank you for the order. I will get out of your hair and on my way so you can get back to your work."

"Jack, if you are staying over night in O'Fallon I can offer you a bed. You see, my wife died last year and so I am alone in this house and would love to have company if only for one night. I have not fought in any wars but can tell some stories about my trapping escapades up in the Dakotas when I was a young lad. You look like you might have a story or two that I would like to hear."

"I think we can make that work if you know how to cook."

He did indeed know how to cook. We ate well. He made German potato cakes and a squash pie that could be served in any hotel in St. Louis. His stories were like listening to Jim Bridger telling of the wide open spaces he had explored and in return he wanted to hear all about the Chisholm Trail and the hardships of the cowboy and his horse.

We talked 'til after midnight before deciding we really needed to hit the bed and get some sleep.

When morning woke us both, he walked with me to the train depot saying we should have some breakfast at a little restaurant he liked to frequent.

Parting at the station, I believed I had met one of the good guys that makes the world go round and round.

CHAPTER 28

Columbia, Missouri was a haven for learning. It had three colleges and Boone County where Columbia was the county seat, had many small farms contributing to the health and wealth of mid Missouri.

After the 85 miles and four hours on the train, I was walking down Broadway Street looking for Providence Road and Ferry Brothers Hardware Store. It was early afternoon so maybe I could get in the store and out before they close. I found Ralph Ferry receptive to adding the Peacemaker to his line and sold him an order for two dozen guns of various combinations and 50 boxes of ammunition within a short time.

I hoped to be in Boonville, which was only 25 miles from where I was, at least early enough to get some sleep before my seeing the local gunsmith there. I noticed a stage company while walking down Broadway. I inquired when they ran west, and they told me that in 20 minutes a stage would arrive that would push on to Boonville shortly thereafter.

Even though it was dark when we arrived in Boonville, I saw a hotel sign in the next block and headed for it. The lobby was warm and felt good after the cool ride in the coach. Fortunately, the restaurant was still serving so after putting everything in my room I had a late dinner and went straight to bed.

In Boonville and Brownsville I located the local gunsmiths and took orders for two guns each and four boxes of ammunition at each dealer before catching the train to Westport, Missouri.

Arriving in Westport and checking with the ticket master, I learned the town only had one hotel not too far from the station. I checked in and settled down for an evening of relaxing and reading. It was Saturday night, and I had just spent 6 days traveling through Missouri and was really tiered of travel at this minute in time.

Sunday morning, the hotel clerk gave me directions to a stable where I rented a horse to ride out to see my friend, Jim Bridger. His farm was on the outskirts of Westport, and it had been over 6 years since I had left him and his family after helping them to Missouri from Fort Bridger up in the territory.

As I rode to the front of the house I saw a pleasant lady walk out the front door to greet me, "Hello friend, please come have a cup of coffee with us." Getting closer, I could see it was Mary, Jim's wife, but she had no idea who was riding up to her home but knows he probably had come to see her husband. "Your face is familiar, son, but you're much older than last time I saw you."

I got down off my horse, took off my hat and before I could speak, she exclaimed, "Oh yes, with the hat off seeing your red hair you're the Knight boy that drove stage for us when we came to the farm! Come in . . . Come in . . . Jim be glad to see you."

Jim was at the table having a cup of coffee. He stood up with his hand out in greeting and says, "Come closer. I don't see as well as I once did, but the voice I hear is familiar. Jack Knight, been several years. What are you doing in Missouri in the middle of winter?"

Taking his out stretched hand, I answered, "Came to see you. Why else would anybody travel to Westport but to see Jim Bridger, the only mountain man living on flat land."

"Wow, mountain man, that was long ago but the memory is still there."

"Well, Jim, how does your garden grow now that you are all settled in?

"Jack, this time of year we set in the house and drink a lot of coffee. The boys keep busy working on the equipment and getting it ready for the next go around, but won't let me in the barn to help. They say I can't see good enough to tell the difference between what you plant with and what you use to harvest with. Not true but close. We do well, and you were right. We sell everything we harvest. It's a good life. I hear about the troubles the banks and some of our financial houses are having but here on the farm, life goes on and I am glad to be here. Now I know you ain't just come here to see me so what else brings you to these parts?"

"As a matter of fact, I'm just passing through on a selling trip. I represent Colt Firearms and am introducing a new line of pistol to the local stores and gunsmiths. It is a .44 caliber copy of the single action .45 caliber they made for the army. So far it has been well received everywhere I've shown it. I have one to give you and know you will probably never fire it, but want you to have it anyway."

"I can still see the broad side of a barn so thank you. It will be given the proper baptism when the time comes. By the way, you need to make a trip up the Missouri to St. Joseph. A man and wife I know have a gun shop there. Both are good gunsmiths. Your friend Diego DeLacruse taught Richard the trade before you came into the picture as I understand. Now Richard and his wife, Sara Falcon, are two of the best gunsmiths on the Missouri River bar none. Richard has gotten to the place he'd rather fish than work so Sara does most of the gun repairing and selling now. Those two would probably sell more of these guns than the Mercantile in the City of Kansas. Last time I went it was less than a day trip up the river to St. Joseph."

"I can do that Jim. How is the boy, Taw, doing? I have thought of him a lot and have high hope for him."

Taw spent a lot of time with me on the trip bringing his mother and father to their new home in Missouri.

"That boy was never going to make it as a farmer so he's at school in Columbia, Missouri studying to be a lawyer. He talks about you from time to time when he's at home. Tell me, Jack, did he really drive that stage as much as he says he did?"

"Yes, in fact, he was a good driver. I never taught him to use the whip, but I think he would have become good at that too with a little help from me."

"I'll be gosh darn, always just passed his stories off as that of a small boy. Should have paid more attention, I guess. You need a place for tonight? Mary keeps a spare room 'cause someone is always showing up just to talk with me, and we end up jawing well into the night sometimes."

"Not this trip, but thanks for the offer. I rented the horse for the ride here and have a room at the hotel. I need to be up early and off to St. Joseph then head back to the City of Kansas and on over to Kansas City, Kansas as soon as I can make it."

Mary served us both a late breakfast and while enjoying her good cooking, we talked about the memories of our times together which seemed to be just a short time ago to me. After 2:00 in the afternoon, I took my leave and promised not to wait so many years before returning.

The trip up the Missouri River was eventful. Some tin horn gambler decided he didn't think I should come into the public bar with a bullwhip on my side even though it was almost hidden by my coat. Several gentlemen besides me had hand guns on their hips and who knew how many were hiding under heavy coats. I really did try to reason with the fellow but he was insistent that I was not going to bring it in the bar. As he reached in his vest pocket and pulled a small Derringer pistol out, I reacted and had him with both arms tightly bound to his body with the whip and his gun on the floor.

"Now sir, you see how much more effective the whip is next to a gun. Some men would have dropped you where you stood, but with the whip you can breath and live another day. You should turn around now and go find a table that will deal you a hand and leave me with my own train of thought." I gave the Derringer to the bartender to hold until he believed the man would arouse no more trouble. The room returned to normal noise after that, and the bartender poured me a sarsaparilla. I took my glass, walked out on deck and breathed a little softer.

The rest of the trip to St Joseph was calm and my meeting with the Falcons was a success. They were everything Jim had said and they bought two dozen Peacemaker's and 50 boxes of ammunition.

The next 21 days before arriving back in Denver, I covered a lot of territory. Two more days in the Kansas City, Kansas area and tickets on the Atchison, Topeka, and Santa Fe railroad for stops in Lawrence, Topeka, Emporia, and Wichita, Kansas that took me five days to complete. On Monday, it was on to Great Bend and Dodge City.

Arriving in Dodge City, Tuesday evening before dark I found the F. C. Zimmermann Hardware store and saw my friend waiting on two ladies buying cloth goods. Looking my way, he gave me thumbs up signal and returned to the two ladies giving them his full attention. After the ladies were on their way out of the store, Fred walked from behind his counter and waved me over, "Jack, what a pleasant surprise. You look like a man with a purpose not someone just passing through our fine town."

"Frederick, you see before you the western representative for the new Colt Peacemaker. I'm sure you have received some notice from Colt that they have built a .44 caliber single action on the same frame they sell to the army with .45caliber."

"Yes, I have been aware of the change for some time and wondered when they were going to release it for us to sell. Is that one of them in your holster?"

I pulled the pistol from my holster, unloaded the shells and handed it to him butt first. He smoothly twirled the piece three or four times, cocked the hammer as he set it in his hand and pulled the trigger.

"Nice feel and weight, probably better balance with it loaded. It's closing time so let's ride out to the farm and have some supper. We can talk about an order later. Matilda will be glad to see you and I'm sure there'll be plenty to eat since the older boy is at his Aunt's home tonight."

The invitation for dinner was not one to pass up. I had heard Matilda was a great cook. Frederick had a buckboard behind the store and hitched a mare to the rig and we took the mile ride to the farm.

We ate well. After supper, Fred invited me to his den for a Brandy, but I begged off for another cup of coffee. We talked of the troubled banks and the state of the country. The west seemed to be doing better than the big cites back East Fred lamented. I related some of Edwin's concerns and he remembered his time with Edwin and said. "I would listen to your brother. He strikes me as the one person that really knows what is going on in our confused world." We retired early since Fredrick liked to open before the town wakes up totally.

Wednesday morning on the ride to town, he gave me a handsome order to relay to Hartford and dropped me at the railroad station.

Having two hours to kill, I did my usual when waiting. I became a drummer for Colt and talked to as many people as would listen about the new pistol.

I now backtracked to Topeka and on to Junction City, Kansas. On my ride back to Topeka, I was delighted to find James, the boy that was my Butler in Milwaukie, Oregon. He was no boy anymore. The fifteen months since he left me to come to work for the Atchison, Topeka and Santa Fe railroad had turned a boy into a man. Tall and straight like his father Orrin; he had filled out and had become one good looking man.

"Mr. Knight, what a pleasure to see you. You look fine. As if the world is treating you well. As for me, I could not be better."

"It's good to know you are happy with the way things turned out, James. I have thought of you many times since we parted."

Our car was full so James and I got little chance to talk. The travelers kept him very busy. I watched as he brought a smile to almost everyone with whom he came in contact.

Leaving James in Topeka with a hearty hand shake, I changed railroads and continued on to Abilene, Salinas, Hays and a couple more small towns before arriving in Denver worn out and dead tired from the almost five week trip.

I was able to finish The Gilded Age novel and was sure I talked to 100 or more people on this trip about the advantages of the new gun available to them now. I took the time to stretch my muscles before heading for the door of the car with anticipation of giving them some much needed rest before starting my next trip.

CHAPTER 29

When I got to the Bendickson stables, one of Harvey's nephews offered to saddle Black Jack for me after giving me a hearty welcome home. It gave me a little time to become refreshed for the ride to the ranch. After riding Black Jack home to the new addition of the bunkhouse made just for me, I saw a letter from Hartford on the desk and opened it. Mr. Jarvis had expanded my territory to include Santa Fe, New Mexico. Seaton Bass, the southern and Texas, Colt rep. said he could not make it to Santa Fe, for more than a year and Mr. Jarvis wanted someone in the area sooner. Mr. Jarvis stated that I needed to contact Jorge Gutierrez, Diego's brother in law, as soon as possible. He had heard that Smith and Wesson was about to make an appearance in Santa Fe to introduce the .45 caliber Schofield.

Well, well . . . . I've always wondered what Margo's brother's name was. I had never asked in all the years I had known her. After a few days's rest, I would go there and put my trip to California on the back burner for now and then be ready to head south. I took a moment to run the trip through my mind.

I can ride rails to Pueblo, Colorado and a stage on to Santa Fe, New Mexico. Need a dealer in Pueblo and Colorado Springs, anyway, so have to find customers there before moving on. Colorado Springs might be a great spot to sell the Peacemaker sinces they cater to a lot of British tourists as old man Palmer financed his railroad and most of the Springs with British investors.

After two days of rest and getting my paper work straight for the Colt Company, I boarded the narrow gage Denver and Rio Grande railroad to Pueblo, passing through Colorado Springs while planning on stopping at the Springs on my return trip. The ride on a narrow gage was not as comfortable as the normal width railroads. The cars swayed and bounced more noticeably than on the Union Pacific, or the Atchison, Topeka and Santa Fe, but it sure beats a stagecoach with horses at full gallop with wheels hitting the bottom of the ruts on dusty trails.

Pueblo had grown since my last trip here. I don't think it even had a post office when I was here earlier. The town was busy and there were people walking the board sidewalks all over town. I saw three general stores from the rail station. Guessed I would attack the largest looking one in the middle of town.

I did well. Marshall Deveroe, the owner was receptive even though he had no firearms for sale in his store. He gave me a nice order and asked if I would find a rifle he could also sell.

I told him I would try and get him information on the Model 1873 Winchester which I felt was about the best all around long gun for his area.

It was still early so I checked for a stage to Walsenburg. It was only forty five miles so I could be there shortly after dark to check into a hotel. I knew Fred Walsen as a customer of JAK Sales and called on him before at his mercantile. He would surely want the Peacemaker since he carried other Colt products I recollected.

The next 200 miles to Santa Fe were bone crushing. It had been quite a few months since I had taken a long ride on a stagecoach. I decided on a stop in Las Vegas and Trinadad on the way back to break the monotony on the trip home.

Jorge Gutierrez was a small man and reminded me of his sister. They walked the same and used the English language about the same. I found he was also a fine maker of knifes like his bother-in-law Diego. I saw a four inch, very slim line blade with a small handle of some animal horn. It had a fine tooled leather scabbard that could attach to a belt.

The hilt was small and made it look like a miniature knife a man could carry concealed. I had to get this for Jane as she could carry it and no one would even know she had it on her.

After Jorge gave me an order for both guns and ammunition, I asked him to sell me the small knife in his case and he took it from the display and handed it to me. "Jack, I made that special for good friend's wife to carry as she taught school at Indian tribal school and walked the mile or so home at night in dark. She never got to see knife as she fell and hit head on a rock one night. They said fall broke her neck and she died at spot she fell. Please, if for female friend take it as my gift and hope she never have to use."

I told him about Little Bird, and he was happy she was to receive the gift.

Jorge would not take no for an answer when he offered me dinner and a bed for the night. His wife, Dolores, spoke a little English and I spoke a little Spanish so we conversed very well. Dolores told me she and Jorge married late in life like Margo and Diego so had no children and she loved to cook for more than herself and Jorge.

As Jorge and I drank our hot tea and Dolores prepared our dinner, I asked him about a whip I had noticed on his office wall.

"Jack my people on father's side from Spain, and you know the bullwhip probably first made by the Spanish. My father's people were leather tanners also made whips before coming to Mexico. My father teach me to make bullwhips I still make one or two a year when business slow. The one you see at shop made this year. Handle is braided over three layers of braided leather. Thong is very thin raw hide braided from piece of leather I trim to make thin at point I join the fall. The fall is raw hide I scrape thin as some paper and has double braid and is a foot longer than most. I made 6 poppers from my black stud tail hair and makes a good sound if used right. You like to buy that whip Jack? I sell to you twenty dollars."

"You just sold a whip Jorge. I think it is longer and lighter than the one I carry now and this one is well over five years old anyway."

Dolores served chili rellenos smothered in some kind of cheese I have not had the pleasure of 'til now and a rice dish to die for.

The next morning, after hugging Dolores and finishing my potato and egg wrapped in a tortilla, I walked with Jorge to his shop. With my new bullwhip on my side we shook hands and I headed for the stage depot for the trip to Las Vegas, New Mexico.

The weather was warm for this time of the year and the ride on the Santa Fe Trail through Glorieta Canyon was nice. For an area that had so much turmoil during the Civil War, it had returned to the natural splendor that some areas of the war had yet to attain.

Entering Las Vegas and crossing the Gallinas River, the hotel I had stayed at before came into view, and it would be a good place to stay tonight.

Climbing from the stage, I saw a drummer who rode from Pueblo to Trinidad with me earlier in the week. Alfred Wilson was a quiet man for someone selling cigars, and tobacco products. He was from North Carolina, had a heavy drawl, and it was hard to understand what he was saying at times. Probably why he was short on conversation.

He looked at me and raised his hands to get my attention, bumping into the fellow next to him. The man was dressed in black, wearing a black Stetson hat, and wore a gun strapped low on his hip. He grabbed Alfred by his lapels and was giving him some lip service I couldn't hear. I ran to help the drummer and the man in black swept Alfred's legs out from under him so that he landed on his back in the street. Grabbing my bullwhip, I suddenly realized the weight and feel were not there like my other whip. Even so the whip reacted right and I was able to pin the man in black to a post on the porch he was standing on with his hand unable to reach his gun.

"What's your beef, red hair?" he growled.

"No beef . . . Mr. Wilson is a friend of mine, and I saw no reason for you to attack him as you did," I replied as I walked close to the man, pulling his gun from his holster. I relaxed the tension on my whip, telling the man in black to sit down on the porch and let's talk with no weapons involved.

In a low menacing voice, the man spoke through clenched teeth, "Okay friend, after embarrassing me in front of the town you think we can be civil about this? This has just begun for me. You can just take your talk and walk to the center of the street for your whipping from me."

I took my gun belt off and handed it to Wilson along with my coat then walked quickly to the center of the street. Turning at the same time, I swung with a right and hit him on his shoulder. He turned fast enough to miss my blow. He quickly came at me with both a left and a right and made contact with the right on my left ear. That jarred lessons in my memory from Diego. I crouched a little and caught him in the belly with the hardest right I could muster. His body folded; then catching him between his eyes with a solid blow, he went down and stayed there.

As he hit the street a big man with a star on his chest walked between us.

"Well, Chester, have you had enough?. Looked like a fair encounter to me. I saw you kick the legs from this fellow's friend and he just stood up for the two of them 'cause you wanted to fight even after he asked for peace between ya."

"Well, Sheriff, I'll go across the river and stay there if he stays on this side of town 'til he leaves."

With the Sheriff listening for my reply, I said, "Sounds fair to me. I'll be leaving on the stage north tomorrow and have no reason to cross the river tonight."

"Fair enough. Now all you folks get back to your business and I'm expecting to have a peaceful evening in Las Vegas tonight."

I invited Wilson to have supper at the hotel with me and he agreed but wanted to clean up before we sat down. We had a good dinner and talked about the success we were having with tobacco and gun sales across the west.

The next day at noon, I left Las Vegas after having a successful visit to the Twin City Hardware store and getting a sizable order.

The rest of the trip by stagecoach and rail back to Denver was boring except for the nice order for Colt products on my stop in Colorado Springs where I had to stay over night since the train left while I was standing on the side stretching my legs. Being close, I camped at the local resort hotel and would probably not do that again. Mr. Palmer knew how to charge for the comforts at his hotel and I could see why his business was mostly dependent on foreign tourists.

It came to mind as I left the hotel that it sure would have been nice to have the expense account like I did at JAK Sales. The train whistle was blowing a warning to board so I hurried. Didn't need to double dip in the profits this trip.

CHAPTER 30

Arriving back at the stable in Denver, Black Jack was ready to go. He headed out of town with almost no reining on my part. I could get my paper work done today, rest Sunday and head for San Francisco Monday morning. I needed to practice with the new bullwhip Sunday because it had a different feel and I didn't need to get caught short like I almost did in Las Vegas, New Mexico.

After an hour or so working with the new bullwhip, I needed to put a new popper on. I liked the feel and the weight of the new whip and had my confidence back that I could defend a situation if necessary.

Art Bendickson happened to see me and came over to the corral and said, "Phyllis has made some squash soup and corn bread for a lunch. Would you like to set with us for a spell Jack?"

"Sure would," I replied and walked with him to get washed up before going into the house.

After lunch, I saddled Black Jack and made a fast trip into Denver and purchased tickets to San Francisco with a stopover in Salt Lake City. I needed to stop and see William Jennings at the Eagle Emporium while in town there. He was a dealer on my Colt list, and I was sure he had heard of the new gun and was waiting to see it.

Monday morning after getting Black Jack to the Bendickson Livery, I went by Booker's Hotel for a breakfast cooked by Ho Sing. Having a short lay over in Cheyenne gave me a chance to take an order for the Peacemaker at a gunsmith shop two doors down from the Union Pacific train station.

With the layover, it took two days to arrive late Wednesday in Salt Lake City.

Walking into the Eagle Emporium, I saw William Jennings with four men at a table near the rear of his store having what looked like a glass of water. William was facing me and gestured for me to come to the table to join them.

"Jack, I didn't expect you until April. Gentlemen, this is the man in the story about the four dozen wool blankets I was telling you earlier. Hope you don't need that many blankets this trip 'cause we are low again on inventory. Jack, these fellows manage the other outlets of the Emporium. This is Jackson Strong from Cedar City, next to him Jason Kerick from Provo, and this is Harvey Olsen. He is from Box Elder, and this young man next to me is my brother, Alec from Payson. They are the reason my orders to you are as large as they are because we cover a lot of Utah from our five outlets."

"Makes sense now that I think about it. Your quarterly orders were always heavy. Nice to have you all here at one place. JAK Sales will still be calling on you but I have another line to represent now. I know you have the Colt Firearms in your stores and I am out and around with the new Peacemaker they have added to their line."

I unloaded my piece and passed it around so they all had a chance to touch and feel the new offering by Colt.

"I guess because I buy so much of the Colt product. Mr. Jarvis sent me a letter letting me know the new gun would be available early this year. He didn't say who was going to bring it around so this was a nice surprise. I always look forward to your visits, Jack."

It was great having the whole group in one place. I ended up with a huge order when all five were finished. Taking my leave, I telegraphed all five orders to Hartford for direct shipping as they ordered a lot of nickel plated guns and I have a limited supply of those in Denver.

My ticket from Salt Lake City to Oakland's ferry terminal had no layovers so I planned on skipping through Nevada on my way back to California.

I was getting excited to see Jane but had a long way to go so I made a trip back to the Emporium before leaving Salt Lake City to look for a book to occupy my mind.

Alright, I walked right to a historic novel about the French and Indian Wars in the 1750's. Old Fort Duquesne by Charles McKnight. Story took place in the Pittsburg, Pennsylvania area and was about Captain Jack. The scout that was bent on killing every Indian he saw. After the second chapter, I knew I would have to finish the book even though I might have disagreed with the main character.

As usual, I was interrupted now and then by a passenger asking about the gun. It was totally exposed since I usually took the belt holster off and laid it across my lap. Most had never seen such a pretty firearm that was not only pretty but deadly. With the attention to the gun and the interest in the book, the 700 or so miles to Oakland from Salt Lake City wasn't so tiring though it took a day and one half to complete. I only slept for seven hours so I finished the novel before we made it to the ferry.

The closer I got to Edwin's home the more excited I became. It could only be the thought of seeing Jane and holding her in my arms again. It was unbelievable that I had let a woman into my life to control my thoughts as much as Little Bird had. It seemed I could recall a thought of her everyday since leaving San Francisco in December last year.

I found a passenger ferry for the four mile ride across the bay and walked the two miles to Edwin's to work out the kinks from the trip.

The front door was locked so I had to knock to announce my arrival. I heard footsteps and felt sure it was Jane since everyone else should have been at work. Opening the door, Jane yelped and jumped closing her arms around my neck and her legs around my waist. Nice welcome as she kissed me hard on the lips.

Hardly taking time to speak, she pulled me into my bedroom and started taking my coat off before I even had time to drop my travel case. We seemed to be suspended in time as we explored each other with an urgent tenderness and I whispered softly between kisses how much I had missed her.

Lying exhausted in each others arms, I began to hear a tea pot whistling in the kitchen. Jane seemed to come to the same realization and jumped up and ran to the stove with only one moccasin on and nothing else. She returned, grabbed her dress and hastily pulled it over her head saying. "Get up Jack and we can have some tea while we still have the house to ourselves."

Now that was a home coming every man should enjoy. Sitting in the kitchen, watching Jane prepare the supper, I became aware that I was relating the total time and travel of the past two months complete with the story of Black Jack and my breaking of that horse. I passed on the encounter with the gambler on the riverboat and my escapade in Las Vegas, trying to keep the conversation as light as possible. Jane seemed enraptured with all my news, and if I hesitated she would ask a question that would cause me to remember another incident.

Finally, when Jane started telling me of her trip to see Father McDougall, I went to my travel case and got the knife I received from Jorge Gutierrez for her to carry when she traveled. She said she knew how to use it but did not feel any need to carry it for protection since she had never had any indication anyone would try to hurt her. But she promised to carry it when she went on a trip.

She pulled the knife from the scabbard admiring the handle and weight. "It is nice. Thank you. I treasure anything from you. Did you know you could shave with this if you needed to, Jack?"

Rose came through the kitchen door and I was surprised at how quiet she was when entering the house. Telling her so she retorted, "Jack, I am an Indian. Remember? We are taught to be silent from a very young age and besides I find out a lot when I am quiet. I saw your foot prints on the porch so I thought I might catch you in an awkward moment and I would have something to hold over you for the rest of your life. But it looks like I was too late this time."

"Edwin will be home soon. Jane, I went by the French Bakery and bought a New York style cheesecake because I figured Jack would make it here today or tomorrow. You can serve that for dessert tonight with some of the Sumatra coffee Edwin brought home last week. That should keep everyone awake long enough to have an unforgettable evening. Just a thought, Jack."

"Rose, you might have an evil mind, but I can live with it as long as Edwin can."

When Edwin arrived he had a folder with him and waved me to his home office on his way through the kitchen.

"Jack, I want to show you why we are so proud of what you started. Rose and I marvel at the growth of JAK Sales in this down turn in the economy. I have January and February sales here and we are up 35% in February over any month last year, and January was up 28%. The customer base you left these boys with is growing every month."

We discussed the successes of JAK Sales and my sales of the Colt over after dinner coffee and turned in for the night.

My late Thursday arrival gave me Friday and Saturday to call on the five Colt dealers in San Francisco with a Saturday trip to San Bruno and Santa Clara.

With the orders I had gotten from the seven dealers I called on Friday and Saturday, I felt I could spend Sunday with Jane. We went uptown for breakfast and had supper at the Franklin House on Broadway. The weekend was going by in a flash as I had made my calls during the day and made sure Jane had my attention every night.

When I left Monday morning, I had spent four days selling guns and making love to a beautiful lady in my bed every night. But every good time must end for a little while and the call of the unknown returned to my mind.

The ferry ride and train trip to Sacramento went by fast, and I realized I left San Francisco without a new novel to read.

After two calls on Colt gun dealers in town, I found a mercantile that had a nice variety of published matter interesting to me. I picked up a book with a familiar author's name. Jules Verne. The book title also caught my eye as it was called The Fur Country. Paging through it had the Hudson Bay Company with the main character, Jasper Hobson. I could tell it had to be total fiction but probably could hold my interest anyway.

In 1874, you could travel by stagecoach from Sacramento, California all the way to Portland, Oregon. I bought a ticket to Shasta, California and on to Jacksonville, Oregon. There I planned to buy a horse to ride through southern Oregon to Roseburg where I would sell the horse and tack and pick up the Oregon & California railroad making my stops in several towns very familiar to me as I made my way to Portland.

I quickly learned that reading in a stagecoach was not as comfortable as in a railroad car. It was fortunate to have two gentlemen riding with me that were familiar with the areas and had some good stories to tell of the people and the country. The timber in northern California would sustain the country for many years, and the areas that had mining were doing well. One of my companions owned timber and the other was a mining engineer for a company in the Trinity area outside of Shasta. The mining fellow was aware of the Baxter Steam Engine and remembered buying from the Shasta Hardware Emporium.

Both appeared to be intrigued with the Colt .44 and were going to purchase one when they found an area that had one available.

The stage was stopping in Shasta for two hours for some work on a bearing on a rear wheel giving me enough time to make my call on Shasta Hardware and Burton Holzgang. After taking a nice order, I was able to continue on to Jacksonville the same day.

We had a full coach and a wrenching ride over the Siskiyou Mountains into Southern Oregon. Not sure I would want to cross these mountains on Ben's railroad after this trip over them. Maybe they could tunnel some of the way.

Entering Ashland, we were pelted with hail the size of grapes. One of the passengers said the area seemed to get a hailstorm every year around this time. Being tired and seeing a hotel, I left the coach and stayed overnight to have a restful night's sleep knowing it was still another 12 miles to Jacksonville.

While in Shasta, Mr. Holzgang referred a gunsmith living in Ashland and said I should look him up on my way through. Richard McKnight was easy to find. His shop was on the next corner across from the Wells Fargo Office on Main Street. Nice fellow and was able to order six of the 5 ½ inch barreled .44 Peacemakers. He gave me a drink of Lithia water, but I liked Sarsaparilla better and decided to not take any of the Lithia water with me.

Richard let me know that I could probably buy a horse and tack from Helman Livery cheaper than in Jacksonville so I crossed the plaza and purchased a fine buckskin mare. He also tossed a saddle and bridle into the deal for 135 dollars. The livery boy said, "Your mare should respond to Goldie."

CHAPTER 31

Following Bear Creek downstream for several miles, I saw a sign pointing left on a wide trail with "Jacksonville 8 miles." Knowing I had found my trail, I pointed Goldie down the hill and on to Jacksonville. I saw a sign that read "Jacksonville, Seat of Government for Jackson County" was hanging as one entered the town limit.

Ray Anderson, my salesman from JAK Sales, said if ever in Jacksonville I needed to stay at the Bella Union. Riding farther down the main street, I saw the Bella Union on the left at the far end of town. I thought it best to check into the hotel before finding a livery for my horse. They would be better able to tell me the closest and best livery to leave Goldie anyway. As I passed the Jacksonville Saloon just a block from the Union, I knew that was the last place I remembered Artimas York had been.

His brother wrote him to come help run the saloon when we shut the Oregon & California Railroad down just outside of Roseburg a year and a half ago. Always thought I would make a trip up here to see Artimas, but another salesman had this territory and I never had time.

After getting checked in and Goldie taken care of, I walked the boardwalk to see Artimas. The saloon was a busy place, and Artimas was covering the far end of the bar. A fellow that looked as if he could be a miniature Artimas York was tending the front part of the bar. I wandered to the front end of the bar between the window and the bar.

There was no stool so I continued to stand, removed my Stetson and swept my hair back. Artimas looked forward, saw me and almost ran to the front of the saloon.

"Jack, my friend. How are you and what are you doing back in Oregon?"

"Bart, come meet my friend, Jack Knight. He and I go back a long way. All the way to Nebraska when I was in the army."

Bart came and shook my hand while Artimas was saying, "Jack, this is Bartholomew York, my kid brother. I guess mom stunted his growth as she says she started pulling snuff while she carried him. Find that hard to believe, but she believed it. When Ma died, Pa sent Bart to live with his sister and her husband here in Jacksonville. Soon after Pa died, our aunt and uncle came down with something and both of them died a day apart. That's how Bart ended up with the saloon. He was young and sure needed help when he wrote me to come and help him. He's doing alright now but I told him he pays me too much for what I do."

When Artimas finally took a breath, I said, "Well, I'm glad to see you haven't missed many meals since I last saw you. I'm just passing through and look to sell a gun or two at your mercantile but couldn't pass up the opportunity to check on what you've been up to. Right now, I represent Colt Firearms Company and am showing the new Peacemaker that they copied from the army .45 single action they brought out two years ago. It's early afternoon. What time can you leave for some supper at the Bella Union?"

Bart spoke up and said, "Jack, we slow down in about two hours, and Artimas needs the night off anyway. Go see George Davis at his store and come back by and pick Artimas up after completing your business with George. Be sure and tell him Artimas and I both want a Colt like yours with his first shipment."

That evening Artimas and I talked about all our meetings and of the adventures we've had in northern Oregon. Of course, Thor made it into our conversation, and Artimas told me to come by the saloon in the morning to meet his Thor. He said his name was Brutus but he would have named him Thor if he knew my dog was dead.

Artimas drank his fill of beer, and I remembered finishing the third glass of Sarsaparilla before looking at my watch to find it was almost midnight. We parted in the lobby of the Bella Union agreeing to get together again before I left his town.

By ten in the morning, was up, checked out of the Bella Union and had picked up Goldie for the ride to Gold Hill. Stopping by the Jacksonville Saloon to see Artimas on my way out of town, I had to find a hitching post on the side street. There were none in front of the saloon. I saw a side door to the saloon and walked in. Just inside the door was a big black dog as big as Thor lying on a hooked rug. He laid his head back down as I closed the door and walked to the front end of the bar.

Artimas was the only bartender with three customers near the front of the room and came to the front with glass of Sarsaparilla and set it in front of me, "Morning, Jack."

At the same time he happened to look out the front window and said, "That's strange. That Bear Creek Creamery wagon parked in front of the bank. He's usually out of town before eight o'clock."

About the same time a big man with a double barreled shotgun walked in the side door and stood in the middle of the room shouting, "Bartender git your dog behind that bar and the rest of ya unload onto the floor and slide all yore hardware off the far end of the bar."

He could see my .44 but had no idea the whip was on my right side where he couldn't see it hanging on my belt. We all followed his wishes and spilled ammunition all over the floor. Brutus was now behind the bar, and it was so quiet you could hear a pin drop in the room.

The front doors were open and we heard a door slam across the street and the big man walked forward, then turned around saying, "Y'all stay where y'are, and no one will feel the sting of this here shotgun."

As he walked through the doors, I pulled my bullwhip and caught him just below the knees and jerked real hard. As he fell forward, both barrels of the shotgun went off when the butt hit the wood walkway. The Creamery wagon horse jumped forward and ran up the street with the wagon, and three men were running for horses tied to the Creamery wagon. Brutus had come around the bar and jumped on top of the man with the shotgun, Artimas had gotten his cut down Winchester repeating rifle from behind the bar and was out the door shooting two of the would be robbers at the same time the last of the three fell to the ground ending in a fetal position. Two men ran out of the Jackson County Bank, scooped up the leather bags from the two shot men and retreated back into the bank before anyone else got unsavory ideas.

Artimas recruited some men that had come into the street when they heard all the commotion to help get the four men to the jail. He was almost yelling, "Sheriff Applegate is up in Grants Pass today so we need help from you citizens to clean this mess up. Albert, please find Doc and have him come to the jail. Two of these guys have holes in them. Hope they don't die on me before he gets there."

"Jack, you remember on your ride north that this mess is your entire fault. If you would have left that bullwhip in its place these guys would have probably rode out of town and it would have taken Applegate three days to track them down. Now I got to go explain to my brother why his saloon sign was shot off the front of his building and laying in the street. Just kidding, Jack, that was quick thinking back there. Me and the whole town owes you a barrel of gratitude."

After all the excitement was calming down, I suddenly realized I'd had nothing to eat since early last night. I was hungry and some bacon with eggs sounded good which Artimas got for the both of us.

Staying on a trail, halfway up the hillsides to Gold Hill I could see the valley spread to my right would someday be very fruitful in agriculture. Artimas said to forgo Medford. So far it has no gunsmith or a store large enough to need firearms.

Goldie had a good gate and was a comfortable ride. We made Gold Hill and the Rogue Mercantile well before closing time and finished writing an order before dark. As Mr. Benson and I walked to the front door, a tall distinguished looking man walked up. Mr. Benson opened the door and greeted Sheriff Clearance Applegate as he entered and said, "Walter, I need a cup of your coffee. Don't rush off young fellow. The coffee is better than you can get anywhere else in this town."

Walter Benson introduced me to Sheriff Applegate and we all headed to a back room.

We had some small talk and the Sheriff pointed to my gun asking, "You handy with that hog leg, son, or are you just trying to impress someone?"

Walter held his hands up and said, "Clearance, he is a representative of the Colt Firearms Company and that hog leg is their new offering of the Army Colt .45 single action they're making available to the public. I just ordered a dozen for delivery next month. Jack, let the Sheriff see what he is going to need soon."

The Sheriff handled the gun skillfully and handed it back.

"Jack, it's late. You got a bed roll? I know a nice sandy beach we can sleep on tonight down by the river, and I have a coffee pot and two cups for coffee in the morning. Good grass close for the horses also."

"Best offer I've had today, Sheriff Applegate."

"Call me, Clearance, Jack."

After we hobbled the horses and got a good fire going, we lay back and just listened to the water running over rocks.

"You know, Jack, we never met but I was a Deputy in Cottage Grove the night the train brought you in with the missing finger. I thought I knew you but until you handed me your gun I wasn't sure. That's been almost three years ago. I had to write up some paperwork on you and send it to Portland."

"The world gets smaller every year for me. I guess I better tell you what happened in Jacksonville today." We both laughed at my story and fell asleep about the same time knowing no one died that day because of us.

With a good night's sleep under the stars, a couple cups of strong coffee and another story apiece we parted company and went our separate ways.

I followed a wagon road down the Rogue River and wished I could be there when the fish were biting. I had spent time on the Umpqua River out of Roseburg but never got this far south.

Goldie and I reached Grants Pass in the middle of the afternoon. I was glad I had bought some cheese and biscuits before leaving Jacksonville. The two stage stops along the river only served breakfast and it was too late to partake of the morning call.

Finding the town gunsmith was a chore. Ben Wooldridge had his shop behind his home and a nice lady that gave me directions left some clarity out of her finger pointing. Still Goldie and I kept the faith and found Ben.

After a story about the town's name and Ben's story that he had been there since year one and had never seen Ulysses S. Grant pass through his town, he never said why it was named Grants Pass. He signed his order and gave me directions to the Applegate Trail, and said if I hurried I could make the Six Bit House in Wolf Creek. I made it to the Sunny Valley stage stop, looked at the mountains ahead and stayed there for the night.

Three days later and several small towns like Canyonville with stores like Colvig's Market, I had four orders for Peacemakers when I rode into Roseburg, Oregon.

CHAPTER 32

I had no trouble recovering my investment in Goldie. The woman running the livery offered me 150 dollars with no hesitation for the mare and tack. It crossed my mind to try for more, but when you better a deal by more than 10% in less than 10 days you probably should just back off.

Having stayed in Roseburg a couple of different times, I was familiar with some of the towns businesses. I remembered using Patrick Forrester's Mercantile and headed for it hoping Pat was still the owner. Sure enough, the tall man wearing his best Stetson was behind the counter giving change to a customer when I walked over.

Before I could say anything, he said with a look that told me his mind was searching its memory banks, "I remember you. Give me a minute and it will . . . Jack Knight. You were with the railroad when it was being built and your bridge guys always shopped here for anything they needed. First, tell me whatever happened to the big fellow Artimas?"

Chuckling a little, I answered, "Pat, he's fine, I just saw him in Jacksonville a couple of days ago."

"Nice fellow even though he was Scotch-Irish. What brings you to Roseburg? You going to finish the railroad to California now?"

"No, that's all behind me now. Riding this way, I remembered seeing your name on some invoices in the JAK Sales office. That was my company, but I've sold it to your salesman and his other partners and started pushing this little toy around the West." I unloaded the Peacemaker and handed it to him.

"Feels good. You think I can sell these in my store? Matthew Driller, our gunsmith might want to handle them."

"Pat, Art Colvig in Canyonville said to bypass Driller. He told me I would probably never get paid doing business with him."

"Yep, I guess that could be true. Most people around here do try to avoid him and his shop 'cause he's hard to get along with. Only a person wandering into town and looking for a gunsmith that ain't never worked with him gets suckered nowadays."

After mulling it over and getting a few tips from me about selling the gun, Patrick gave me a nice order, and I headed for the Oregon & California rail station.

Over the next eight days I spent nights in seven different towns on my way to Portland.

In the Portland area, I made seven calls and hit pay dirt six times. Talking with store owners, I heard Ben Holladay was no longer associated with the Oregon & California railroad. Henry Villard came over from Germany representing many of the German stockholders and ended up in control of the railroad. Because the conversations had taken so much of my time, I decided not to bother Ben and took a ferry to Fort Vancouver across the river.

Taking a steamship ride to Kalama farther down the Columbia River, I transferred to a railroad going to Olympia and New Tacoma where I boarded another steamship to Seattle and then headed south on stagecoaches. After another three weeks of travel, I found myself on a side wheeler leaving Crescent City, California for San Francisco. It was now the middle of May, 1874.

I stayed around Edwin's home for two days making calls in Oakland, San Pablo, and San Rafael, spending as much of the evenings as possible with Jane. Not forgetting it took sales to get that paycheck, I took a Wells Fargo stage to Santa Rosa, and stayed overnight stopping in Petaluma the next day on the trip back to the house.

Jane and I experienced two nights of passion before I left for a six week trip to southern California. She would be a gentle reminder in my thoughts of what awaited my return.

Traveling down the central valleys and on to San Diego and finally heading home, I rode the Overland and Wells Fargo coaches as close to the coast as they went. By the time I left Santa Cruz, I was tired of people, stagecoaches, guns, and just wanted to make it to San Francisco by the 4th of July. It was getting dark but the driver said we will make the station before July 3rd was gone.

Independence Day fell on Saturday this year so we would have a long weekend to relax and overeat some good home cooking. Traveling left a lot to hope for when it came to eating. I ended up with a lot of biscuits and cheese with a little bacon thrown in. Good thing I liked to walk whenever I got the chance.

Saturday, Edwin gathered all four of us for a surprise boat ride to Black Diamond on the Sacramento River delta. His firm now represented Black Diamond Mining Company, and they needed a lot of legal help setting up the water front to enable them to move coal out of the bay area to other ports. This was a curiosity trip for Edwin but ended up a pleasant day trip for the four of us. We unexpectedly were served a delicious lunch on the boat.

By Wednesday, the 8th of July, having made all the calls in the Bay area, I headed back to Denver. It was getting harder to leave Jane, but the expectation of my trip to the Dakota Territory already planned put one foot in front of another with little afterthought.

My plan is to ride the train to Omaha, Nebraska and take boats to Fort Abraham Lincoln up in the Dakotas to show the Colt and take orders in that territory. Sometime after arrival, I'll buy a horse there.

Putting that plan into action consisted of several layovers on the train and six different river boats on Monday, July 27th before I arrived at Fort Lincoln. Having made 12 very successful sales calls on my trip to here left me a lot of telegraph work as soon as I got settled.

I was told the Fort was about empty of soldiers. The 7th Cavalry with over a 1,000 men and officers had left for the Black Hills country. Word had it that gold had been found, and men were starting to pass through this area chasing the bright colored metal.

Alonzo Stringer, the owner of the general store, said, "I guess with what's going on up here I better have you send me 50 of those critters and a 100 boxes of the ammunition to give us a chance to keep at least a few fellows with some protection from them Sioux, and Crow Indians as they head southwest to the Black Hills country."

Asking how far to the Black Hills, I got answers from 275 miles to 325 miles. Just head southwest and you will run into Custer and the 7th cavalry somewhere down there I was told.

Crossing the river to the settlement, my first task was to look for a livery to buy a couple of horses and some tack. Seeing North's Stables, I opened an empty corral gate and walked to what looked like the office.

A young boy chewing on a yellowed straw and standing in the doorway drawled, "Ya look like a man needen a horse. Name's Buck and my pa lets me do sum of the tradin' so whatcha' got to trade? We'uns got horses or mules but cha got the look of a horseman. Ya know how to use that whip on yore side thar? Pa showed me some 'bout bullwhips. He use'ta drive freight over in Minsota, afore we came hare."

Out of the corner of my eye, I spotted a small rat chewing on some spilled grain just inside the stable door. I walked a couple of steps forward and pulled the whip at the same time and caught the rat before he could scurry off. The popper split him open, and a big gray cat had him in his mouth before I replaced my bullwhip on my side.

Buck said, "yep, ya know what that thang's for alright."

"Buck, I'm Jack, and yes, I need two horses, a saddle, bridle, and a pack rack with blankets for both. Suppose you can scare all that up?"

"Jack, tha's a pair of mares back hare ya cain't tell one from 'nother 'less ya look'em in the face. Ones got a star 'tween the eyes, and the othern's got jes' a table top white spot the same place. We call'em Star and Bar. They'uns jes' three years old an jes' been shod for the secon time. Ya kin ride'em or hitch 'em to a buckboard."

"What say I give you seven 20 dollar gold pieces and that's if you throw the tack in."

"Com'on, Jack I wuldn't do that ifen I put that old McClellan saddle over thar on one uv'em. For 225 and ya kin have that western saddle in the corner thar, both mares and pack gear for 'nother silver dollar."

"Okay, Buck but you're taking advantage of me because I'm from out of town."

It really was a fair deal. Both horses were in good shape, and for the walk I was taking them on they needed to be in good shape.

It was early in the day so taking my purchase back across the river, I bought some grub and a heavy bed roll; trying to limit my gear to 50 pounds. I expected to change horses at least once a day on this trip.

Going back in the general store, Alonzo pulled me to the side and said, "Jack, pays to be careful down around the Cannonball River country. Just south of there is good buffalo hunting for the Indians. I also heard that Elmer "Texas" Dumont and his black breed buddy, Serinto, stole four cases of repeating rifles from a fort down on the Missouri River and are looking to sell them to some Indians in that area. Forty eight repeating rifles shouldn't fall into any tribe's hands."

"How did the law miss finding them before they got this far into Indian Territory?"

"What law, Jack? The army is 'bout the only law around here. That's what I mean about being careful."

"I'll be careful, Alonzo. Thanks for telling me. I'll stay away from the high spots and keep a watchful eye. Probably won't be noticed by hunters or the two men you speak of."

On the trail, Star might have looked like Bar, but when it came to horse sense there was no comparison. Star was sure-footed and alert to her surroundings, and Bar just took you for a ride.

While riding Star, she and I both seemed to have a feeling someone or something is following us. Her ears were working back and forth like she heard something, and I looked back several times when her head and ears turned to the rear. I finally saw out of the corner of my eye what was following us. When riding out of Fort Lincoln I noticed a large gray dog lying near the flag pole. It was that dog Star had been hearing and probably smelling.

The second day out, I camped on what must have been the south side of the Cannonball River and picketed my horses in some lush grass. Looking across the river I saw the dog hunkered down near the water. He didn't make a movement toward me and I didn't feel it time to try for a new friend.

Close on to dark, I heard a wagon coming up the river and having a smokeless fire, I walked several yards away from camp and into a clearing to see what was coming. I saw two men in an old Conestoga wagon hitched to four horses. They pulled up and stopped when they spotted me. One man was white and his companion was black.

The white man spoke, "Smelled yore far. Got any coffee for a cuppel drifters? We're headed fer the Black Hills and the gold strike. That whar you headed?"

I sure didn't need these guys knowing what I did or that I have six more Peacemakers in my belongings so I replied, "Yep, thought I would chase that shiny metal myself."

"Names Dobber and this here's Catch. Mind ifen we put our horses over with you'rn? Should be 'nuff grass for all of 'em. Got some can beans and kin heat enuff fer all us and we even got air own cups if'en you got some coffee. We sleep in the wagon and will be gone afore you git up in the morning. That shore is a fine looking gun yore carry'in. Mind if I git down and have a look at it?"

"Dobber, you do a lot of talking . . . awful fast for me. You and Catch come on in and use my fire and have some coffee, but I'll just keep the gun holstered. Thanks for the offer of beans but I had biscuits and bacon already. It's been a long day so I'm turning in for an early start tomorrow. That's a good spot where you parked the wagon so you're welcome to share the campsite if you like."

"Ok, friend. Got the lay of the land. Soons we heat our beans we'll retire to air wagon. Thanks fer the invite."

I propped my saddle against a large rock and opened my bedroll and laid down. Dobber and Catch finished the coffee and took their warm can of beans to the wagon.

It had been along time since I'd had to keep one eye open for trouble at night, but tonight that feeling had crept up my spine and was stuck in my gut. It didn't take long. I had a match in my left hand, my gun in my right and the fire was down to white ashes. I smelled him first and adjusted my eyes as much as possible to see where he was. As the breed stepped next to my feet, I raised my left hand, lighting the match with my thumb nail to see he had a knife in his teeth; his eyes as big as coffee cups. My gun pointed at his chest got his attention as I spoke firmly, "Now open your mouth and let the knife drop and let's find your partner and get your rig hitched up and out of here . . . . . NOW!"

CHAPTER 33

A gnawing feeling that this was not the last of my contact with those two, I laid back down with my mind churning out a plan together for the next day. *Sure this is Sioux country. I need to hug whatever hills are available.* As I ran this through my mind, I thought about the four dozen rifles in that wagon and decided if I didn't stop these guys no one would.

Following them is easy the wagon being heavy and leaving deep marks wherever they traveled. They stayed on level ground and wanted to be seen by the Indians. Seeing them ahead before noon, I maneuvered to get in front of them to try and stop them. I spotted my tail, the gray dog, and wondered why he continued to follow me. Making a wide circle to avoid them took three hours. I came to a stand of trees with a creek running by and figured they would head for it. *Sure hit that one right.* They were headed straight for it causing me to think this was to be the spot they had set for a rendezvous with whatever bunch of Indians they were dealing with. Looking around the country, it was the only place not wide open for any eyes to see what was going on.

Some high brush and trees to the south hid my animals from the trail. The wagon tracks along the creek ran close to the tree line where I took shelter from being seen as they were drawing close to the grove of trees. They pulled the wagon within twenty feet of me and both climbed down from the wagon and headed for the creek. They were down getting a drink as I quietly walked up behind them with my gun drawn and asked them to get up slowly.

"I know you're not Dobber and Catch. You're Elmer Dumont, and the half breed, Serinto. If you'd have left me alone last night instead of trying to kill me and steal my horses, I possibly would have rode on and let the army handle you. On the other hand, if I was real honest with you, once I figured out who you were and what you were doing out here I guess I would have stopped you from your mission. These Indians don't need repeating rifles by the dozens to protect them. The Indians you're dealing with are renegades."

Dumont said, "Friend, you ain't got no idea how much trouble yore in. My Injun people'll be here within the hour making you a dead man."

With that he pulled his pistol to shoot at me. My reflex on the trigger beat his shot and he dropped his gun with a bullet in his shoulder. Serinto was getting ready to throw his knife and I cut his right ear off with the popper of the bullwhip. He dropped the knife and grabbed his head with both hands. I quickly hit them both just above the neck with the butt of my pistol before they could recover from the shock of surprise. They lay sprawled before me, out for now, but I had decided what needed to be done and done quickly to leave this place before the Indians arrived.

Dragging Dumont to the rear wagon wheel, I tied him spread eagle to the spokes with rawhide from my saddle bag. I picked the breed up and carried him to the other rear wheel and tied him spread eagle to those spokes just like Dumont.

I wasted no time unloading the rifles in the wagon and one by one, removing the firing pins, and slid them into my saddle bag. Finishing the last one, I took a bucket to the creek and filled it with water and threw it on Elmer Dumont.

"Dumont, when your friends get here I'm sure they'll take good care of you both and have their medicine man fix your shoulder and Serinto's ear."

"Whoever you are, they'll hunt you down and kill you."

"Not with any of these rifles. They have no firing pins. Have fun explaining that when they find they fail to shoot with the bullets in the gun."

"Wait . . . wait . . . they'll kill the breed 'n me ifen them rifles don't shoot."

"Better them killing you than me. By the way, just in case they know how to count, hope you can explain why there's only 47 rifles in those cases. Thought I'd hold on to one. Oh yes, it has the firing pin still intact. Ya'll enjoy this beautiful day now."

I ran through the woods and mounted Bar and headed southwest with Star on a long halter rope so she could maintain solid footing when we started our climb halfway up the side hills on our right.

Late in the day, after traveling ten or so miles from the small stand of trees and the wagon, I found a dry camp site on a side hill and could see much of the valley just covered. I saw no movement so started a small fire and made coffee. The gray dog walked from behind a rock and wagged his tail and lay at my feet. He started licking Dumont's blood from my boot. I moved my boot and the dog went to the edge of the camp, lay down quietly and just watched as I moved about.

I had gotten little sleep last night so the soft sand in the camp area helped me relax and fall into a deep sleep. When I awoke it was the next morning. Moving slowly, I started a fire and decided on hot bacon and hard biscuits for breakfast. Dog had stayed in the camp area so I passed him a hard dry biscuit and he ate it slowly like he savored it. *I really don't need another mouth to feed but this guy is really alone except for me so welcome to my table.*

Cleaning my small frying pan with sand I looked north and saw a cloud of dust coming my way. I got my glass and saw a column of army soldiers maybe three miles out. As they got closer, I could see they had the wagon that Elmer Dumont was driving. They followed the valley floor, but three of them left the column and climbed to my camp.

A Major and two corporals rode up and dismounted. "I'm Major Warren B. Clegg, 7th Cavalry. Saw your camp and had a feeling you might have some coffee for the three of us."

"Come on over, Major. I'm Jack Knight from Denver just passing through on my way to Cheyenne from Fort Lincoln."

"That's a mighty long trip for a man by himself."

"Well, there is a little more to the story. I represent Colt Firearms and their civilian copy of that piece you wear on your side and stop in any place people sell pistols to other people."

"Tough job . . . Not something I would want to do. Tell me Jack Knight from Denver did you see a couple of fellows with that wagon down with my troops?"

"Possible. I went around a wagon yesterday back ten or so miles north of here."

"Well, you must have missed their fight with some Indians. Funny happening, I guess, but not for them. We knew they were in this area to sell some repeating rifles to the Indians and thought we knew who they were. Texas" Dumont and his side kick stole some guns at a fort down on the Missouri River, and we thought they came this way."

Major Clegg got a cup from his saddle bag and filled it with black coffee from my fire. He found a rock and sat down right next to the rifle I picked up yesterday.

"We found 47 of the stolen rifles but there were four empty cases near the wagon so we missed one some where. You know every one of those rifles had the firing pin missing. Must have been what made the redskins mad because they were not kind to those boys. They had spread-eagled them to the rear wheels and tied them with rawhide to the spokes. We found the wagon with the horses gone about a half mile from the guns, and those boys were hard to look at. Not a lot left after the turning wheels against the ground wore off the flopping body parts down to the iron rims."

"You know, Jack, the strangest thing about those rawhide ties, they were treated with something and each arm or leg had three loops around it and tied to the spoke with a Bolin knot. My father taught me that knot when I was a young boy. Never gave it a thought about Indians knowing how to tie that knot."

Major Clegg got to his feet saying, "Jack, I like your hat band of rawhide and the Bolin knot on the side is a nice touch. By the way, are you a gunsmith by any chance?"

I just snickered and shook the Major's hand wishing him good luck as he mounted up and rode off with a warning to watch out for Indians with bows and arrows.

My new charge needed food and I needed all of what I had so I had to snap some heads on rabbits and prairie dogs from Star with my bullwhip and roast them over the fire at night for Dog. Bar wouldn't have anything to do with the whip and wouldn't get me close enough for the kill.

My map showed the closest settlement to be Belle Fourche just a few miles from Wyoming Territory and north of the Black Hills so over the next eight days I rode and walked to Bella Fourche. They say that was French and us westerners called it Bell Foosh. Wiley Comstock had a small store there and we ended up putting together an order that I had to tell him I had no idea when he might receive it.

For two days I skirted the western edges of the Black Hills and headed for Fort Fetterman in the Wyoming Territory which was familiar ground to me. I never saw Custer or the 7th Cavalry but a lot of hopeful fellows following one another all over the Black Hills looking to get rich.

Reaching the south end of the mountains, the land leveled off. Looked like I had reached the Wyoming Territory. I came up on a group of men who said they were headed for the Black Hills and a fortune in gold. They also told me I was about 150 miles from the North Platte River and Fort Fetterman. *All right 7 more days and I get a hot bath. That should put me at Fort Fetterman by the 18th or 19th of August. Have only taken one order in three weeks but should have better luck at the Fort and on into Cheyenne. I had expected more settlements or small towns in the Dakota Territory But in the next two years that will change.*

I was still two days out from the Fort and saw people setting up cattle ranches and building farm houses. This was a far piece from help if it was needed. I guess the main thing is water and there were creeks in abundance in the lush grass land. Last time I was here, the Indian called this his hunting ground.

Dog must have found what he was looking for at one of the farms we passed. He hasn't been trailing me for sometime. Not much loss to me as he never would let me pet him anyway.

The Fort had been expanded since I was here but that was one of the reasons for the large delivery of lumber we brought up when I worked with Harvey Bendickson as a Wagoneer.

The store was busy and I spent a short time with the person running it because he was very busy. He still gave me a good order while waiting on his regular customers though. Outside I saw a face from the past but couldn't place it. He saw me and came over." Jack Knight, remember me? William Comstock . . . I rode with you and Bill Cody out of here several years back. I still hunt buffalo for the army and scout sometimes."

"Sure Bill, I remember. You have put some age on you so I knew you but did not pick up on it immediately. Sorry."

"What brings you up to our fine country again?"

I showed him the Peacemaker and explained my position with Colt.

"Jack, let's ride down to Douglas. It's only five or so miles. I want to introduce you to Ben Frolick. He has the Mercantile there and I bet you will sell him more than you did here at the Fort if they even bought any. I was headed down there anyway to get a hot bath before I bed down for the night. There's a good café, too, next to the barber shop if you've a mind to join me for supper."

"Ok, you planning to bed down close to the river tonight?"

"Yep. You'll find that's the best sleep you'll ever get on the trail, Jack."

CHAPTER 34

Ben Frolick was a small man with a large presence, and when you met him you knew he was in command of his territory. His store was so large and busy enough he had two people on the floor besides himself helping customers. He would remind Tim to be sure to show Martha the new buttons from St. Louis and yelled to Raymond to be sure Art saw the new grain sacks in the corner. When finally finishing with his lady customer, he went to William's side and greeted him.

Bill introduced me, "Ben, meet a friend of mine. Jack Knight out of Denver. He's going to sell you on a new gun made by Colt that you need for sale for some of these fellows passing through to Oregon."

After a hearty handshake, I unloaded the Peacemaker and handed it to Ben explaining the differences from the older .36 caliber.

Ben remarked, "Had a fellow from somewhere in Missouri pass through this week with one of these. You bet I want some of them. Jack, the fellow said he saw three different barrel lengths. Tell you what. Send me 12 of each and 50 boxes of ammunition for them."

Ben let me know he had to get back to tending his business, put his hand out and was on to another customer. I wrote the order and had him sign it as Bill and I passed him on the way out.

Leaving the mercantile, Bill asked, "Jack, you want a hot bath before we eat or after?"

"My mother always said, don't go near the water just after you eat so we better have our bath before, huh?"

While were enjoying our meal, I asked Bill if he remembered the time we lost Able up near Chugwater Creek.

"Sure, Jack. I pass his grave at least once a year since it happened."

"You know where his grave is?"

"Yep, it's just off the trail this side of the Chugwater cliffs. I'll ride with you that far. I can head over into Nebraska from there. If we ride 30 or so miles a day, we can make it by the third day before sundown."

'Bill, I saw a stone cutter when we rode into town. I'm going to see if he can have a small stone with Able Roby carved on it by morning to take to mark the place."

"I know that fellow. Let's go. His name is Eric Griffith, and I bet he can get it done in time. Years ago we hunted together, and it comes to mind he was a crack shot. If he had been in the contest with Bill Cody and me when we shot buffalo for the title, he would be Buffalo Eric Griffith and Cody would be just William Frederick Cody now. You know Cody only beat me by 24 buffalo in eight hours."

We camped next to the river for the night, and by 7:00 in the morning had met Eric Griffith and picked up the stone.

Bill was right. By the middle of the third day, he had led me right to Able's grave site. The wooden cross we'd made from the extra wagons tongue was about to turn to dust. I buried the rock in the dirt at the slight rise on the valley floor and shook William Comstock's hand in parting as we headed our separate ways.

It's still 40 miles from Cheyenne. Looks like I'll be spending one more night on the prairie before having a hotel room and a soft bed. I need to find a hardware store or mercantile to sell the Peacemaker in a town the size of Cheyenne.

It was Thursday afternoon, the 27th of August when I rode into Cheyenne. I found a livery that would buy my stock and sold the whole outfit for 200 dollars. *If I didn't have Black Jack I would have kept Star. She was a keeper. Bar . . . she never settled in as a partner like I think a horse should be. I got spoiled early in life with Powder, I guess.*

Finding Beckwith Hardware was a stroke of luck. I had left the livery and was heading into downtown when I turned the second corner on

Broadway and there was the hardware store. Henry Beckwith was your typical store owner. Slightly jolly and a little heavy through the middle and wearing glasses on his nose.

"Mr. Beckwith, I hope," Speaking as I walked up to his counter.

"Yep, that's me. What can I do fer you on this fine afternoon?"

I went into my regular speech after introducing myself.

"I already have a Colt Navy .36 and have had it for several years. No takers. I heard about the one you got there but they tell me you can buy it at Frank Bonner's gun shop. What makes you think it would sell in this here store?"

"Well, if you hide it like the .36 it probably won't. But try displaying the Peacemaker and the Navy model and I bet they will both sell."

Showing renewed interest, Frank said, "Boy I will take that bet for a dollar. Send me three of those, and I will put all four up on the wall right here, You come by in 60 days, and if all are still there, you owe me a silver dollar."

"I can do that. I come through Cheyenne quite regular so I can collect my dollar before November to help buy my winter coat off your rack over there."

I wrote the order and let him know they would ship out of Denver Monday.

Heading for the train depot, I passed the Golden Eagle Hotel and remembered hearing it had a good cook in their restaurant and decided to stay there tonight.

I purchased my ticket for the early morning ride to Denver. After I finished my paper work for the last seven weeks, I needed to head for San Francisco and plan a trip into eastern Oregon as well as the Idaho Territory.

Finally, getting back to the ranch, I picked up a letter that had come from Richard Jarvis. He congratulated me on my first six months of business and stated that with the reorders and all of the additional ammunition ordered my sales had reached in excess of $80,000.00. He had a request due to a letter he received from a prospective customer in Carson City, Nevada. The letter stated: *Please take the time to make a trip to Virginia City and Carson City as soon as your schedule will allow.*

Look for Leo Carson Hardware and introduce yourself. Thanks, Jack. As always, Richard.

On Wednesday, September 2nd I arrived in Truckee, California and bought tickets on the Virginia and Truckee Railroad to Virginia City and Carson City.

In Virginia City I found a hotel and mercantile next to one another. Harry Setzler accommodated me with a large order and invited me to the rooming house where he lived for supper at seven this evening. Walking to the front of the store, I spotted his book section. Not having a book to read and several train trips at hand I needed a new book. Picking up Lombard Street, by Walter Bagehot, I remembered Edwin talking about the 1866 London panic and Lombard Street as its center.

Then following Harry Setzler's directions, I walked into Miss Lillian's boarding house five minutes early. Harry greeted and introduced me to several locals. Walking toward our table, a man got up from his seat at a table, pulled his gun and pointed it at me.

"Remember me? I'm Vern Logan; you shot me in Wells last year. Now it's my turn to shoot you. You want it in the leg or some where else? Don't reach for the gun. I got you covered. You just walk outside. I don't need Lillian to have to wash blood off'en her floor. Now jes' you back out the front door onto the street."

"Vern, you need to back off. Didn't you hear me telling the judge if I'd wanted to kill you, I would've shot you in the head. We both know I shot you because you attacked me. We're both alive now so let's just be peaceful, settle down and have some supper."

As I was backing away from him, my right hand had grabbed the bullwhip from my side and his gun was on the floor before he knew what had hit his wrist.

He dropped to the floor to pick up his gun, and I dropped the whip and reached across my body, pulled my gun and aimed it at his head while he was still on the floor.

Vern said, "This is not over, boy." He turned and exited the front door.

Looking down I knew I was lucky because Vern never noticed that I had failed to cock the hammer on my gun.

After supper, I passed on the offer to set in on a poker game, shook hands with Harry and headed to the kitchen to thank Lillian for the great meal.

Sitting at a small table by the rear door was Vern Logan eating his meal.

"Watch your back, son, because I will find you again somewhere sometime."

Deciding the next morning to settle the Logan problem permanently, I walked to Lillian's front door and waited for Vern to come out. One of the men at the table last night came out, saw me and said," If you're waiting for Vern, you have a long wait. He was hurt last night in the mine and lost his right arm in the mishap. He's in the mine hospital and will be for several days."

Well, that should take care of that. I will be out of this territory by day after tomorrow.

In two hours I was on my way to Carson City and a better day, hopefully. Leo Carson Hardware was in the center of town. We passed it as the train continued through town to the station. When I got off the train and checked on departure times, I discovered if I took care of business in three hours I could make the return trip to Truckee today.

After a very successful one hour encounter with Leo Carson, I took my leave and walked back to the station, opened the book I bought in Virginia City and read for an hour.

By Sunday afternoon the 6th of September, I was back with Jane in San Francisco having coffee and conversation with the love of my life. She never complained about my long absences and greeted me each time I arrived home with such an air of happiness at my being there, it was no wonder she filled my mind while I was away with anticipation of my next return.

Tuesday would be here much too soon to suit me. I would be leaving on an eight week trip through northeastern California, eastern Oregon and on into Washington territory, over to Missoula, down through Boise ending up in Seattle. I would then take a side wheeler from Seattle back to San Francisco arriving on Sunday, November 1st.

CHAPTER 35

With winter settling in, I decided California was a good place to work for the next three months. *I'll work out of San Francisco all the winter of 1874 and the first month of 1875 covering the eastern most mining towns in the desert areas of California and southwestern Nevada. Seeing Jane for a couple of days every few weeks is getting comfortable even though in the back of my mind I know I'll need to leave the area for Colorado, Nebraska, and Kansas for an extended period shortly.*

The first week of February, 1875, I returned to Denver and my little home on the ranch of Harvey Bendickson's. I took Black Jack to Charles' blacksmith shop and had him shod with new shoes before he and I took a short trip to Pueblo, Colorado and back. I would have to make four stops on each leg of the trip of six days.

I gave some thought to taking Black Jack and another horse on a trip through Nebraska, but the weather is cold this year. I don't need to suffer the cold and wind so I'll plan a trip to Omaha . . . hit all the towns in Iowa to Cedar Rapids . . . go down the Mississippi River to St. Louis cross Missouri to Kansas City, Kansas . . . make the trip to Dodge City . . . back to Topeka on the Atchison Topeka and Santa Fe Railroad. Returning to Denver by rail, I'll stop by the horse farm on the Solomon River. If I have every thing right, I should be at the farm in Ottawa County by Saturday, March 27th unless the trip down the Mississippi has something I fail to know about.

I stepped off the train in Abilene, Kansas on the 26th of March having had a successful trip with over 50 orders sent to Hartford by telegraph in the last 30 days. I walked from the station to Joseph McCoy's office and begged a horse and tack. It had been over two years since the last time I walked into his office with my bullwhip and tamed a riled customer, but that was the first thing out of McCoy's mouth as he said, "Jack Knight, you still carry that whip?"

"Yep, Joe, still right here. Any chance to rent a horse for a couple of days?"

"Don't have one to rent but we can fix you up for a day or two. Heard last year you were selling guns now. I bought one of yours at Jacob's store, and he said you were the one taking orders for Colt now. How is that working out for you?"

"Great, Joe. Just made a trip all the way to Grand Rapids, and down the Mississippi. I was looking for adventure and sure have found it with Colt Firearms Company."

We walked to Joe's barn and he brought out a pure white mare saying," Jack, she is a good one, you will enjoy her gate."

He tossed me a saddle and blanket as he fitted the bridle for me.

"Have a nice visit at the farm, Jack. I'll see you in a couple of days."

I stopped at Abilene Hardware Store and took a large order from Jacob Faulkenbury on my way out of town.

The farm had a lot of activity going on as I rode to the barn to put the white mare away and feed her.

Father was with a customer, and I saw Uncle John showing a pair of geldings to another customer so I walked to the house and knocked on Mother's kitchen door.

"My wayward, son," Mother exclaimed as she opened the door." Come in and have a cup of coffee and tell me about this little Indian girl you've been hiding from us all." Seeing my look of surprise, she said without giving me a chance to reply, "Yes, Edwin wrote to us. He only said how happy you seem to be with Jane though. Can you believe he even sent us a picture they had made just for you when you return home from this trip?"

Mother scurried to the front room and returned with a picture of Jane in her white dress and squash blossom necklace with her hair in one braid pulled over her left shoulder. She was as pretty in the picture as in real life. Mother had another picture of Edwin with his beautiful wife, Rose, posing sitting on Edwin's lap.

"Jack, those are both beautiful women. How did you boys find such wonderful girls to fall in love with?"

"Mother . . . that was not luck. Just look at what they had to choose from. Edwin and I are the pick of the litter so you should not be surprised."

Father walked in the back door as Mother laughing gleefully served me coffee and apple pie.

"Hi, Jack. Saw you ride in but was busy with Andy Farthing. Sold him a four-horse team to pull his combine this fall. Say were you in Dodge City lately and hear anything about Lone Wolf and his band of Kiowa down in the Red River country?"

"Yes, Father, the weather has been so bitterly cold I heard he surrendered to try and save what is left of his tribe. Guess there is only about 500 of them left. Also some other tribes want to join him on the reservation the army has set up around Fort Sill."

"It's been cold and wet around here this year too. More rain than usual. The river rises and recedes every day or so. By the way, Mother and I sent money to my brother, James, in Hillsboro, Oregon to purchase ten acres next to his farm. We've given some thought to moving out there next year. From what I've been told, the weather out there just might be easier on our bodies, and James said farm labor is reasonable if we want to farm the land."

"Uncle James is right. I spent three years out there, and it's a lot warmer there than here and the wind is totally different in that part of the country."

Next day I rode the white mare over to the Wheatley farm and visited Mary Alice and William in their new home. Bill was right when he told us back when Brother and I thought we could explain the facts of courting our sister from this spot. You could see both farms and a lot more from their site.

Asking Mary what she thought about Mother and Father moving to Oregon she explained simply, "Mother is very happy with her home here but says she might like the climate better there and she is sure Father would like it better." Then she added her own feelings about moving, "As for me, I have a good life here and William and I love the land too much to want anything else. We are making a life here and Father and Mother have to do what they believe is best for them."

After another cup of coffee, a hug from Mary Alice and a hand shake from Bill, I rode back to Mother's home and some good food for a change.

By Saturday, April 3rd, I returned the white mare to Joseph McCoy and headed for Denver, making my stops in Salina, Russell, Hays, and Strasburg, Colorado for more reorders. I ended up with a layover Sunday in Hays as the mercantile was closed on the Lord's day.

Arriving at the ranch on Tuesday, Art saw me riding up to the barn on Black Jack and before I could take care of my horse, said, "Jack there is a telegram at the big house for you. Mother is there, and you can get it. It came last week sometime.

Telegrams were usually about important events and happenings so I secured the reins on a hitching post and headed for the main house.

Betsy was at the front door when I reached the porch, "Jack, this came last Thursday for you. We didn't open it. It's from your brother Edwin and, we figure it's personal."

Opening it, I read: Jack. Come to San Francisco as quickly as possible. Stop. Please make arrangements now. Stop. Edwin Knight.

CHAPTER 36

I had to put my orders together and send the ones that I still had from the trip after leaving the farm. I changed into some clean clothes and went to Denver for the train tickets.

The train would leave tomorrow morning. I sent a telegram to Edwin telling him I would arrive in San Francisco Saturday noon if he wanted to pick me up at the ferry terminal. After sending the orders to Hartford, I headed back to the ranch still wondering what was so vital for me in San Francisco.

I packed and asked Art to take me into town the next morning. I had a book to read that I had gotten earlier in the year and would need it since I had no calls to make on the way. It was another Jules Verne novel The Mysterious Island.

The novel kept my mind off of the thoughts churning through my head. Edwin was keeping something from me and I had a sickening feeling it had something to do with Jane.

Weather was good and the train was following the schedule closely to the posted times. The ferry arrived at the San Francisco terminal fifteen minutes behind schedule but that was not unusual. Edwin had a buckboard waiting for me.

I greeted him and he shook my hand and put my luggage in the back of the buckboard waving his arm for me to get on board. He pulled away from the crowded area and stopped the buckboard on a side street.

"Jack, I'm glad you made it here this quick. I had no idea when you would get my telegram." Edwin sat quietly for what seemed like an eternity with a strained look on his face. He spoke so softly I wasn't sure I was hearing right, "Jack, there is no good way to put this so here goes." Then he blurted out, "Jane has been murdered. She was found floating in the bay Monday, March the 29th."

"Edwin that's not possible. Are you sure it was her?" I replied in disbelief.

"Jack, I had to meet the coroner and identify the body after seeing an article in the paper and a telegram from Father McDougall saying Jane did not arrive at the Mission as pre-arranged."

"She left Saturday, two weeks ago for a five day stay at the Mission to do her regular help week teaching Indian culture to the girls there. Tuesday morning, I read in the *Examiner* that a body of a young Indian girl had been found floating in the bay between Fisherman's Wharf and Alcatraz Island. Police said if she had not been found when she was, the tide would probably have taken her on out into the ocean. I never gave the article another thought until later in the day when I received a telegram from Father McDougall asking if Jane was sick. He had not seen or heard from her and this was her regular time to come to the mission."

"Knowing she had left and not arrived at the mission, I went to the police and they sent me to the Coroner's office. When I told them the story, they showed me the body they had pulled out of the bay. Jack, believe me. It was Jane's body there. She had been strangled but the Coroner felt she had not been molested and thought she died instantly as the person that strangled her was strong and crushed several vertebras and the spinal cord with his very large hands. He also told me that she had been in the water for at least two days when found."

"Jack, I'm sorry to have to tell this story to you but we need to get over it and remember Rose and I have to heal also. Jane was like my daughter and always will be. Rose is going back to her office Monday. She has not left the house since the knowledge of this crime came to us."

"I don't know what you can or will do about this but I can tell you there will be little help from the police as Jane was an Indian and they have a low priority just like the Negro, or Chinese people here in San Francisco."

I had sat stunned and wordless until, at last, Edwin stopped talking, leaning back in the buckboard seat like the wind was knocked out of him. "Edwin, I have no idea where to start but after this all sinks in, I will do something even if it's wrong. Let's go home and see Rose now."

Walking into the house, Rose greeted me with tears in her eyes, reached out toward me and I held her for just a minute.

Edwin said, "Jack, we have made some arrangements but have held off as long as possible waiting to hear from you. Father McDougall has a spot at the mission for her grave if that is acceptable to you. I have paid the Coroner to keep her body cold but Monday is the last day he will oblige me on that. Tomorrow is Sunday. We can take a casket to the morgue and claim the body and carry it to the mission then if you wish. Or wait till Monday, if you feel that's better."

"No Edwin, let's do it tomorrow and get it over with."

Rose added, "We have a casket at the JAK Sales warehouse and could pick it up and have Jane put in it for the trip to the mission. It's about forty miles to Mission Santa Clara so it'll be faster and smoother to use the train. There is one early Sunday for people going there for services."

"Thank you guys, for waiting for me to arrive before putting together and completing funeral plans for Jane. I would be at a loss at where to begin to get it done though I know both of you knew Jane and I were more than friends."

"Jack, you stay here and rest. I will go to the warehouse and pick up the casket and make arrangements to pick the body up in the morning before the train leaves. Rose, please check the train schedule so we're not late for the first trip of the day."

Sitting down alone at the kitchen table with a cup of coffee, I realized what was happening and what had happened to my life. What an empty feeling overcame me . . . Suddenly, my body started trembling and I began to sob until my body felt drained of all feeling. Then I got mad.

Father had taught us all that emotion was one thing that could kill you so it must be controlled whether it was good or bad. Remembering this, I somehow brought calm to my jumbled, racing thoughts and started the process of self control.

Rose returned with the train schedule and told me we needed to have the coffin at the station for loading by seven the next morning.

I asked Rose. "What have you taken to the morgue to dress Jane in?"

"Edwin has taken her best white buckskin dress for them to put on her as the one she had on was almost gone when she was found."

"I would like for her to wear the squash blossom necklace I gave her also," I remarked before she could say anything else.

"I guess she was wearing her necklace, Jack. When I was getting the dress, I looked for it because I knew it meant a lot to her and it was not in her room. It's probably on the bottom of the bay somewhere."

Two hours later Edwin returned and joined us in the kitchen. He said. "Everything will be ready to be picked up from the morgue after 6:00 in the morning. I also sent a message to Father McDougall to have a buckboard meet us at the train station there around 10:00 in the morning."

"By the way Jack, Jane will be in a private room before they nail the casket lid and Keith the Coroner said you could have a few minutes with her before we pick her up for a final remembrance and farewell."

Ray Anderson, my original salesman for JAK Sales, pulled up in front of the house at 5:30 a. m. with a buckboard to take us to the morgue and on to the railroad station.

Everyone stayed outside for me to have a couple of minutes alone to say goodbye to the woman that was the first true love of my life. Having rehearsed over and over in my mind on the trip to the morgue, I said everything I had to say and put a rawhide necklace with a twenty dollar gold piece around Jane's neck, kissed her lightly on the lips and closed the casket in less than five minutes.

Father McDougall had a wonderful ceremony with twelve Nuns and fifteen of the girls from the mission school. He related to Edwin and Rose as her adopted parents and called me her one true love in her short life. As part of the service, the Father asked if we all had been Baptized and once confirmed served Communion to the three of us and the nuns.

When we had something to eat and coffee in down town Santa Clara, everyone seemed lost in their own thoughts and had nothing to say 'til we boarded the train for home. When we had all sat down I broke the forlorn silence. "You know, it has been several months since I made the rounds in San Francisco. I think if I work a few days it will help me, and something might turn up to show me a clue of where to start."

"Jack, you ought to let sleeping dogs lie. Knowing you like I do, I didn't think you would so I have contacted my friend at the Pinkerton Office. He said he would give you any support you need if you get any evidence pointing to someone."

"Thanks, Edwin. We will see what happens for awhile. I can't just leave and go back to Denver without trying to do something."

By Wednesday late, I had covered my walking and buggy trip customers and had enough reorders to keep Richard at Colt off my back for a couple of weeks.

That night, while we were enjoying an after dinner cup of coffee, Ray Anderson came to the house with a big surprise. Rose brought him into the kitchen and he had Jane's Squash Blossom Necklace swinging from his hand.

"Hey, Jack. I was making a call on Port Hardware in Oakland and after I left, I was walking toward the wharf area and saw this necklace in a Pawn shop three doors down from the Hardware store. They had a display window in the front of the store and this was in it. I went in and asked if it was for sale and it was. I bought it for thirty-five dollars. I asked the fellow how he came to have it and he said this guy brought it in and didn't want to pawn it but sell it and he gave him twenty dollars for it. I didn't push him for more information 'cause I figured you would know better how to address the situation than I. I was sure this was Jane's. I remembered seeing her with it on and had never seen another like it."

Rose told Ray to have a chair while she got him a cup for some coffee. Edwin took the necklace and handed it to me. Straining to keep my composure, I said, "You were right. That is one of a kind and it was hers for sure." I reached into my pocket for some coins and handed them to Ray, "Here are two twenty dollar gold pieces. Now where did you say was the location of that pawn shop?"

Ray gave me the location once again. I turned to my brother and said," Edwin, Rose now, I have someplace to start. Can you believe the luck?"

CHAPTER 37

Finding Port Hardware in Oakland was easy, but when I walked down to the pawn shop, I discovered it wouldn't open until 10:00 A.M. The morning breeze was a little cool and since I had to wait about an hour, a café on the water front that opened early accommodated me with some heavy black coffee. I left there with enough time to be looking at the goods in the pawn shop window as the owner approached to open for the day. After he entered he re-shut the door so I knocked to let him know I would like to enter.

Meeting Boyd Dalton just as he opened the front door was memorable. He had a Peacemaker in his hand and was not sure he wanted me to enter his shop. "Mister, yore packing a lot of iron to want to jus' walk into a pawn shop this early in the morning. What can I do for ya?"

To put him at ease, I replied, "I will hand you my piece butt first if you invite me in off the sidewalk."

He waved my gun off as he opened the door wider for me to enter. He introduced himself after I let him know who I was and that I represented Colt Firearms Company.

He let me know he was not interested in handling new guns and that I was wasting his and my time and opened the front door to let me out.

Not moving, I explained, "Mr. Dalton, I'm not here as a salesman or customer. I'm looking for some information about one of your recent customers. I was told you purchased a Turquoise and Silver necklace in the last week or so and I need to find the gentleman that sold it to you."

Mr. Dalton looked at me warily and said, "Have no idea what you are talking about."

I pulled the necklace from my pocket and held it for him to get a good look. "Boyd, my partner bought this from you yesterday, and you said you had bought it for twenty dollars just lately. I need to find this person and you won't be involved I can promise that."

Relaxing somewhat, Dalton said, "Oh that trinket. Yep, we dickered for quite a while. He thought it was worth a lot more but I figured I would be stuck with it for some time so yes I ended up with it for the gold piece. I believe your partner would have paid double what he paid but I had not figured he wanted it so badly until after I sold it to him."

"Tell you what I am going to do. I will triple your money if you give me a good description of the man who brought this in."

Looking thoughtful, he replied, "I can do that. He's a big man. Looked to be six foot four. Probably weighed around 270-280 and I couldn't help noticing he had huge hands. Oh yes . . . he had a fresh scar from his left ear to the bridge of his nose. Should be easy to spot if you get in seeing distance. Come to think of it, for another gold piece, I believe I can tell you where you just might find him."

"Okay, you got it. Make me comfortable and I'll give you five shiny twenty dollar gold pieces for your time."

Hearing that, he added, "He smelled like fish. I'm sure he is a fisherman. To get more specific he smelled like Dungeness Crabs like those guys around Fisherman's Wharf over in Frisco."

I dug five gold pieces out of my pocket and handed them to Boyd, told him I was much obliged and ran back to the ferry building in time to catch the next ferry to San Francisco.

Getting off the ferry, I walked the waterfront to Fisherman's Wharf and saw the boat basin where all the fishing boats were docked or at anchor. The realization hit me that this might not be as easy as I had thought. There seemed to be well over a hundred boats there and empty spots for more. Stopping to think for a solution, it came to me that all the boats had to sell what they caught. First, find the place they went to sell their catch and ask them if they knew of a man fitting Boyd's description.

I spent the rest of the daylight hours talking with fish buyers and came up empty but felt I was on the right track. Afterwards walking home, my body was so stressed and tired; I went straight to bed and fell asleep with no supper.

At breakfast, I told Edwin and Rose what had happened yesterday and of all the clues gotten and what I had done for my follow up.

Edwin asked, "Jack, do you want to see the Pinkerton man yet?"

"No Edwin I need a couple of days to look around to do some more checking on my own then maybe next week if I hit a brick wall we'll talk about that."

Friday was a dry hole. I found no one that could help me. Not ready to ask for help yet, I started out early Saturday morning. A woman selling crab bait at the end of a dock west of the boat basin told me about a man on a boat named "Roxy" that bought bait from her usually on Monday and Thursday and had a hand on board that could be the fellow I was looking for.

I looked the basin over and didn't see any boat with "Roxy" on it so headed for home to wait 'til Monday with hopes the "Roxy" would buy bait as she usually did.

Edwin and Rose had replaced Jane's position with a nice Chinese lady who used to work for one of Edwin's customers. She came to the house each morning but did not live in the house. Her name was Fenfang Chun which meant Fragrant Springtime in English so we all agreed to just call her Fenfang. Although she knew how to cook western cuisine, I was also learning to eat food with different spices that I was not used to and discovered it was very good.

I arrived at the bait dock well before daylight on Monday wearing clothes for the type of work being done on the dock. I had already decided to go back to the place of the old lady who gave me the information about the boat named" Roxy". After I introduced myself as James, I asked her to let me help load the bait on her customers' boats this morning. She told me her name was Ellie, and I was a welcome sight since it looked to be a busy day.

She was more than happy for me to do the heavy lifting and the third boat to pull up for bait was the "Roxy". She called to Roland, the skipper, asking how many pounds he wanted and after he answered told me to load four of the wooden boxes from a stack next to the boat on board. Glancing over the crew, I saw my man but just loaded the four boxes and walked back to the shack she called her office. After loading 20 some boats, daylight was with us and no more boats come by for bait.

I asked Ellie how to find out the crewman's name on the "Roxy" and she said." I think Harry Kind, the tender at the boat basin, knows most of the fisherman that have been around any length of time. Be prepared to listen a little when you go to see him. He likes to talk on and on."

Finding Harry was no easy task. He moves around a lot so I was sent from one dock to the next and then onto several large boats before I corralled the man. Then I understood quickly what Ellie meant. Starting a conversation was easy but getting a word in edgewise was a problem. Harry liked to tell about how the boat basin would not exist without his presence and yes he knew most of the fisherman by name.

"Harry, I would like to know the name of a man on the "Roxy "you know any of them?"

"Shore know 'em all."

"Harry, I have a couple of twenty dollar gold pieces if this conversation never happened. Do you understand what I just said?"

"Yassir."

Passing him the two gold pieces, I asked about the man with the big scar across his face.

"Okay, thet'un is Slidell or Lydell Walsh. One or tuther, I ain't never got straight on thet furst name. He ain't had thet scar long, but prob'bly deserved it. He ain't no good so I'd stay 'way from 'im and, yep, never seed you afore in my life."

"Harry, any idea where this guy hangs out when he's not on the boat?"

"I mite 'member to forgit whut I'm 'bout to tell ya fer 'nuther gold piece."

"Ok, Harry, one more time." I said as I handed him the gold piece.

"He's of'en the boat on Wensdy and Saddy's. I seed him at Vic's Place, Paul's Port, and Fast Eddie's mos' ov da time. He shore kin hold his liqqer. He drinks straight shots 'n I seed him down seven or eight in an hour."

"Wow, careful. Not too much information I can't afford any more. Much obliged, Harry."

When I got back to the house, my brother, Jay Parker, was having coffee with Rose and he was a sight for my sore eyes. Now, if I could just talk Jay into an evening of drinking and carousing, I just might meet Mr. Walsh without making Walsh suspicious of my intentions.

After a brotherly hug and slap on the back, I joined them with a cup of coffee. I began explaining what happened to Jane and also why I needed him to spend some time with me to meet this fellow. He was more than ready for a joint venture as usual.

Tuesday, Jay had to make a trip to Petaluma and I went with him for company and to discuss how we were going to begin fitting in with the locals at the wharf.

Wednesday afternoon, both of us dressed as dock workers. We made our first call at Vic's Place. With no gun or bullwhip, only a knife displayed like a lot of dock workers, I really felt naked but the hardware would be out of place.

Jay could hold a lot of whiskey, but I told him this could be a long day so to pace himself. After an hour Jay remarked, "You know any other place he would go?"

"Yes let's wander over to Fast Eddie's and hang around."

When we came inside the door, I saw Walsh standing at the bar and alerted Jay by look and gesture who he was. Strolling to the bar, Jay stood next to Walsh with me next to Jay.

Jay ordered two shots of whiskey and turned to Walsh," Hey pal, I'm Peter and this is my partner, James."

The big man put his hand out to Jay, "I'm Lydell Walsh. I ain't got no partner, but let me buy you both a drink."

Jay had downed his shot so I slipped the empty glass next to me and pushed mine to Jay. The bartender put three more shots on the bar, and

Lydell offered to sit at a table after shaking my hand. He picked up his drink and we followed him to an empty table at the side of the room.

As we were sitting down, Jay said. "We work the docks wherever we find work. You look like a fisherman to me.

"Yep, I've been on the "Roxy" for two years now. Saw you the other day, James. Loading bait for Ellie off her dock."

Got to be careful with this guy. He's an observer and has a good memory.

Jay picked up on Lydell's statement also and followed with, "Lydell, how do you get a spot on one of these boats? You crab guys make better money than we do chasing work on the docks seems to me."

Jay had Lydell talking and telling us what to do to get a boat job while I continued to switch glasses and faked drinking the shots. Jay bought more shots and also pushed his shot to Lydell since he just drank what was in front of him. After several rounds at the table, I told Jay we had to meet Earl soon. Didn't he think it was time for us to get going?

Jay agreed and stood up putting his hand out to Lydell. I did the same. We sauntered out of Fast Eddie's and headed for home.

Walking home, I thanked Jay for spending the time helping me get to know Lydell. We both marveled at how much liquor he could drink with no visible effect. After talking about how the evening went, we both felt I could handle the situation alone now. Lydell seemed to be receptive to the idea of making the rounds with just me this coming Saturday.

CHAPTER 38

I had taken care of all my customers in the San Francisco area and close towns and had lots of time on my hands. My mind kept churning with plans that would bring justice to the harm that was done to the first love of my life. Waiting for Saturday afternoon was hard and I had to keep a patient demeanor since I didn't want Edwin and Rose showering me with questions. They thought I was still working at overcoming my grief and I couldn't let them be involved with my plan to right the wrong done to our household.

Saturday afternoon, I told Edwin I was going for a walk to get my mind settled enough to go back to work. He asked if I would like some company and I told him I would like to be alone with my thoughts right now.

I started looking for Lydell at Fast Eddie's but after nursing a sarsaparilla for an hour I moved to Vic's Place and the bartender told me he had left some time ago. *If he goes to Paul's Port that would be perfect for my plan. He's a big man so I sure can't haul him around and the beach I have in mind to complete my revenge is close to Paul's Port.*

Walking into Paul's, I saw Lydell at a table all by himself. Perfect. As I moved toward the bar, Lydell saw me and motioned for me to come to his table.

"James, how ya doing? What happened to Peter? Set yourself down. I think I can get one of you guys on the "Roxy." Roy, one of the hands,

217

got on a steamer run to Alaska making us short one person. You want the job?"

Over the next three hours, we talked about crabbing and what I needed to learn to be good help to the crew. The bartender kept the shots coming and I was able to keep him distracted so he had no idea he was drinking his and my shots. It was now dark outside and if Lydell got any more in the tank, I wouldn't be able to handle him.

"Lydell, how about you and me going over to Vic's Place and having something to eat before we get too far gone to enjoy a good meal."

"Thas a good idea. I'm 'bout half in the bag a'ready. Les' go."

As Lydell got to his feet, I wasn't sure he could walk. He straightened up and finally got one foot ahead of the other and we were out the door. I suggested a short cut down the beach to which he slurred it'd be easier to walk on the sand anyway. By this time, we were staggering to move down the beach. I asked off handedly, "By the way, Lydell, how did you get that scar on your face?"

"One aft'noon, I wuz walkin' in town and tried to git this little Injun girl to talk tu me . . . and you know what she did? She ignored me. She was a little thing . . . prob'bly 90 pounds or less. I grabbed her from behind when she was trying to walk by; picked her up, carried her to the beach Ya know . . . to have a little fun. When we gets to the beach, she wouldn't stop yelling. I couldn't unnerstand a word . . . Must've bin some native tongue. I tried to set on her and she pulled this little knife on me and afore you knows it; got me 'cross the face."

He then pulled the little four inch blade I had given Jane out of a shirt pocket. Now I was sure I had the right guy. We were getting away from the lights and to the spot I had left a cache of items. He staggered in front of me with just enough time for me to quietly pull a heavy knife from it sheath on my belt and rap him on the back of his head with the handle. He was out like a snuffed candle.

Spreading him out on the sand, I went to work to bring my plan to fruition before he woke up. I reached in his pocket and retrieved the small knife before continuing my plan. It was a half hour job before I threw a bucket of water on him to make sure he knew what was happening. His eyes were wide in the moon light, full of fear as he realized he could not move his arms or legs. He jerked his head from side to side as much as possible making gurgling noises.

For a moment, he stopped to listen as I said, "This might take some time, Lydell, but the sand is soft so you won't be too uncomfortable for a little while. You may have enough time to make peace with God unless you want to join some of your friends in hell."

By the time, I walked ten feet from him, I could no longer hear his muffled noises and knew the sock in his mouth with the raw hide thong holding it in place would keep him from alerting anyone. The walk to Edwin's was an easy one even though the beach where I was had to be close to four miles from home.

Edwin and Rose were both reading when I entered the living room and Rose told me they had saved some supper for me but knew it was cold now. She got up and went into the kitchen to reheat the food for me and asked if I enjoyed my evening walk. I thanked her and explained that yes, I had done a lot of thinking and decided to leave in the morning. She asked if I knew how long I'd be gone and I told her no I had not a clue when I would return but would let them know when I settled someplace.

I notice Edwin looking at my right side for the bullwhip but he doesn't say anything about it not being there.

Sunday morning I took the ferry across from San Francisco and was on my way to Sacramento to work all day Monday. I felt light not having the bullwhip on my right side as usual, but the Peacemaker would suffice from now on.

Tuesday morning, April 27, 1875, I picked up the San Francisco *Examiner* and read the following story:

Monday, a body was found on the beach just off McDowell Avenue. Officials have identified the body as that of local fisherman, Lydell Simpson Walsh. It is without a doubt a homicide. The Body had been spread eagled with four foot iron stakes driven into the sand and his legs and arms had been tied with rawhide thongs to the iron stakes. One of his boots had been removed, and his own sock was stuffed into his mouth and secured with a rawhide thong around his head. Officials have followed the footprints of two men back to Paul's Port where it was reported that Mr. Walsh and another big man, possibly with the name, James, had spent several hours drinking Saturday night. Police feel James is also a fisherman as the knots used to tie the victim are usually used by seamen. Further investigation found that earlier in the week, Lydell Walsh and this same fellow, James, with another possible fisherman that the bartender at Fast Eddie's Tavern heard Walsh call Peter, spent an hour or so drinking heavily before leaving that bar. Captain Worthington of the crab boat "Roxy" that Mr. Walsh had served on for two years said he has no crew members named James or Peter so the companions are from other boats. Cause of death was from strangulation. Lydell had four wraps of a cut up rawhide bullwhip fall and thong that had been soaked in water and stretched and tied around his neck. As the rawhide dried, it choked the victim to death. Wrapped inside the bullwhip next to the victim's throat was another piece of rawhide with the words "FOR JANE" burned on the piece. Officials checked records back for two years finding no Janes's involved in crimes that would merit this kind of revenge. No relatives have been identified, and no one knows if Mr. Walsh has anyone in the San Francisco area that should be contacted. Police are taking this case very seriously. Citizens should be protected from this kind of violence whatever their status in our community. If you have information about this crime please contact your nearest police station.

Well this sounded like a great case of good old bullwhip justice to me. Now I could begin a new life with new adventures with no regrets.

THE END OR IS IT *A NEW BEGINNING?*

ACKNOWLEDGEMENT

Anyone that takes the time to write a novel finds a host of people that become involved in or at least part of the writers thinking and so become part of the process. I am fortunate to have a large family full of support and constructive criticism to further my endeavors. After completing my first novel, a friend, Jerry Vermillion, started a biography of his productive and fun life and has now published the results. Just knowing my work encouraged Jerry to produce such work is gratifying. Of course, I have to thank my wife, Yvonne, for her support and the time she awarded me away from her at the computer to finish this offering. Also, my children and grandchildren that almost demanded a return performance about our family and their travels.

Many thanks are required for my stepdaughter, Dorcas Branham, who took the time from a very busy schedule to do the final editing and putting her several degrees to good use for my benefit and Judi Lin Huffman, another daughter, also gave advice when asked about computer applications.

I may not have given everyone just credit for their help but omission is not my intent. Thank you all.